I0630089

HANGING TREE

ALSO BY TONY MASERO

HANGING TREE
A WESTERN NOVELLA COLLECTION

TONY MASERO

WOLFPACK
PUBLISHING
— EST 2013 —

Hanging Tree: A Western Novella Collection
Paperback Edition
Copyright © 2024 by Tony Masero

Wolfpack Publishing
1707 E. Diana Street
Tampa, FL 33610

www.wolfpackpublishing.com

All rights reserved. No part of this book may be reproduced in any form or by any electronic or mechanical means, including information storage and retrieval systems, without express written permission from the publisher, except for the use of brief quotations in reviews. Any use of this publication to train generative artificial intelligence (AI) technologies is expressly prohibited.

This book is a work of fiction. References to historical events, real people, or real places are used fictitiously. Any similarity to real persons, living or dead, is purely coincidental and not intended by the author.

All brand names and product names used in this book are trademarks, registered trademarks, or trade names of their respective holders. Wolfpack Publishing is not associated with any product or vendor in this book.

Cover art by Tony Masero
Editing by My Brother's Editor

Paperback ISBN 979-8-89567-050-7
Ebook ISBN 979-8-89567-049-1
LCCN 2024950066

HANGING TREE

HANGING GIRL

CHAPTER ONE

N o one can say for certain where Mrs. Irene Dunn and The Wichita Kid first met.

Although in a statement made in old age by Irene's elder sister Beatrice, she claims they met while Irene was out riding and The Kid was surveying the coach route while planning his next robbery. It was a high place, so Beatrice tells as it was described to her, amongst ponderosa pines and overlooking a rugged fall to a deep valley and the road into town far below. The view stretched away across miles of green forest to a distant range of mountains, mauve in the haze, they stretched across a horizon alive with pillared clouds of gold set against a blue sky as aquamarine as the ocean. Irene had paused in her ride at the edge of the ravine to feel the fresh breeze against her face and smell the clean tang of pinesap from the trees around her. She closed her eyes and drew a deep breath and when she opened them again he was there before her as if he had risen from the ground.

At that first sighting she claimed, inexplicably, that her heart swelled in her chest and she knew undeniably that she would love this man.

It is not known if this was in fact their first true sight of each other but it is for sure that it did happen in some form or other and as with what followed after it surely could have happened in just such a manner.

———

Irene was an heiress and socialite who at twenty-four years of age had moved out west to oversee a small cattle ranch left her by a distant cousin. Known for her adventurous and often daring behavior by friends and family in her Boston home it was not surprising that during her time in the frontier town of Big Tar she met and married in headstrong fashion—a circumstance frowned upon by her father who strongly forbade it—one Sheriff Joseph E. Dunn, an impressive lawman, built, they say like a hairy mammoth and with a certain woolly temperament to match.

Reading between the lines of various reports from the Texas Ranger vaults and with a surplus of hearsay, Sheriff Joe Dunn had led a varied and wild career. He came to notice at a young age as a questionable trader in suspect horseflesh but was better known as a cattle rustler along the Mexican border. Then he flipped his card entirely to earn a five-Cinco badge and become a Texas Ranger with a name for ruthlessness and an expeditious manner in dealing with perpetrators. There was no quibbling with Joe, so the word went; he would as soon as put a bullet in a suspect's brain before asking whether he was guilty or not. With this kind of resumé, he had no problem in being elected law officer for the town of Big Tar and had served there for six years before he met and married Irene.

Not surprisingly, his ruthless rule and harsh results brought relative peace to the county, and the locals were pleased with his success and when Irene stepped down that first time from the Overland Stagecoach she found herself in an uncommonly safe and placid environment for the Texas panhandle of the day.

Old photos show Joe as a plug-ugly son of a gun, a broad face battered and scarred with his nose bent out of shape by past disputes and seated on a no-neck chest built from a solid six-foot tall, round, and a muscled barrel of hard body. No one could dispute his lack in the looks department and his loud presence in a room was always notable for his great size and elephantine behavior.

How he came to impress a fragile lady of Irene's status is indeed a mystery and yet so he did. Some suggest that her gentile Bostonian upbringing under wealthy parental guidance was so swayed by Joe's demeanor that it proved to be a challenge to her niceties and she misguidedly intended to make a gentleman of him. Others, more impolitely, suggest that his known physical attributes and prowess in the bedroom had something to do with it. It was common knowledge amongst the soiled doves in Madame Beau's relaxation establishment where a frequent visitor such as Joe proved to be more affectionately known, not as sheriff, but more secretly as "King Dong."

Irene for her part floated on a cloud of wealth and indifference far above the dust and sweat of the cow town. With the slender grace of a ballerina she was a pale-skinned beauty with a long neck and vapid blue eyes under a fringe of silky blonde ringlets. Never seen without her finery and a small parasol held against the sun's searing rays she would promenade the boardwalk and hoary cowpokes would make way for her in deference to her obvious display of royalty.

According to Mrs. Cynthia Johnson, the renowned journalist and dime-novel writer, Ben Downs, also known as The Wichita Kid, was at that time a veritable thorn in the side of the sheriff. Ben originally came from Wichita Falls in the east of the panhandle and that was how he had earned his name. He was a lean figured young man with ruggedly handsome features, often solemn but with an open innocence to the eyes that repudiated his chosen trade. Ben cut a rakish figure in his tight denim pants, sweeping silk bandanna and a short poncho cut to the midriff where a single action Colt showed it bone handle set in a high holster. Unusually he carried the Colt not fastened to the thigh but, when off his pony, it was swung to the front and hung between his thighs and might be considered as some psychosomatic emblem of his own prowess in that region. In such manner this display of sexuality was equal to the sheriff's but in a wholly different and more overtly dangerous style.

With only nineteen years under his belt, he

earned the soubriquet "Kid" but his experience was
that of an older man. Raised by hardscrabble folks
in a dingy trackside hovel he had learned thieving at
an early age by helping his pa steal goods from the
passing boxcars as they slowed for the grade outside
their home. There was a dash to him though, a
natural charm that held a winning way with the
ladies helped on by his good looks. The reserve he
displayed and that appealed to so many was in actu-
ality a secret concern for little more than for himself.
But Ben was wise enough to use this perceived attention to good use and would often make a display of
sharing some small part of his stolen rewards. In
such, a name grew around him, and he was favored
by many simple souls for this apparent generosity
that duly overlooked his criminality.

Ben continued his raiding ways with the help of
another, a partner, one Billy Jay Castana a part
Mexican young man of equal age and interest. Billy
Jay was also not unhandsome with his Spanish
looking tanned skin and curled black hair the color
of tar that always seemed to be as if it were oiled.
He was the quiet type but his conservative appearance belied his natural inclination for the speedy use
of his gun and he was a renowned sure shot. Always
in reserve he backed Ben's play and was devoted to
him as a wiser and more cunning companion on the
outlaw trail. The opposite of his virile partner
although of a fair disposition he appeared thin and
stooped in body and often racked by a weakening
cough that was the result of a passing brush with
tuberculosis acquired in the poverty of his childhood. It was recognized that Billy Jay most often

kept to the background and was no more than a mere shadow to the more dashing figure of The Wichita Kid.

In the town of Big Tar, it should also be noted, lived Ben's older brother, Donald Downs, who ran the mercantile store. A burly, balding fellow tending toward chubby comfort but far removed from the lawless activities of his younger brother so that Don apparently had nothing to do with his activities. He was a churchgoing, honest and hardworking family man with a wife and three infant children. A pillar of the community he served on the town council and was one of the foremost members in electing Sheriff Joe Dunn. This strange dichotomy was ignored by most of the local population who laid no blame or guilt at Don's door despite his brother being a known road agent and nefarious villain.

In retrospect, there was no doubt that The Kid and Irene met secretly on many occasions, the first being that moment on the cliff edge when the attraction became known to both of them. Was their love fulfilled at this early stage? With her being a married lady and him a wayward outlaw, it is hard to consider but not unreasonable. Difficult to say, but we were assured Irene suddenly took on a lighter disposition and displayed benevolence toward the townspeople. There was brightness to her and demonstrations of good cheer as she met and greeted folks, she was happy so we have been told.

Our best report of their consummation came from one Arthur Weesley, a deputy sheriff serving under Joe Dunn. In a letter to his mother, to whom he held fond attention, Art, as he was more commonly known, recorded a moment that tells of such an event. Many misspellings, lack of punctuation, and use of vernacular appear throughout the missive so some attempts have been made to clarify the text for readers.

"Hi, Ma. Knowing how you like a good tale, here's a few lines to tell you of this uncommon experience I have recently enjoyed." Being seconded by Sheriff Dunn to accompany his wife and act as bodyguard on a trip where she intended to visit her bequeathed ranch, the lady being a fine rider we took saddle horses and two supply mules and set off early.

"It was a couple of days ride through some flat and pretty boring prairie country with nothing much to comment on, other than me being held to task on frequent occasion by her highness before we finally got to our destination. On arrival there was not much left of the place it being in want of maintenance and fallen some into disrepair. Only a cabin was habitable, and this surrounded by a few dugouts, sheds, and outhouses, and a small corral. No sooner had we set up in the cabin when we was undertook by bandits. They caught me unaware and that treacherous villain The Wichita Kid and his partner, a dog-eared lunger called Billy Jay, overcome me by force.

"They put me in this outhouse shed and chained me to a post—the chain was old and rusty but the padlocks were new, so I reckon the whole matter must have been planned previous. The Kid grabs Mrs. Dunn and tells her he will 'see to her' instantly. I didn't know quite what the Kid meant by that, but it didn't sound too good and I feared the worst. Strange thing is although Mrs. Dunn made noise of objection and beating on his chest as he carried her off saying, 'No, no, you brute, unhand me,' even so there was something odd, almost a smile on her face as if the notion appealed, despite this terrible act of assault that she was confronted with. I guess it was just the awful fear as to the outcome that was showing on her face.

"You just sit quiet," Billy Jay told me. "There might be some noise but don't you pay it no heed."

"What will he do to her?" I asked. "The sheriff will be mighty upset if she's harmed."

"She'll be fine," he promised.

"Sure enough, pretty soon after this, a heck of banging and crashing begins. A whooping and a hollering like you never heard. Such a sobbing and screaming, my heart went out to the poor woman and all her suffering while that beast is laying into her.

"Later, when all was quiet, this Billy Jay come to me with a sandwich and some water. He brings a board and sets it down to play some checkers with me. The damn half-breed keeps on winning and I ask him how he cheats so and he reckons he's smarter than me and that is all. Ma, you know my feelings on that score, I never heard such lamentable impudence, how some greaser wetback can think he is so much better, so I tell him he ain't nothing but a cup of half and half and should watch his mouth when speaking to a white man of American blood. The cheeky dog just grin at me, starts on coughing his lungs out like he's about to pass over and then calm as you like resets the board.

"Next morning the lady brings me some coffee and breakfast and here's the surprise of it, she looks fine, not distressed at all but chirpy and shiny. I mean fresh, you know, like she's just stepped out of her boudoir. Not that she don't always look as if she is top dollar but this was real spritely. So I ask her how she does and she says she is most well. I ask about all the awful noise and terrible screams and she says that I must have heard wild animals out on the prairie and that she was being well treated and there was no need for concern.

"I tell you, Ma, it was a strange affair and when the pair of villains had rode off Mrs. Dunn was nice as pie and set me free humming a right nice tune like she was taking the washing in."

CHAPTER TWO

I n all probability Sheriff Dunn got to hear of the matter on Weesley's return as it is certain his mood changed for the darker, people said that it was as if black storm clouds were gathering on the horizon when they saw him around town. Irene was held to question by her husband about what had occurred but she dismissed the matter as of little importance. But by now Joe Dunn's suspicions were aroused and there is no doubt that he kept a careful eye on Irene after that time and his suspicious hatred of The Kid redoubled.

The Kid did take leave off his romantic inclinations for a short with just sufficient time to rob the Overland Stage some miles outside of town and still inside the sheriff's purview. It was almost as if his intention was to cause the sheriff irritation and make him appear foolish and incapable by taking the stagecoach down so close to the lawman's area of influence.

The Division Robbery Reports for the Butterfield Overland Mail in that county prove that The Kid demonstrated gallant form by taking off his hat and with a bow giving good day to the lady passengers. According to the account register the strong box held little in the way of interest, only a few hundred dollars, a surveyor's report concerning the building of a bridge and a few lawyer's personal documents referring to land sales. It became all too apparent that these were of no interest to The Kid and his companion as they only took the money and the other papers were thrown to the wind once the box was opened. The Kid relieved the male travelers of their pocket watches and wallets, the ladies of their rings and necklaces, although the passengers tell that he returned one engagement ring to a young lady as she pleaded for it, claiming that her fiancé had given it her only a day since on his bended knee at the proposal.

An unfortunate incident did occur at that time though when Billy Jay was suddenly brought down by one of his coughing fits. The guard, a young, eighteen-year-old boy called Tom Hard and new to the job rashly brought his shotgun into play and would have killed the incapacitated Billy Jay as he was bent over and incapacitated by his hawking. Sadly, The Kid saw his move with the shotgun and before the boy could fire, he was brought down by a shot from The Kid's revolver. Sorely wounded the youngster lay thrashing on the ground for a while but very soon expired of his injury. The Kid lost his temper with what he considered the boy's foolishness and proceeded to kick at his inert form cursing and denouncing him for his stupidity.

Billy Jay recovered and pulled The Kid away leaving the shocked passengers in a state of dismay at sight of this unpleasant display. As one of the passengers was later to sagely remark, "You can't expect to take up the occupation of road agent without somebody at some time getting bent out of shape."

When news reached Big Tar, a posse was immediately organized and with Joe Dunn in the lead they set off to track down the bandits. To see Joe on a horse was an impressive thing, him being such a large individual so that only a shire workhorse of sturdy proportions could manage to carry him. Set up on the great beast he set off at a ponderous rate followed by the others, who could have set a faster speed but were forced thereafter to keep pace with Joe's slower moving animal. From this observation it may be incurred indeed that size isn't everything.

It is here that The Kid pulled a clever stunt, once the posse was clear of the town and the sheriff out of the way he saw it as an opportunity to have another fond assignation with Irene and with this intent he crept slyly back into Big Tar. It was there on Main Street that he ran into his brother, Don, who cried on him to leave immediately before a calamity should fall on his head.

The Kid, being of a wild and carefree nature, merely kissed his brother sweetly on the forehead and asked after his nephews and nieces. Don admonished him soundly and said it was well known that Joe Dunn was already suspicious of his friendship with Irene and would do him harm if he was captured. At which, The Kid broadcast his passion for the lady and that it was in his mind to carry her off if she was willing, which he was certain she was. Many in the street were listening to this noisy interaction and would later verify the adulterous exchange.

Don begged his brother to leave off such considerations but The Kid would not be moved and said that their trysts were a certain evidence to him that Irene loved him to the death and cared not a fig for the sheriff, that big lummox called Joe Dunn. Don openly wept tears of anguish and was sure that The Kid's attitude would be his undoing but notwithstanding this his outlaw brother strode off to find his beloved at the hotel where she had preciously taken rooms.

Safely ensconced with Irene, they were in the throes of a passionate embrace when, unbeknownst to them, the posse had been forced to return.

As it turned out even the sturdy animal that carried Joe Dunn struggled with his weight and at a steep rocky scree it cast a shoe and fell lame and it was for this reason the troop of lawmen returned. Billy Jay, who had been set to keep careful watch on the road in case of such an event, rode post-haste into town.

Even as the posse clattered down Main Street, Billy Jay was hammering on Irene's room door with his loud shouting heard over the whole hotel and certainly by the clerk at the front desk.

"Hey, Kid, get the lead out we gotta go, the sheriff's back in town."

There was so little time, as it proved the sheriff was on his way up the stairway to see his wife directly. His booming voice was a match only to Billy Jay's recent wailing alarm. "Hey, honey, I'm back," cried the sheriff. "Damned horse threw a shoe, so we got a while."

Seeing no way out, Billy Jay burst into the room before the sheriff arrived, only to find both Kid and Irene shocked and in a general state of undress.

"Get out of the window," begged Irene. "He cannot find you here. Go quickly, my love, save yourself."

So both companions, The Kid with his shirttails hanging out and without his boots, and Billy Jay urging him on, squeezed through the window and onto the hotel's porch roof. No sooner had they exited and stood balanced on the thin shingles outside than Joe Dunn burst through the door. He took one look at the partially clothed Irene and a lascivious grin spread across his ugly face. "Why, you sure is looking a peach, Irene. I can see you is all ready for some loving and I'm here to oblige."

Below the porch, the posse stood around idly chatting and smoking as they waited for the sheriff's horse to be re-shod and to take up the chase again. Creeping with as much care as they could manage, The Kid and Billy Jay made their way along the front of the building over the fragile roof. They had almost reached the far end when the sunbaked tiles as crisp as biscuit gave way under Billy Jay's feet and in a cloud of dust and splinters he crashed through and landed heavily on the boardwalk beneath.

"What the devil?" cried a posse member. "That you, Billy Jay, what the hell you doing here?"

Balancing on bare feet on the porch edge, The

Kid tried to avoid the widening hole in the roof as more pieces dropped and the whole construction creaked dangerously as it began to give way.

"Look here!" cried the posse man in a moment of awe. "That's The Wichita Kid up there."

They all stood gaping for a moment and then the entire porch decided to slide down in a rolling wave that fell with an awful noise of crashing and slamming and exploding a great cloud of dust far out into the street. Before you could say "escaping felon," Billy Jay and The Kid were on their feet and running. Behind them chaos followed, the terrified posse horses squealed and bucked in terror and any mounted men were thrown from the saddles while the rest of the livestock stampeded away down the street. Dogs barked and men cursed in the rending sounds of destruction as the entire front of the hotel was remodeled.

Billy Jay and The Kid were overcome with the excitement at their narrow escape and hollered and screamed in delight as they ran. Laughter followed with them as they raced away down narrow alleys and past silent houses making for the edge of town.

The impassioned Sheriff Dunn was caught abruptly by all the noise with his pants around his ankles. Irene could not resist the sight of him struggling with his fallen trousers as he headed for the door and squealed with unladylike laughter. Joe Dunn glowered at her before he slammed the door open and headed for the stairway.

"I shall see to you later," he roared in warning.

CHAPTER THREE

The journalist Mrs. Cynthia Johnson, an eyewitness to the whole proceedings, reported the entire dreadful scene in comprehensive detail in the Columbus Gazette next day. Once again The Wichita Kid had made a complete fool of the law and escaped, an item that caused Joe Dunn great embarrassment. He rumbled about the town unsure of how to handle the repercussions in any way except by bloody murder. From his own pocket, he advanced a reward of two hundred dollars for sight of The Kid or report of his whereabouts. His oath was proclaimed loudly in drinking parlors and about town that he would seek revenge on The Kid and his associate with diligent approbation and once taken he would see the outlaws duly sentenced as the lawless pestilence they represented.

In such a state of heated disarray he took out his anger on Don Downs, The Kid's brother, by accosting him in the street and accusing him of aiding and abetting the outlaw. At which accusation Don was obviously upset and proclaimed loudly that the sheriff was outside his jurisdiction in confronting a town councilor in such a peremptory fashion. Joe Dunn's only response was to lower his eyebrows, hunch his powerful shoulders and promise due recompense in his most crude and unmannerly fashion. Shocked and distressed, Don returned to his store fuming at the false charge laid against him but also unmanned by the terrifying prospect of the sheriff that left him fearful for his own life.

Joe Dunn did not rest there though and now believing that he had been cuckolded and that all previous clues to his wife's adulterous behavior were true took out his spite on the lady. From that day, it was said that Irene appeared in public sporting a serious black eye and although trying to maintain an upright pose, displayed an obvious limp.

An uneasy quiet settled over the town with the sheriff lumbering about snapping at people and displaying more of his earlier unforgiving traits as a rough Texas Ranger.

In this manner, he paid more frequent visits to Madame Beau's in such a desperate manner that it seemed he was intent on proving his manliness against any charge of the horns laid on him. He would indulge himself with one or many of the prostitutes in a single visit, staying until all hours in desperate demonstration of some kind of masculine indifference to his wife's behavior. There was no doubt he was a formidable man and proved he could consume great quantities of alcohol and at the same time satisfy any number of soiled doves.

However, the women tired of his aggressive advances and complained to Madame Beau that he was losing them other custom with his continuous demands. Madame Beau was forced to ask her guardian to step up and attempt to discretely advise the sheriff that he should desist. This task fell onto the broad shoulders of Mr. Oliver Langoustine, a French national who had been brought across by Madame Beau to act as protector for her establishment. He was affectionately known as "Shrimp" but the name in no way epitomized a representation of that small ineffectual creature. Built like a stone edifice, with a shaven head and solid proportions. His face was laced with scars that he had earned as a convict on a prison island off the shore of French Guiana known as Île du Diable more commonly called Devil's Island. Oliver said little and when he did his accent was so thick that his few words of English were barely comprehensible.

So when he approached the bellicose sheriff with the phrase, "No good, you go. No come 'ere." The sheriff roared with laughter, he was by this time well into his cups and with a floozy on each arm was not about to be deterred by a man he dismissed by considering him not only as a foreign but also a lowly immigrant.

"Hey, Shrimp," he called. "Go take a walk, will you?"

"No, you feenish," stressed the Frenchman. "You leef."

"I *leef*, imitated the sheriff. "What kind of language as that—*'you leef?'* No, buster, you're the one leaving, I'm busy here."

"You go," said Oliver threateningly. "Or I take."

With that, the Frenchman laid his broad hand on the sheriff's arm and attempted to pull him from his seat where he lounged with the two women. There is no doubt that all the past weeks of Joe Dunn's distress had built up in him and his meanness was an explosive bubble in his brain that was about to burst. The sheriff came up easily enough but fast and like a rocket he delivered a massive punch that sounded, so other clients have retold, as if a great hammer had slammed into a side of slaughterhouse beef.

The hardy Oliver was undimmed but thrown back a step by the sudden savage and unexpected assault. He lowered his scarred head and rolled his shoulders from side to side in the pose of a fighter who had learned his trade in the fiercest of rings.

Joe Dunn sneered at the Frenchman and called him out, challenging the man to try it on and best him if he could. Oliver obliged and with a swinging blow as if delivered from a mechanical arm, he landed one bunched fist as hard as a rock hammer on the side of the sheriff's jaw. With blood drawn, Joe saw that he was into a fight with a tough character and not one of the lowly disposition he had imagined.

They battled in the middle of Madame Beau's parlor, trading blow for blow like two prehistoric Neanderthals forty thousand years before. Each strike shook the room and sounded as if it were the hits of an axe as it strikes the tree. Blood flowed from both men but there was little sign of either surrendering such was their enormous strength.

Chairs were broken, tables overturned, mirrors and glasses smashed, and uneasy clients thrown to one side. Never before had such a show of fisticuffs been witnessed except in epic bare-knuckle contests where the Marquess of Queensbury ruled, only here no such law applied.

It ended only when the sheriff caromed across the room to where his gun belt hung beside his hat on the rack next to the door. In one swift move, Joe pulled out his forty-five and placed one bullet accurately between Oliver's eyes. Like a great tree felled in the forest Oliver tipped over and slowly fell as stiff as a post to the fine wool-carpeted floor.

Joe Dunn wiped his bloody nose across the back of his wrist, pulled a wry twist of his split lip and said, "Settled his danged hash but still not a bad show for a dago." Saying that, he next did the most intemperate thing and grabbed Madame Beau by the neck of her décolletage and booted her from the room.

Unwavering in her devotion to The Wichita Kid, Irene used a signal lamp in her room window to tell The Kid when the coast was clear and her husband was reveling in the arms of one of his ladies of the night. Her lover would enter the hotel through the rear door while Billy Jay kept the clerk quiet and watched for any interruption to the couple's tryst.

Seeing his true love's beaten body on these occasions infuriated The Kid and he vowed revenge for the sheriff's cowardly act of brutality and thought to devise a scheme to demonstrate Joe's ineptitude for office and shame him before the town.

"Why so thoughtful?" asked Irene, safely

enclosed in the cradle of his arms as they lay together in the bed with their recent lovemaking leaving them warm and contented.

The Kid wrinkled his nose. "It's nothing, give it no mind."

Irene shook her head. "You're always doing that, hiding your thoughts. I wonder sometimes what goes on inside your head."

The Kid turned to look at her and brushed a strand of golden hair from her forehead. "What are you doing with me, even so. You had all them fancy attributes that I never knew, a proper upbringing, a fine education, the best of everything and here I am just a down-at-heel no-account thief and you a lady with class and manners. What the devil are you doing with me?"

She ran a finger down his cheek. "It seems to make no sense at all, does it?" She shrugged. "I just know how I feel that is all."

"Sure," he agreed, staring into the darkness of the room. "That's it, how I feel too. Maybe it don't matter what clothes you wear it's what's underneath that matters. All I know is I care for you, Irene. Damned if I know why, but you is the brightest and best I have ever known."

"Have you known that many then?" she teased with a twinkle in her eye.

The Kid smiled at her. "Not so many, I bet you got a better score."

Irene compressed her lips. "They were certainly not anything like you."

"That's a given." He chuckled.

"You're not as rough and ready as you make out,

Ben. You're more gentle than all the so-called gentlemen I've shared company with."

The Kid raised his eyebrows in faint disbelief. "That so?"

"It is, the society fellows I knew back home were not so different as many of the roughnecks here, they had money and fine tailoring to disguise them that's all. The rich may live in a different world but they are human just the same and their tastes and inclinations are not so different if you're a banker or a bartender."

"I find that hard to believe."

"All I know is you've changed me," she confessed. "I was wild and spoiled I think, hard to believe I had no purpose but my own indolent pleasures."

The Kid frowned. "Changed you, how does that work?"

"I want something else now, something steady, stable. I feel like I fit here beside you and have no desire for anything else."

He bent his head close and his lips brushed hers. Irene sighed and swung her arm around his neck to bring him closer and they kissed.

He pulled away. "One thing that beats me is how you could marry a knothead like Joe Dunn."

Irene twisted her lip. "That was merely because I knew it would upset my father. He is such a proper fellow, strait-laced and distant. I guess it was meant to be a way of shocking him. You see they had such plans for me, it would be the sort of wealthy man with a high standing in society that I should marry. They wanted my life to fit into the expected niche of tea parties and balls and I just balked at the notion and coming here was my opportunity to escape, it was rebellious I know but I was desperate."

"How about the rest of your family?"

"My mother? Well she follows in a similar path to Father and plays at being a queenly duchess in the all the respected salons of Boston. My elder sister is already a part of it, married off to a stockbroker and with two little ones in tow. Their life is fine dresses and jewelry and always wondering how they look."

"And here you are in bed with a low-down villain, that's quite some show of rebellion."

She affectionately nibbled his ear. "And I love every minute of it."

He mused a moment, deep in thought. "It cannot last though you must be prepared."

"Don't say that." She frowned. "Why, we shall run off together and be nothing but happy."

"There ain't a fine day that don't come with some cloud in it at some time."

"Yes, there will be troubles, there always are but we shall have each other to rise above them."

"For me," he said, drawing her close. "I can't see much further than right now and I aim to make the most of it."

"Here, here," she breathed, wrapping her hot body around him and with her long limbs drawing him close in a tightening hold. "So stand and deliver, my handsome highwayman."

According to all reports, Ma Weesley was a reclusive woman who dwelled with her deputy son in a single-story house outside of town that had been invested by her loving son with every modern appurtenance possible. A woman not much given to any show of kindness or generosity, she accepted all her devoted son could give her with the expectation that she believed was her right. After all had she not delivered her child with all the painful trials and tribulations of birth and had she not raised him as a single mother after the father had left, in all probability, it was said, to escape her tiresome demands and critical admonitions.

A thin graceless woman of unlikeable looks with gaunt graying features and a loss of hair that gave her pinched face the decayed look of a month-old orange. She had no friends to speak of and any conversation she might indulge in with an unlucky passerby often turned to criticism or sharp remand.

Only her son lighted her life and she made sure that he was permanently tied to her apron strings.

She preferred her isolation and spent her days constantly cleaning her treasured display of china figurines that filled every corner of the house. Small shepherdesses sat on idealized tree stumps, owls peered from leafy branches or jolly farmers danced a jig with their buxom wives. Each gleaming ceramic shone in the darkness of the rooms highlighted with random blobs of color that gave them an air of unreality. These small additions were to her a life that she had no knowledge of, and yet fulfilled a fantasy of taste and simplicity that endowed her home with an invented flavor of discrimination. It also kept her busy with daily dusting.

When The Wichita Kid came calling, he took her by surprise. Flustered, for she was unused to visitors, she answered the door and saw him standing there with a very large and heavy sack in his arms.

"How do, ma'am," he said, puffing with exertion and setting down the sack to remove his hat. "Your son, Art, told me to bring you this."

She eyed him suspiciously. "You know my boy?"

"Indeed I do, a fine upstanding servant of the law. It seems he is unable to come himself, being in duty pursuing some reprobates at present, so he asked me if I would deliver this statue to you."

"*Statue?*" She frowned.

"Indeed, I am to bring it over and place it somewhere where you might admire it."

"I suppose you'd best come in then, though I don't know what that boy will get up to next. A

statue of all things! A fine thing, what am I to do
with a statue as big as this?"

"It is an angel, ma'am. A divine figure standing
in a peaceful pose with a finger raised heav-
enwards."

Ma Weesley screwed up her already screwed-up
face even more. "Sounds more fitting to a graveyard
than a house."

If she did but know it the gift was in fact the very
same, an item of remembrance removed only that
day by The Kid from the local cemetery.

"Well, bless me," cried The Kid, struggling in
with the heavy package and resting it gratefully in
the center of the parlor floor as he looked around.
"Will you look at all these splendid works of art?"

"You like them?" asked the woman in disbelief.
"Not many folks do."

The Kid took his time studying the collection
that filled every corner. "So delicate," he sighed in
admiration. "So pretty, you have a damned good set
of these tiny figures here. If you'll excuse me
saying."

"Yes, sir," she agreed, being somewhat won over
by his appreciation of her assortment of figurines.
"They are my babies; I treasure them above all
else."

"Except for your fine son, I'll be bound."

"Oh, him," she said dismissively. "He has no
appreciation, more trouble than he's worth, I can
tell you."

"Dearie me, is that so?"

"It is, I have to say. No consideration for my
frailty, you know? Expects me to wash his clothes

and tend his needs like a baby, it is more than a body can stand sometimes."

The Kid was considerate. "That is most unmannerly indeed. Why, I would not allow my poor mother to have to carry a load like that, I can tell you."

"Your mother is in poor shape?" she asked with the raised eyebrows of a curious gossip.

The Kid downturned his lips and squinted as if tears were about to fall. "Sadly departed this mortal coil now, ma'am. I miss her so, she was dear to my heart. She really was."

"I wish my boy were like that, appreciative of all I do for him."

"Tell me, ma'am, would you like to see this gift of his, then tell me where you would like it placed?"

"I suppose we had better," she replied. "Though Lord knows where it will go."

With that The Kid whisked off the canvas sack and displayed the graveyard relic. Ma Weesley walked around it, studying the angelic vision with a deep frown upon her brow.

"I don't like it," she said. "Don't like it at all, too morbid by half."

"Sometimes," said The Kid. "Sometimes unpleasant things are best kept covered up."

Ma Weesley opened her mouth to reply but in a single swift movement, The Kid brought the sack down over her head and caught her around the waist and lifted her over his shoulder.

She squealed in surprise and then began bellowing blue murder in a muffled shriek.

"Now you calm down, lady," said The Kid as he

made for the door. "We ain't going to harm you, just keep you safe for a while."

Billy Jay had arrived at the gate with their two ponies and after lashing the sack securely, The Kid tossed it with Ma Weesley inside over one of the saddles.

"Hold on here a minute," he said to Billy Jay as he headed back for the house.

"She sure is making a kerfuffle," complained his partner.

"She'll run out of steam soon enough," said The Kid, hurrying back inside.

In the parlor he took a sheet of paper from inside his jacket and pinned it over the pointing finger of the heavenly angel, then left leaving the front door wide open.

A handwritten receipt still exists from one Jacob Von Larst, a local prospector, who rented a shack in one of the Palo Duro canyons to The Kid at about this time and we can only suppose that this is where they carried Ma Weesley. Having ensconced her there with water and supplies and the warning that nothing lay nearby only many miles of arid land and that to escape was to mean certain death, they left her with the promise that she would be returned to her home soon enough.

They then returned to Big Tar to await the outcome.

Art returned home after his day's labor to find the strange sight of the funeral statue in his mother's parlor with a note attached. After desperately searching the whole house in vain he rode as fast as he could back into town and the sheriff's office.

"They done took my ma!" he bleated on entry, waving the sheet of paper. "Look here, it says, if I don't find five hundred dollars, they would leave her to die on the Palo Duro."

"Who did?" roared Joe Dunn.

"Them two lousy thieving varmints, The Wichita Kid and that half-breed partner of his, see they signed the damned letter."

The sheriff snatched the sheet and studied it, his jaw working furiously with rage.

"There ain't nothing out there but dust and snakes," he snarled. "We'll get us that Indian, what's his name, Two Horse something?"

"Two Horse Rides."

"Yeah, that's him he knows that area all over. He'll know where she is, go get him, Art."

"If they've hurt her," wailed Art. "I mean, she's a poor old woman, who in their right mind would do such a thing?"

"Just go get the Indian and don't worry, boy, we'll get her back for you."

"I pray we do, Sheriff. I couldn't bear to be without her tender care."

With that he left at the run to go and find the old Indian who lived in a shabby tin-roofed dugout on the outskirts of town.

Two Horse Rides was of Apache blood, and as a young warrior had raided with Victorio, and was now of an age where he had seen most of the unpleasant things that had been done to his people and only wanted a quiet life. He manufactured his own *tiswin*, the corn-brewed alcohol Indian's preferred and drank himself to dull extinction regularly with the beverage. A shrunken man with features cratered and lined by time and searing sun, his hovel was often oppressively hot inside and with a rather rank smell due to a urine problem that had beset him in old age.

When Art came running up, the old man was lounging idly outside and avoiding the dense air inside. He rested on blankets with a long-stemmed a corncob pipe between his seamed lips and a mug of *tiswin* within reach. It took some arguing to convince the Indian, albeit with the promise of fifteen dollars for his services, to undertake the task.

Next morning, Two Horse Rides packed his mule with gourds of his favorite liquor and presented himself to the sheriff ready to scout for the mission.

Joe Dunn was loath to leave town, especially for the miserable harpy he knew Art's Ma to be and here it was that the change was made that later brought disarray to The Kid's plans.

The Wichita Kid's intention was to wait until the sheriff had left town and then to take all he could steal in the Travis Transcontinental and Loan Bank, whose offices were situated directly opposite the jailhouse. Such an audacious act in the middle of town, he hoped, would shame the sheriff in front of the whole place and so pay back the grievous assault he had laid on Irene.

But the sheriff cried off.

The continuing irritation had festered in Joe's brain; his state being such that his wife and her dalliance with the outlaw had aggravated his already sensitive frame of mind with all calumny she had heaped upon him. The insult was profound and rubbed against Joe's picture of himself as a manly figure of righteous order and a stud without comparison.

They were not far out of town when Joe Dunn complained about sickness and moaned he was in pain and that his stomach was in uproar with the flying trots so he begged off the rescue attempt leaving Art with the Indian and two other deputies. Art whose frenetic behavior had already reached such a level of excited anguish over his kidnapped Ma left the sheriff convinced he was doing the right thing. A search through the dusty sunbaked ravines and canyons of Palo Duro was bad enough but having a neurotic deputy along weeping and wailing over his lost mother was tantamount to walking barefoot through cactus. The place in Spanish meant "Hard Stick" and Joe was sure he needed that particular rod to his back like he needed a second nose.

In this way Joe Dunn, feigning illness, turned about and returned to town.

Mighty relieved at avoiding the tiresome trip he removed himself promptly to the saloon for a refreshing glass of cold beer and settled in to an afternoon of drinking with his posse friends who usually spent their days similarly engaged.

Later editorials in the *Columbus Gazette* told how events played out.

Without any expectation of trouble once they had witnessed Joe Dunn's departure, The Kid and Billy Jay rode into town. Dismounting outside the Travis International and Loan Bank they tied off at the hitching rail and with a satisfied glance up and down the deserted street made to enter the bank. Once inside they moseyed casually up to the clerk's cage and presented him with a withdrawal notice in the form of two Colt pistols. Unfortunately at just this moment one of Sheriff Dunn's deputies passed by outside on his way to the saloon and glanced through the bank window.

He could not believe his eyes as he recognized the two inside both with guns drawn and he set off at the run to advise the sheriff.

The bank clerk was most amenable and handed over dollar bills with alacrity.

"You ain't going to shoot me, is you?" he asked nervously.

"I reckon not," supplied The Kid, leaning casually against the counter. "Just be sure to tell the sheriff who it was broke in and took all the money directly across the road from him."

With a sack full of cash in hand, Billy Jay grinned at him and said, "Well, that was real easy."

With a tip of the hat to the nervous cashier, The Kid headed for the door but Billy Jay was blocking his way. "Come on, move it along," he complained.

Billy Jay stood frozen. "I thought you said he was out of town."

The Kid glanced over his shoulder to see that the street opposite held a line of five grim looking men with stars on their chests and pointing rifles at him.

"Get back in the bank," ordered The Kid and both of them stepped quickly back inside.

"We going to make a fight of it?" asked Billy Jay.

The Kid felt the sudden draft at his back and then heard the click of hammers being drawn on two shotguns. Joe Dunn and one of his deputies stood holding leveled shotguns with the back door standing wide open behind them.

"Try it, Kid," threatened the sheriff through clenched teeth. "I'd sure like you to try."

"Ain't no way out, Billy Jay," advised The Kid, raising his hands. "They got us cold."

CHAPTER FIVE

Tentatively Irene entered the sheriff's jailhouse. "I would like some time with Ben," she pleaded nervously.

Joe Dunn eased back in his chair; he was facing away from her looking into a corner of the room and the disdain showed all too evidently on his face.

"And why should I allow that?"

The sheriff rocked slightly in his office chair allowing an unfortunate squeal like nails on a slate to fill the room. They were in his outer office, a foyer that gave way to the cells through a connecting door and it was dark inside the room and smelled of oiled leather and smoldering cinders from the pot-bellied stove, there was the bloom of warm coffee in the room coming from an enameled pot sitting on the stove. Aging wanted posters and civic notices were pinned to the wall beside a chained rack of rifles and shotgun and a boxed pendulum clock that ticked noisily.

Irene was appearing as supplicant, standing

before him with hands clasped one in the other before her and biting her lower lip nervously. "Because I'm asking you, Joe."

The sheriff turned to look at her, his ugly face impassive. He shrugged. "So what you going to say to him?"

"Just share some time is all."

"He's heading for a rope's end, Irene. He don't want no company."

"Can't you send him to prison instead?"

"He robbed the bank and killed someone, Irene. Shot down a young man, Tom Hard, the stagecoach guard. There were witnesses that saw him kick the dead body afterward, now that's some special kind of spite, don't you think?"

"I have money, you know it, Joe. I'll pay if you'll amend the sentence," she begged desperately. "I'll recompense the family, pay the witnesses, pay the stage company, I'll even pay you."

"And what would that do?" he said, swiveling the chair with its annoying squeal. "That would set the standard, then every dumb ass with a gun would think he could come in here to rob and steal and get away with it as long as he has some cash money to hand." He shook his head. "I don't think so. The Kid is a killer and people saw him do it, it's a clear-cut case. Besides, I ain't taking no bribe money from the likes of you."

She paused, then drew a ragged breath. "What about the Baranquillo brothers?"

He froze momentarily, the glitter in his eyes sharp as he peered at her across his desk. "What do you know about that?"

It was a story that The Kid had told her and one that she had held in reserve for just such a moment.

"I know that they were two Mexicans working over on the Simons place and you went there to see them off."

"Sure, I did, they was illegal, I sent them on their way."

"Then how is it that Mr. Baranquillo turned up six months later saying his sons had never arrived home?"

Joe spread his hands innocently. "How the hell should I know?"

"That's not the story I heard," she said with a touch of venom in her voice. "No, I heard that Simons upset you somehow and you meant to pay him back. Didn't he confront you in the street one time and tell you to your face to leave those two Mexicans alone. That you were no longer a Texas Ranger and should stop behaving like one. I believe those two boys are still on that ranch somewhere, out there in a patch of ground lying buried under flattened earth."

Joe pouted and raised indifferent eyebrows. "Believe what you like, they is gone. Look, Irene, I'm sheriff here, I represent the law and folks in this town don't want to see nothing or hear a thing about what I do, just so long as I get it done. That's all they care about."

"But that's still murder just the same."

"So, you say. If you're accusing me then where's your evidence, all you got is hearsay?"

"Can I go see Ben, please?"

"Aw, hell," puffed the sheriff, tiring of it all. "Go ahead, you got five minutes."

Irene hurried around his desk and over to the connecting door.

"One thing," said Joe, with a warning edge to his voice. "Once this is done, we're through I hope that's understood. You get on the stage, and you get out of here, disappear. I don't give a damn where you go, I don't want to see you around here no more or, you know, I just might not take it too kindly. We clear on that?"

She nodded acquiescence, not wanting to make a reply that would send him into any anger and spoil her chance at seeing The Kid.

She opened the heavy door that swung easily on oiled hinges and went on through.

"Ben," she whispered.

He looked up at her, a faint glimmer of a smile showing on his lips, "Irene, why it's real good to see you."

She rushed forward, pressing her face up against the bars. "How did this happen?"

"Ach! It just did, that's all."

"But why, Ben, why, right now, when we have so much between us?"

"It's the way of things when you do what I do. I liked this life, Irene. I never knew you would walk into it one day."

She shook her head in despair. "How can you want this, I don't understand?"

"Why am I like I am?" The Kid said, sitting down on the bunk with his clasped hands between his knees and looking at Irene through the bars. "I'll tell you."

In the corridor outside the cell Irene's face crumpled in despair and she clutched at the bars desperately with both hands.

"It's like this," he began. "They had the preacher come see me the other day, I didn't want him, but it turns out he was a reasonable man. You know, someone you could talk to, not a body all concerned with sin and damnation like most of them. I asked him the very same question, why and why now, and he told me this story and I guess it figures real well. Leastways I can understand it, see it's like when a farmer comes out seeding his field. He has this sack full of corn and walks the rows tossing the seeds out by the handful. Most goes into the acreage but some of it ends up along the borders, like outside the tilled ground. Well, I'm like that. I get to be raised in that spot alongside the road, where the wagon tracks have dug their grooves and pushed up a ridge and it's all poor soil. You got rocks in there and weeds and briars, now that corn can set down roots but it ain't in good earth so it still grows up, forces its way through and for a while it shines.

"But soon enough the danged thorns and wild-flowers come crowding in and bury it over. The rest of the field flourishes and you got a crop of grain getting all gold and ripe in the sun. 'Cept them that had a hard start finds it difficult to make a go of it, they wants to survive so they struggle to be what they're meant to be but the trash around them have other ideas. When you got a bad beginning you tend to wither, now that's a natural law and it's how I get to end up in here waiting on a hanging rope."

"But you have someone that loves you now, it could have been different," Irene said, tears forming at the corner of her eyes. "I love you so much."

The Kid smiled. "Me too but it's just a step too late, I guess. You're my sweetheart, Irene, can't say no less and I'm glad we got what we did. Maybe if it had been in earlier times, who could say how it might have turned out."

Irene's knuckles whitened with her grip on the bars. "What can we do? I know you can shed those old ways."

"My pappy raised me to rob and steal, my ma attended mostly to herself and a bottle like she learned to do from her loneliness. I never knew anybody care for me like you do, honey. I come out like that and learned the trickiest way to be, how to be sly and cunning and when that failed then to follow the gun. You do what you can to survive no matter what it costs."

Irene sighed. "I have never known anyone like you."

"That's 'cos you're in that field, you're all golden and straight and will do precious things. You growed up on chosen ground."

"It seems so unfair."

"Maybe so, but who said it has to be fair, only suckers with some misguided virtues that's who. *Fair!*" he spat. "There ain't nothing that's fair."

"Unlucky then," she modified.

"That's more like it, you throw the dice and play the hand you're given and it pans out how it will."

"But why now, just when we have found each other?"

"We found each other, ain't that enough."

"No," she sobbed. "I want more, I want all of it."

"You already got a whole heap, Irene. More than you can handle, it's all there waiting on you."

"It doesn't feel like that at all."

"Not right now but you'll see."

"I don't want to lose you, Ben."

"Shame to say it but you lost me the minute I was born. It's a sad fact and I wish I could change it but that's the way it is."

She sighed and then leaned forward a light of eagerness suddenly lighting her eyes, "I've sent for my father's lawyer, he's the best there is and when he gets here, we'll see this charge overturned I'm sure of it."

The Kid shook his head. "Won't happen, they got me here on a killing dead to rights. It's plain and simple and won't change no matter what fancy lawyer speaks his piece. I'm bound to go, you'd best accept that, Irene."

"I don't want to." She broke down with tears streaming down her cheeks. "I don't want to."

"This is the frontier, girl, where it's wild and dangerous. It's free too, Lord knows it's free and I been like that. Short, sweet and free I guess, and all the more sweet by knowing you for this short spell."

Joe Dunn appeared in the corridor behind her, his looming shape stopping out the light from the doorway. "You had your minute, Irene," he growled.

"Lord knows why I give you that, but your time is up now, so come you away."

He took her arm to pull her away, but she clung onto the bars not willing to leave and with an annoyed shake of his head, the sheriff grabbed her around the waist in his brawny arm and easily forced her free.

"I'll always love you, Ben Downs," she cried out as Joe carried her bodily down the corridor. "Always, Ben, always."

"Shut your mouth," rumbled Joe. "Fancy dame with less morals than an alley cat. I should put you in a sack and drown you."

The Kid was left with only the echo of her words before the sheriff slammed shut the connecting door. He hung his head sadly and then turned to look up at the patch of clear blue sky he could see through the small-barred window high up in the cell wall.

Early next day, with the sun barely raised but showing as a silver disk through thinning cloud while the tree line below was lost in milky wreaths of departing mist, the people gathered. They came quietly like silent ghosts making not a sound but appearing only in gray form as they gathered together.

The tree was large and black with its leafless branches spreading out in a stark pattern against the pale sky. It was a solitary place, and the tree grew on a slight rise, it was a dead tree struck at some earlier time by lightning and never recovered so the bark was burned and blackened. From a single broad limb hung the two cord nooses that hung unmoving and remained still in the lifeless air.

They brought out The Kid and Billy Jay with irons on their wrists and ankles leaving them hobbled and unable to walk freely. Around them were gathered the sheriff's deputies, all armed with rifles and grim dispositions. The crowd of silently voyeuristic townspeople stood around in a loose semi-circle kept in check by the deputies.

"Howdy, folks," called The Kid cheerfully, attempting to put a lighter frame on the event. "How y'all doing?"

"Way to go, Kid," called a voice from the crowd.

"I sure ain't going far this day," joked The Kid.

"No, you ain't," sneered the sheriff, pushing both men roughly forward.

The Kid spotted the concerned face of his brother in the crowd. "Donny, good to see you."

Don shook his head sadly, his face pale and worn.

"Yeah," growled the sheriff. "You step out here, Don Downs. Come on, come forward. I got a task for you."

Tentatively, Don stepped away from the others. "What is it you want?"

"Well," said the sheriff, vindictiveness evident in his tone. "You say you is a law-abiding man and you had nothing to do with your brother's misdeeds, ain't that so?"

"I fear it is," Don agreed and then turning to

The Kid he said. "Oh, brother, why did it have to turn out this way?"

The Kid smiled. "I done what I done and it ain't no skin off my nose."

"Stand aside and wait here," said the sheriff, brushing Don away. "Put them ropes on them now," he ordered his deputies.

The Kid turned to Billy Jay as the noose was pulled over his head and tightened at the neck. "Sorry about this, Billy Jay. You been a good friend and a true partner for sure, if I misled you in any way, I'm truly sorry."

"See you on the other side," replied his companion, his face remaining impassive as he too was roped up.

"I'd shake your hand if I could," said The Kid, raising his manacled wrists. "But take it as read."

"So long, pal," answered Billy Jay.

"So here we go," rumbled Sheriff Joe Dunn, loudly playing at rough performer as he brought Don forward by tugging on his sleeve. "Now is your time, Don. You got the job of raising these two thieving killers up."

"*What!*" Don gasped. "Never, no, he is my kin, I can do no such thing."

"It's the law," rumbled the sheriff, leaning threateningly over Don. "You take the rope's end and if you is any kind of lawful citizen you'll play your part and see judgment carried out. See, I got my doubts about you and I'm thinking you got more of a part in this than you claim. Might be that you should be standing there next to your brother. Bless me, I don't see why not."

"I won't—I can't," said a round-eyed Don.

"You'll do it," the sheriff whispered in his ear and Don felt the hot fetid breath on his cheek as if the very devil himself had risen from hell and was offering him choice. "Or I promise you'll be going down next to them."

"No, no," whined Don. "Please don't make me do this."

"Get it done," barked the sheriff, buffeting the man hard on the shoulder.

"Best do it, brother," said The Kid in a calm voice. "Or this mean pig will see ill of you."

Don was forced around to where the rope's ends hung down and with shaking hand he reached out and grasped the one belonging to Billy Jay. "I'm real sorry," he said in a broken voice. "God forgive me."

Billy Jay made no answer but only steadied himself, expecting the jerk of the rope. Don pulled the loose end over his shoulder and turned away.

"Get it done," shouted the sheriff, with one hand on the grip of his pistol. "Right now or I'll plug you for the miserable cur dog you are."

Don began to walk away, tightening the rope and hauling it across his back as if he were a haulage ganger working on a freight load. Slowly Billy Jay rose up, his feet struggling to touch the ground and relieve the tightening noose. Don's feet were slipping on the grass and he was almost bent double as he struggled away heaving on the rope.

"That's it, go on," barked the sheriff. "We got him lifted off now."

Billy Jay was beginning to make gagging noises and his features reddening as he swayed higher.

"Damn you, Joe Dunn, you ain't worth a plugged nickel," snarled The Kid.

The sheriff smiled slowly with smug satisfaction. "You're next, sucker."

Billy Jay was now swinging at the rope's end some three feet off the ground as a sweating Don struggled, his face swollen and the breath panting in his chest.

"Tie it off," the sheriff ordered the watching deputies. "Go help him wrap it around the trunk."

Willingly, almost gladly, two eager deputies rushed forward, leaning their rifles against the tree trunk as they took the rope from Don and with a savage pull that hoisted Billy Jay higher began to circle the trunk. Billy Jay was kicking now, his face changing color to a bluish tinge as the air was choked from him.

The deputies had the rope tied around the tree trunk and then with an almighty crack the dead limb supporting the ropes suddenly snapped and fell away and Billy Jay came tumbling to the ground.

A great sigh rose from the watching townsfolk and the sheriff let loose with a curse, "Hot damn! Can you believe it?"

He looked down at the ragged end of broken timber, splintered and stark white against its dark bark and at the squirming figure of Billy Jay as he lay on the ground gasping for air like a fish out of water.

The Kid burst out laughing. "Woo-hee! Lookee here, the sheriff can't even arrange a hanging, let alone keep his wife. You surely is one miserable excuse for a man, Joe Dunn."

"Find another branch," fumed the sheriff, with bunched fists held tightly by his side. "Give me a good one and we go again."

As the ropes were laced over another firmer limb, The Kid looked around hoping to find Irene in the crowd but he could see no sign of her. It emptied the already hollow place in his chest and he was sorry for it but sure that she could not face to see his demise and was hiding herself in some sorrowful place. It was better this way, he thought and gazed around at the misty distance beyond the rise where the trees fell away into a gray haze and the distant mountains stood faded and solid on the horizon as if cut from card. There was no stopping it now; certain death was approaching as fast as a Brahma bull released from the chute. He was glad though, glad he had been here and glad that he had known Irene, that had been worth all the rest.

"Lift 'em up," bawled the sheriff. "Let's see 'em swing."

There was no more to it The Kid thought as the noose tightened, his string had finally run out.

A PICNIC WITH THE CONFEDERATE DEAD

CHAPTER ONE

The level clearing crests perfect pastureland and with its lush grasses it slopes away from the flat land into the surrounding woods that lay in the hollow below. Woods untouched for years that are full of variety and color, ancient oaks grow here beside ash, leafy elm, and slender beech. Buttercups are spread across the pasture like yellow stars and cast a gentle carpet over the fresh green grassland rolling away to where blossoming blueberry and cranberry bushes flourish in sentinel rows along the boundary of the forest.

The day is slightly overcast and brings a certain gloom inside the forest but even so the Lyons family has decided on the picnic.

Normally theirs is a quiet and stately Indiana home, built in solitary yet rural splendor to the north and east of this, their neighbor's farmland and set beside one of the races running down from the St. Joseph River. A two-story rambling clapboard building raised over a hundred years before but now showing its age with white paintwork sadly in some need of repair around shutters and small square-paneled windows. It is a sight that distresses Father and yet the war's exigencies had meant that provision of certain necessaries is in short supply.

Father brings the open-top carriage around to the front of the house for the ladies while he and James will ride to the picnic spot of choice on saddle ponies. James's young sister Ellen can handle the carriage horse and Mother and Aunt Jenny will sit inside the gig with Grandpa. It is a little cramped with all that they carry but they manage with only a slight fluster of arrangement from the ladies.

Their destination is known as the Lower Field and is a part of the large hundred-and-twenty-acre Joshua Farm. The owner, Mr. Levi Joshua, is away at the fighting since earlier that year having raised a company and called it, not surprisingly, The Joshua Brigade. He is that kind of fellow, a flamboyant individual and unable to leave his connection hidden from any grand gesture without an overly demonstrative show. Right now, by letters received from the enlisted son of his cowman, they are believed to be in Pennsylvania and chasing Rebels wildly across the whole state.

As Mr. Joshua was as far away from North Indiana as the rest of the distant war and it had been decided that being the Easter weekend the Lyons family should have a short holiday and celebrate with a picnic on the missing owner's land. Not that he would have objected, for although a bit of a blowhard and somewhat larger than life he was not generally considered an unkind man. His farmland covered sixty-three acres of forest and brush with fifty-nine left for agriculture so the temporary use of a corner would not be missed.

The Lyons family had all attended church service that morning in the North Bend Chapel and the minister, Parson Villiers, had taken time from his sermon to read out the latest lists of those who had succumbed or were reported missing. Mother thought this a little unnecessary on this particular holy day but as the reverend had insisted; "Our Savior died on such a day for our benefit so let us remember those that give their lives so boldly in honor of our great and noble cause."

Parson Villiers was not a local but a Northern gentleman from Washington and, as mother pointed out, his son was at present riding in the train with General Grant as one of his headquarters officers. So she believed that he had a vested interest in calling on the Lord in such a manner. Mother could be overly strict in her observances sometimes.

———

Once the horses were tethered and the two ladies escorted down from the gig, Grandpa has to be eased from his place with tender care. He was a very frail ancient with pale wrinkled skin that lay over his bones like tissue paper and a long white and pointed beard rising from his prominent chin. The chin is so prominent that it almost rises up to meet his beak of a nose that drips incessantly and Mother will have to wipe continually. His age was unsure although Mother insists he is nigh on one hundred and five years old and a man who in the past had played a great part in the Revolutionary War. She assures everyone that he had in fact created the battle cry "*No Taxation Without Representation.*" Whether he had or not was immaterial as his mind now wanders and only occasionally will he spout some relevant idiom concerning that distant period of the nation's history.

Young Ellen, the sprightly sixteen-year-old daughter, pays close attention to the horses as for such she holds a tender affection. She pets and strokes them incessantly and makes sure that they munch contentedly on the sweetest grass. She is a pretty little thing with sky-blue eyes and pink cheeks brightened by her outdoor life on horseback. With her rolls of lustrous blonde hair that she keeps in place with a blue straw bonnet she can appear either doll-like or tomboy by turn depending on mood. A mimic and a tease, she will pester her elder brother James unmercifully whenever she holds the upper hand, as she often has ever since their earliest times together.

James, for his part, attempts the role of wistful nineteen-year-old daydreamer who fancies himself something of an artist, being both a poet and nature lover. His attention on this day is far away from his present environment as he dreams of a certain young girl and the mere thought of her will bring a flush to his cheek. In display, he will habitually throw back his head and brush at his brown hair that is parted on one side but allowed to drape across his brow in what he considers a display of thoughtful consideration. Try as he might, the small mustache and beard at his chin is a feeble growth and yet he persists despite all that Ellen might jibe at this inadequate hirsute adventure with her sharply critical observations.

———

From the backs of the horses Father and James bring the rolled carpets and rugs for sitting on and spread them around the unfolded crisp white linen tablecloth. A wicker chair has been brought for Grandpa and he is settled there, quite vague and unsure of where he is but happy still in his ignorance. A low stool is set for Mother and she spreads her portly form under her wide dresses, fusses with her bonnet and shawl and settles rather as a hen might rest upon a nest of eggs. Beside her and never far away is her younger sister Aunt Jenny, a small and rather mean-faced diminutive woman with tight, center-parted brown hair fastened at back in a bun and wearing a mournful black Bombazine dress. Self-effacing and bright-eyed she pays close attention to all that goes on around her but very rarely participates with more than a few carefully chosen words.

The rear of the gig holds the great woven wicker hamper; all of two feet deep and three wide and from it pours a veritable cornucopia of all that is necessary for the celebration. A cooked chicken, cold cuts of ham and cheese, wine and cider and a jug of strong Brandywine for Father. A baked apple pie, a bowl of syllabub, crusty bread fresh from the oven, cutlery and jugs, napkins, water and cups. There is even a macramé sack of gaudily painted hard-boiled eggs that Ellen has provided in celebration of the festival and each is named for them in small neat Spencerian script.

So they settle, each of them involved in their own and in the real world.

James demonstrates his academic knowledge by regaling them with the origin of the word "picnic" taken, he claims, from a French play entitled *Frères Pique-nicques* where the protagonists had an excessive abundance of food.

Ellen eats too fast and is complained at by her mother for doing so but the girl skips away sure of her status in the family circle and picks buttercups while gnawing on a wedge of cheese.

Grandpa eats little but sips on the jug with Father who carves up the chicken and enjoys great slices of moist breast meat.

Mother who complains of her digestion is finally coerced into a glass of cider and that brings a light into her eye. Her sister, Aunt Jenny, picks at her plate like a blackbird, a raven, or carrion crow and eats little so that no one can accuse her of any excess.

James who is entrenched in his role as lovesick poet also eats little but sighs often, hoping that someone may notice his distressed longing but nobody does, not even his sister.

The girl he loves to distraction is the person who has manufactured this feast and yet plays no part in its consumption. She is their colored serving girl Misty, a young, pretty, and hardworking girl, humble and quiet and in no way intrusive into the family's life. So inconspicuous in fact that she is barely noticed as she washes cleans and cooks, except that is by James, who has become enamored of her from afar. A forbidden love, of course, given the times and yet he yearns for the unobtainable with truly impossible zeal. How else might one be considered an artist unless defeat lingers somewhere in the background?

But who is this that comes?

Five men in the dusty gray of the Confederate army stand in shadow at the edge of the forest, they are quite still and interested as they observe the family group.

"Say?" asked the sergeant, Jubal. "Anybody know where we are?"

The two other soldiers dressed in uniforms lined at collar and cuffs with the red braid of artillerymen, take an interest and look around themselves.

"Looks like we're down in the woods," observes Private Linus, who, carrying a shovel over his shoulder and as not too bright he states the obvious.

"We was in a battle though," supplies a frowning artilleryman called Brack, standing somewhat at a loss with an Enfield rifle held by his side. He is the only one that is armed but he knows that he has no ammunition for the gun and it puzzles and embarrasses him. "Sarge, ask the captain, he must know where we are."

The captain is a figure standing slightly apart. He strikes a pose; one booted foot before the other and in true Napoleonic fashion one hand is placed inside the open buttons of his tunic. He is a man short in stature, a sallow-skinned drawn-featured white-haired and bearded man who wears a uniform with polished brass buttons, gold Austrian Knot braid on his sleeve and a saber at the red sash on his waist. His sweeping broad-brimmed hat bears a plumed feather in its band.

"Captain, sir," Jubal begins. "Forgive me asking, but what exactly is our position?"

"Form a steady line, boys. Stand ready by your cannon," mumbles the distracted captain, drawing his saber and standing stiffly with expressionless features that stare into some unknown distance. "Where's my good horse, Sergeant? I cannot be expected to command on foot."

"Sir," presses Jubal. "There ain't no horse, and there ain't no enemy. Lord know where we is, 'cos I sure as hell don't."

"No good axin' him," said the fifth member of the group, a Black man called Caesar who is dressed in a ragged frock coat and a buckled stovepipe hat. Caesar, not one to mince his words, is servant to the captain and therefore accepted on that basis as a regular member of the unit and his broad speech suffered with assurance.

"Why's that?" Jubal asks, frowning at the Negro.

Caesar taps a forefinger to his own coal-black temple. "'Cos he gone crazy, that's why."

"No, he ain't crazy."

"He's right," agrees a murmuring Brack. "He was already spouting out dumb things a week since. Cannon fire got to him, he ain't been right since them last barrages. Forty-seven cannon firing in sequence all day; do that to anyone. Surprised I ain't gone stupid myself."

"Nobody could accuse you of that," observes a sardonic Jubal.

"S'right though," says Caesar. "His brain be fuddled."

The captain, a man called Jesamine Riley Coultry, is a plantation owner who had suffered the severe loss a month before that has unnerved him; by report his house and property were burned down, his wife and children murdered by rampaging Union troops and his field slaves dispersed. The news has left him a broken man and when he is not weeping at night over his loss, he feels the great opening of a dark wound living inside himself. It is only the facade of duty that keeps his broken heart intact enough to function.

"What's that out there, Sergeant?" the captain asks, pointing his saber at the picnickers. "Some kind of enemy skirmish line?"

"No, sir. That's just common folk eating out, they don't mean us no harm."

"Very well," said the captain, his voice is airy and vague and comes from far away somewhere deep in the ashes of his mind. "We'll leave them be then although can't say I abide this fashion for non-combatants overlooking the battlefield. Smacks of an unsavory observation, one might say in the inappropriate manner of men secretly watching young ladies bathing, if you can grasp such a notion? Watching from cover, you understand? Hidden from view, behind bush or from tree limb."

"Yes, sir," agrees the sergeant with a querulously bemused smile.

"Distasteful," the captain continues with a deep frown crinkling his brow. "Such observations of pure young virgin flesh, not to be considered a gentleman's style, I should say. Round full bosoms and shiny bottoms washed fresh and pink from the bath. Should not be allowed, forbidden. That's right, it is not to be suffered."

He is breathing heavily and his pale skin flushed and Jubal wonders what he is implying by the rant. But then officers are a race apart and there is no telling what goes on in their minds.

"Yes, sir," said Jubal doubtfully. "What shall I tell the men?"

The captain puffs his cheeks and slides the saber back in its scabbard. "Tell them to be ready, man. The enemy will descend on us at any given moment. Be ready, always be ready. I shall sit under yonder tree and consider the placement of our defenses, Sergeant. See I am not disturbed."

"Very well, Captain, sir."

———

Misty, the serving girl, is coming from the house at the run; it is a fair lick so the sweat beads her brow. She bursts through the edge of the forest and heads for the group of picnickers bearing a large rolled umbrella.

"What's this?" cries Ellen with a small frown on her brow.

"It is Misty," observes Father.

"Indeed," adds his wife. "She brings my umbrella, I had forgotten it."

"Ah!" sighs lovelorn James, his eyes glossing as he sees the pretty young maid approaching. Quickly he sits up straight and tosses that errant lank of hair back in an extravagant gesture. James feigns interest in the book of poetry he always has to hand but secretly he watches the nubile young Misty from under lowered brows. How he burns for her in virginal fashion and in his imagination he enfolds and cossets her with thoughts of impressing sonnets upon her panting breast in some innocent and clandestine meet.

Breathless, Misty runs up to her mistress and with a small curtsy presents the folded umbrella. "Here you is, Mistress Lyons. I brung dis umbrelly."

"Bless you, child," says Mother. "I clear forgot, it will be a gracious respite from the hot sun."

There is no such sun on this overcast day but Mother treasures the paleness of her white skin above all else and knows it is a favored attribute amongst gentlewomen of her stature. It is mark among her society of a lady above common work and one who favors gentility with little else to concern herself above needlework and the maintenance of her household. As she has fulfilled her other duty, namely that of giving birth of her prodigy and what remains is a tranquil existence into the softer years of memory and satisfaction.

Perhaps one mission remains on her horizon and that is the successful marriage of her children to suitable partners and the production of grandchildren that she might cherish in her later years.

Misty stands, unsure if there is more required of her.

"You may run along now, child," dismisses Mother.

"Wait, Mother," says Father. "Might not the girl serve us as she is here?"

"Ach!" says Mother dismissively. "Surely this is a family affair, Father. A time for us to enjoy each other's company in seclusion for once."

"Remoteness is a delight giving quiet pleasure to the soul," adds Aunt Jenny in solemn remonstrance.

Just then Emily sweeps in and takes Misty by the hands, whirling her around in a playful circle. Of similar age they have known each other since childhood and although the difference in status is maintained still the two have a tender association akin to sisters.

"Lordy! Miss Emily, you done make me spin," cries Misty a broad grin of perfectly white teeth lighting her brown face as the two dance off amongst the buttercups.

"Look at that," says Father, smiling benignly. "I do believe that the two sweet girls are as alive and happy as a pair of gamboling foals. Such a joy, oh, such a joy to behold."

James suffers a bite of jealousy as he sees Emily clasping Misty's hand as they whirl across the pasture. He would clasp that hand to his breast and swear undying devotion if he could take his sister's place. This misplaced attention lives solely in a fantasy, for the forbidden prospect of any such association in reality is something that he maintains in mind alone and any attempt at reality would vanish the dream as if it were a puff of smoke.

It is an illicit craving and extends no further than soft thoughts and impressions written secretly on his romantic heart. For although it is not unknown for many young men in his position to take a serving girl in a sexual rite of passage, for James the inaccessibility of such a prize is beyond him. He is inexperienced in such carnal matters and it is doubtful that if the occasion ever should arise, in all probability he would fumble through the matter until it became an awkward shadow of the dream he has constructed.

Mother has opened her umbrella and Aunt Jenny holds it above in protective subservience, while fans are produced and fluttered against some imaginary heat.

"James, my boy," says Mother. "Will you perhaps read to us? I do so enjoy the sound of your voice at moments like this."

Emily and Misty are squealing noisily as they turn themselves about in dizzy circles on the slope and finally tumble to the ground to roll in the grass.

"Oh, dear!" cries Aunt Jenny, causing Mother to look up. "I trust they will not hurt."

"I despair!" says Mother crossly. "I really do. Father, that child of ours is misbehaving. This is not the conduct befitting a young lady; will you not reprimand her? Look there her skirts are in the dirt and her bonnet all awry."

"Ah, my love. They play that is all, let them enjoy. I fear that all too soon our little girl will be presented with the true onerous factors of existence."

"But no one will have her," cries a forlorn Mother. "Who would wed such a tiresome female? I swear she is more boy than girl the way she rampages about."

"Let them be, dearest. All in good time, all in good time."

Mother turns to her son in despair. "James, my boy, do you not agree that your sister is indeed too boisterous to ever find herself a suitable beau?"

James shrugs indolently; he has no interest or concern for his irritating sister. "She is a wanton child, Mother and will always behave as such."

He is haughty and dismissive for he feels no association with Emily beyond the mere fact that they occupy the same household.

———

"Look there," leers Brack, nudging Linus with his elbow. "Ain't that a pretty sight. My word, I tell you I'd like to step out with that young miss for a jig any day."

"Sure is pretty," agrees Linus, resting on his shovel.

"What you carrying that spade for?"

"I dunno," says Linus, looking down at the implement. "I think I was digging a trench."

"You don't know—you dummy. Hellfire, Linus, I reckon you only has half a brain I really do. Maybe you was set to bury the other half and that's why you has that thing."

Linus shakes his head. "No, I don't reckon so. I do 'member we was digging out some lunette placement for the parrot gun though I did find some body parts buried there. Must have been that last fight in the fall rain, them fellas died and was swamped over."

"Now there's a happy thought," says Brack, taking out his stubby pipe and thrusting it churlishly between his lips.

"They did look poorly though, Brack. Weren't nothing but skin and bone."

"That will have been infantry, just thank the Lord we ain't in that particular situation. Marching out in parade rows, one behind t'other to be shot to all hell and gone by ball and canister."

"Yessir, I do thank the Lord each and every night we ain't in the infantry."

"Amen to that."

———

Sergeant Jubal is crouched down on his haunches and watching the family and girls at play and recalling his own kin back home. His eye is wistful as he remembers days such as this when he and his brother would return with hunted jackrabbits hanging on a string. To cut the carcass skin and pull it off as one might a long jacket and prepare the meat for the cook fire. It saddens him to think of them still at home without him and a latent fear lives within him for his younger brother and that he might answer the call and go for a soldier. For now Jubal knows the full truth of soldiering and has seen the reality of warfare and all its false glory.

Jubal is a torn man, one side a brave and courageous soul and on the other a wary disbeliever in the value of it all. He has witnessed bravery beyond any call of mere duty, has seen youngsters offer up their bodies to take some abstract sacrifice set upon them by a distant command. Such passion was hard to witness and it ate at the forthrightness of his nature.

Yet he was obedient and prone to take direction as presented to him by better and more capable minds. His faith in the noble class was adamant and ingrained by long years of perceived inadequacy. Of limited schooling, he could read and write but only so far as to understand the written word without any expression or calculation of a sole concept higher that instruction. A simple man, he was happy with his lot within the military and had not actively sought advancement only reaching his promotion by default, as those above him had left their post for one reason or another.

Now he felt his duty to the others in his unit with some compassion and cared for them as he might have done his younger brother.

The Negro, Caesar, stands beside him and shuffles his weathered boots where the flapping soles and loose laces leave him uncomfortable. He watches the young Misty and thinks of the women in his own life, his mother and sister, now lost to him by the indifferent movement of the plantation's will. One sold away and the other sent to wait at table as the young girl before him.

His father had been a man beaten and driven so low that any ounce of resistance had been lost to him long before. Caesar could find no association with his father, with his gnarled hands and scarred back, who ground through each day in sullen silence. Rising each morning only to find his tools and then work the hours from dawn to dusk in the fields. The repressed violence his father owned against such injustice lived hidden within his breast and held no outlet except against those near to him and as such brought only fear and antipathy with it. Leaving the youngster Caesar with all too often a cracked head instead of a soft kiss and a brutal shove instead of a warm embrace.

Home for Caesar had been a broken-down wallow among the other slave cabins. A dark place within, a crudely fashioned table and stool over a beaten earth floor with scurrying rodents living amongst the cobwebs and sagging eaves of the roof. Immunity from sensibility had come with such a despairing existence and left Caesar with callousness equal to that of the masters that ruled him.

He spat a stream of spittle from between his teeth. "They sho' look like fine folk, don' they?"

Jubal nodded agreement, his thoughts still lost in his own hearth.

"Wouldn' mind me some o' them good things there," Caesar continued, studying the spread. "Y'all tink they might share some, Sergeant?"

"Well you can always go down there and ask them if you've a fancy."

"No, sir. Not me, they ain't likely to take kindly to the likes o' me."

"Nor any of us, Caesar, civilians don't take kindly to any military."

"Only 'cos they done all that taking of their horses and livestock."

"It's a fact," agreed Jubal. "We have quarter-master command to feed ourselves where we might."

TONY MASERO

"So, why don' you go down there and git some o' that fine foodstuffs."

Jubal shook his head. "I don't reckon so."

70

CHAPTER TWO

T he two girls sit giggling and exhausted on the slope, lying together and plucking the flowers around them in abandon. James's cautious glance rises and watches them from moment to moment as he scribbles in a notebook.

Father is attacking the cold roast chicken again slicing at its breast with a long kitchen knife. Aunt Jenny sips her glass as a bird might, tossing back her head to swallow. Mother squats immobile amongst her dresses with a vague faraway look in her eye and only awakens to wipe an errant drip from Grandpa's nose.

Grandpa sees everything through a glass dimly, the movement and color of his family around him appears distant and removed from his experience. If a thought occurs at all it is generally centered either on a bowel movement or appetite. The vague flutterings of his mind are gradually descending into the slow and abstract void that awaits the end of his days. His body is tired, the exhaustions of a well-used machine past its prime and progressively running down leaving him in a distracted state of daze.

His hooded eyes are glazed with a sheen like cataracts and the mind only focuses on a rising need at any given moment and then is as easily forgotten.

But in this obverse moment he sees things with an unknown clarity. Experiences from his distant youth that memory will scatter through the corridors of his failing mind and yet give prevalence to visions forbidden to others. He sees the soldiers standing watching them and frowns in recognition. They are so close to his own declining condition that like some childhood recall he envisages the troopers in a past that still lives within.

Chewing his toothless gums, he studies the Confederates and tries to ascertain their relevance. With one shivering hand, he indicates their presence.

"What is it, Father dear?" asks Mother, seeing his shaking finger. "Is something wrong?"

Distracted, Grandpa glances across at her. "Militiamen?" he murmurs.

"No, Papa." She smiles fondly. "There are no militiamen here, only trees and bushes. You are dreaming, my dear."

But as with all ancients, the moment is impressed on his immediacy and he jabs the air with his finger frustrated that the words will not come. It is a long and slender digit that points the way with curled brown nails that are long past the need for a trim.

"Perhaps it is something else," ventures Aunt Jenny. "You think it might be a call to nature?"

"Oh, dear, I hope not." Frowns Mother. "Such an odious task."

She leans forward to stare into her father's face. "You need a pee-pee, Daddy. Is that it?"

The thought appeals and Grandpa nods affirmation, almost as if the words alone have raised the urgent demand from his bladder.

"Edward, dear?" Mother turns to her husband.

Father's mouth is full of chicken and he mumbles his reply.

"It is Grandpa," explains Mother. "He needs to attend a call to nature."

Father swallows noisily, "Oh, dearest, not now?"

"I fear so, we must attend him, you know what happened last time."

Father is enjoying this self-indulgent relaxation of feeding on such delicacies and does not want his mood disturbed.

"We shall get Misty," he realizes with a gratified smile. "She will deal with it."

"Very well," replies Mother, all too eager to take the easy route. "MISTY!" she calls.

The serving girl jumps up at the call and runs up the hillside brushing grass from her apron, "Yes, missy?"

"Grandfather needs attention, girl," explains Mother. "I believe he wishes to make water, will you take him to woods to allow some privacy and assist him if you can."

Misty lowers her head, it is a moment of dismay but she must fulfill her duty and she begins to lever the old man from his chair.

"I shall assist," said James, leaping to his feet and

seeing where he might at least press close to his secret love for a moment.

"Bravo," cries Mother. "James, you are such a gentleman. Do you see, Father? Your son is indeed a master, is he not?"

Father who is working on a loaf of white bread nods indifferently.

Close to her now, with the frail old bony character between them, both young man and girl ease him toward the tree line. Misty has her eyes downcast and studies her feet placing them carefully so as not to jolt the tottering old man. James breathes hard, his lips full of words he cannot utter while Grandpa stares intently at the approaching forest as if some mysterious splendor awaits him there.

They are amongst the trees and no longer visible by the family. Releasing the bowed figure of Grandpa, he stands alone and swaying slightly. Both James and Misty have stepped back expecting the old man to attend to himself, but he is content to suck his gums and stare directly ahead at the tree before him.

James coughs awkwardly. "Is this all right, Grandpa?" he asks doubtfully.

The old one makes no movement.

"'Em," begins James, glancing sidelong at Misty. She is most lustrous to his eye, the dim light reaching through the trees sending soft shadows across her rounded features. "What do we do?"

Misty shrugs. "Best he be unbutton, Massa James."

The thought of exposing the old man's pale

decrepit vessel does no appeal at all to the young poet.

"I think you should," he ventures.

She glances at him for a long moment with liquid brown eyes and the breath catches in James's throat.

"Missy," he begins weakly. "There is something—"

But she is moving and already behind and encompassing Grandpa around the waist and working on the buttons on his sagging pants. Discretely, James turns his head aside.

"Go on then, suh," urges Misty. "Yo gotta go do it, be right to let it pass."

James cannot resist, he turns and studies the girl, who stands with the ancient's fly wide and his rumpled long johns flowering. But James's eyes are for Misty and he sees her bounty as only his lovelorn eyes can. She is so small and gentle with her hair held up under the turban. Her round features and smooth brown skin with molded lips so marked he can almost feel them on his cheek. The words of praise tumble in his mind and are likely to confuse him his chest is so tight with desire.

"I'd best go back," he says hurriedly and turns to flee.

"What yo' doing, suh. T'ain't nothin' but no dribble," persists Misty, peering over the old man's shoulder.

Grandpa is chuckling deep in his throat, the Adam's apple bobbing in his scrawny neck and fluttering his white beard. Whether he smiles at the close embrace of this young woman with his member exposed or it is the memory of some forgotten earlier encounter with another, only he will know.

"Come on now," says Misty, fumbling with his buttons. "We'd best get yo' back wid your folks."

She takes it all in her stride as she does equally with all her other tedious household tasks of a personal nature. The chamber pots and outhouses redolent with night soil are all just mess and bother to her but all of it par for the course if she will put food on her table and a roof over her head.

James makes his way out of the woods and stands a moment in thought as he tries to catch his breath and still his pounding heart. He is a coward; he knows it but for a moment he has retreated and given way to consider what might have happened if he had exposed his thoughts to the Negress. He tears the page from the notebook, folding it carefully before crossing to the tree where the captain sits.

James sees nothing but carefully looks about to see if he is being watched before tucking the sheet in the cleft of the tree branch. He will tell her, he is sure of it now. He will tell her to collect the paper and see what he has written. No spoken words will pass between them but only understanding will follow he is convinced of it.

"Here comes James," cries Ellen, humor alive in her voice. "Are your nursing duties done, brother?"

James is haughty. "Would that you might help as a granddaughter should instead of mocking me, sister."

"Is Grandpa all right?" asks Mother.

Throwing back the tail of his coat, James takes

his seat again and answers hurriedly, "Yes, yes, Misty is seeing to everything."

———

"You see that?" asks Brack. "Them walk right by us without a word. Not even a how-do, mighty uncivilized."

"He put a paper in that tree, I seen that," added Linus.

"What might that be?" mused Brack. "Here, Sergeant, you think that boy is some kind of spy leaving a message for the foe?"

"What's that?" asks Jubal.

"We seen him," says Linus. "He went over by the captain and left a note in the tree."

Jubal frowns. "That's mighty strange, seems to me everything around here is strange. Those folks been avoiding us all along, almost like we was never here."

"I'm going to see what's writ," says Brack determinedly. "If that boy's giving out on our position I'll bust a cap on him."

"Not with that Enfield, you won't," sneers Linus. "You ain't got a single ball for it."

"Go fetch it," orders Jubal. "Let's see what's said."

Obediently, Brack strides across to the tree and the disturbed captain watches as he snatches the paper from the fork.

"What's that? What are you about, trooper?" asks the captain.

77

"Possible spy missive, sir. Young fellow there's like to advise our position to the enemy."

"Damned impudence, show me."

Dutifully, Brack hands over the folded sheet and the captain climbing to his feet, retrieves his pinz nez spectacles from inside the breast of his tunic.

"Hmm," he mumbles as he unfolds the paper and studies the writing. "Is this some sort of code, I wonder. Here." He hands the paper across. "What do you make of it, soldier?"

Rotating the page in his hand, Brack is silent.

"Can you read, fellow?" asks the captain.

"Sorry, sir," answered the embarrassed Brack.

The captain tusks in irritation. "You there, Sergeant, come here. Can you read this, my man?"

Jubal takes the note, and frowning, squints at the words.

Then he reads aloud.

> *"The bruise that marks the heart*
> *Lies within my darkest flower*
> *Kept in this shuttered house apart*
> *With tasted sweetness yet so sour*
> *Behind a door I write for mine*
> *Alone and in this distant tower*
> *Holding your vision to my breast*
> *Where only fearful symptoms cower*
> *Awaiting for the surest sign*
> *Misted in love's eternal shower."*

"What do you make of that?" asks the captain. "Some sort of coded information to the enemy, do you think?"

Jubal pulls a face. "T'ain't nothing but a poem to my way of thinking, Captain."

"You think so?" The captain tugs at his beard. "As plain as that? A lovelorn scrawling by yonder fetching scribbler."

"Indeed so, sir."

"Let me see it again."

The captain ponders for a long moment while Brack exchanges amused glances with Jubal.

"Yes, yes," the captain finally admits. "'Tis indeed a sonnet of the heart. This young man is enamored of his inamorata. Reminds me of my own dear wife's particular fancy for such things." He muses distantly, "Ah, my sweetest Caro indeed so, eternally the romantic. She was always this way, the same with china baubles and fine lace, ach!" He pauses, then sadly. "'Tis indeed hard to warrant she is no more."

"What shall we do with it?" asks Jubal.

"Replace it, sir. I will not come between any man and his desires. Yes, put it back in its hiding place."

Moving away from the captain, Jubal replaces the missive and Brack nudges him as they return to the others. "What do you make of that?" he asks, glancing across at the seated James.

Jubal shrugs. "Got hisself hot and bothered over some female, for sure."

Linus and Caesar join them with a curious frown on their brows. "What was that about?"

"Just some love scrip that long lank over there is holding out," says Brack.

"Hush," hisses Linus. "He might hear you."

"Appears to me," says Jubal. "None of them hear nothing of us."

"He have a love bug?" Grins Caesar. "Who that be, t'ain't no one here fo' sure. Just ole women and childers."

"I ain't so sure," murmurs Jubal.

"Thass right," agrees Brack. "He have eye for that Black gal, allus sneaking a look in her direction, I seen him."

"How can that be?" asks a confused Linus. "No White man will fancy a nigger gal."

"Not in *your* life," sniggers Brack. "There's plenty back home takes a liking for dark meat, you ask me."

"That a fact," agrees Caesar solemnly.

"Nah," says Linus. "He's a fine upstanding young white fella, he wouldn't be writing no love letters to some serving girl."

"Maybe they's Northern sympathizers," ponders Brack. "Those people ain't above any sort of unusual behavior."

"I tell you," says Jubal. "You watch him, that boy is smitten I'm telling you. He's all hot under the collar for that little gal."

"But he's holding out, ain't he?" Chuckles Brack. "Lookit him, all fancy like his leavings don't stink like the rest of us. He's got this thing but him and his position ain't up to making a thing with the pickaninny. Phew-wee! Give me half a chance an' I'll show him what it's for."

The captain is marching up and down across their front, his hands are behind his back and his saber clashes at his side. He is deep in thought and occasionally glances down to the distant forest edge below the hillside.

"Sergeant!" he calls. "Where exactly is the brigade now?"

"I don't rightly know, sir," answers Jubal.

"We have no scouts? I need to know our position, we have to bring up the twelve pounders, I want a line along this rise."

Jubal looks around and chews his lip doubtfully. "I don't know where they are, Captain. Fact is, I don't know where we is at all."

"We have our placement, don't we? Surely, we are ordered here."

"Maybe, sir, but I don't rightly know. Last thing I recall is standing ready to let loose on the Yankee advance."

The captain rubs his chin and strokes his beard. "Well, we need to know. Go and find out, will you."

Jubal raises his eyebrows. "Yes, sir, but where to go?"

The captain huffs irritably. "I don't know, boy. Dammit! Just get it done."

Jubal salutes then with a shrug wanders toward the tree line. "Come on, the rest of you," he orders. "Come seek out our lines."

Leaving the captain alone except for Caesar they all disappear into the forest.

CHAPTER THREE

Tired and with his mind wandering the captain sits down cross-legged on the grass and looks out over the treetops. He has registered the picnickers in a distant manner and then turned to Caesar.

"Fetch me a drink, Caesar. I am dry."

Caesar standing attentively and slightly behind looked down at the captain. "We don' hab nuttin', suh. No water nor nuttin'."

"Nothing?" pondered the captain. "The commissary wagon has not come?"

"No, suh, Captain."

"Look there, Caesar. You see those people? Go ask them if they might spare a drop of something before I expire through dehydration."

"Yes, suh."

Dutifully, Caesar approaches the group below them on the rise.

Replete, Father rests back and drawing a cheroot from his wallet he lights it and draws on it contentedly. Grandpa's chin has dropped to his chest and he snores gently in his wicker chair. The chair has softened over the years and now forms no regular shape but encases the old man as if he were wrapped in a nest. Mother, who has not moved for one half hour remains steady, her only attention fixed on Ellen, who is lying full length on her stomach and studying the ants running through the long grass. In this position, her hooped dress rises up behind her and exposes her kicking legs with lace-fringed drawers and underthings. Mother frowns at such abandon but says nothing.

James lies dreaming, his head resting on one hand as he watches Misty through lidded eyes as she busies herself collecting dishes and cutlery. Aunt Jenny looks skywards and gives a little gasp of pleasure.

"You see there, sister." She smiles, which is an unusual expression from her normal stern demeanor. "There, a red-winged blackbird. You see it settles in that tree? Oh, how pretty."

Mother half-turns her head not really interested and sees the bird flutter onto a branch of the same tree that the captain rested under and the posting point with its forked trunk that holds James's poem.

Caesar drifts up and takes his battered hat from his head and stands obsequiously.

"'Scuse me, gentlefolk. My Massa up yonder, begs you to spare some refreshment for him, if yo' will be so kind?"

He is ignored and the Lyons family continue with their lazy mental meanderings. Caesar frowns and wonders if he was heard or if they just choose to ignore a Negro.

"The captain he be dry, might yo' spare a drop?"

Still no response and Caesar stands bewildered.

Then Ellen starts up, "Look there, I do believe a military rider comes."

Caesar jumps at the cry and follows her gaze down the hillside to the edge of the forest in the hollow below. There, a Union officer bursts from the trees and comes out proudly riding a fine bronze-colored stallion. The officer is smartly dressed in the uniform of an infantry lieutenant, with tasseled red sash and saber, square buckled belt, heavy round brass buttons that gleam and epaulets with a single bar. A forage cap covers his brown curls and side-burns with a chin strap wrapped to his jaw. Beneath his dark-blue frock coat he wears pants of paler blue and tidy lace-up shoes.

Quickly, while they are distracted, Caesar reaches down into the wicker hamper and snatches a bottle of wine, tucking it into his deep pocket before he hurries off running at full speed up the hill.

"They coming, Captain," he pants. "The blue-bellies is here."

"Really," breathes the captain. "Well, we are ready. Did those people part with something?"

"Got yo' a bottle of wine, suh."

"What is it?" Dutifully Caesar shows the label. "Ah, a claret, commendable. An 1861 Anaheim Zinfandel, I suppose that will have to do. Pour me a glass, will you?"

"We ain't got no glasses, but Captain, I be telling you there's a Union man down there."

The captain snorts. "No glasses? What are these people, savages? How many blue coats can you see?"

"Jist the one, suh."

"Then there's no problem, I'll drink from the bottle."

———

"I do believe that is young Haywood," says Father, peering at the horseback rider.

"You mean Ernest, Eugene Haywood's son?" asks Mother.

"The same, indeed it is."

"So fine, so fine," breathes Aunt Jenny as she admires the upright rider.

"Heavens!" says Mother. "He has a mustache now, I barely thought him old enough, what a bold figure he cuts."

Ellen is surprised to find her heart is beating fast at sight of the approaching soldier as he canters up the hill toward them with his horse spitting divots of earth behind him from the hooves. The animal is strong and a good-looking creature with a shining coat and it manages the slope with little difficulty.

"How do," cries Ernest, offering a wave as he pulls to a standstill.

"Why, Mr. Haywood, how good to see you." Smiles Father. "Pray come down and join us. As you see we are partaking of a holiday picnic."

"Glad to, sir." With a smile, Ernest dismounts and sweeps off his cap to place it under his arm. "Greetings to you all." He offers a polite bow.

"And to you," says Father. "Misty, take the lieutenant's horse, will you?"

"No, I will do it," says Ellen pushing her way forward. She grasps the reins that Ernest hands over with a smile.

"What a fine animal," praises Ellen as she strokes the horse's neck.

"My favorite, my pretty war horse," replies Ernest. "He is called Copper and I intend to take him into battle."

"Oh, my!" breathes Ellen. "How I so wish I were a man."

"Why so?" Frowns Ernest.

"So I could ride, to charge like the wind and fly so gallantly into the fray."

"Ah, no, no, no," sighs Ernest, fixing her with a steady gaze. "You are better here, so pretty, so soft. War is no place for you, dear Miss Ellen."

A flushed Ellen cannot believe the pounding of her heart and she is sure the beating sounds loudly through the material of her chemise. In embarrassment, she quickly leads the horse away, feeling its soft flanks under her hand and smelling the horse smell of the animal.

She is unsure of what is happening and why this response should fire at sight of Ernest in his uniform. She has known him in the village school, of course but he was older than her and seemed like all the other country boys. The ones she could tease and irritate so easily, the ones she could run faster than and climb any tree better than. Suddenly, Ernest is making an impact and she finds herself left

in an unusual position, she feels unsure for the first
time in her life.

Mother and Father are fussing over Ernest,
tempting him with food and drink. He smiles
politely and nods at their hurried conversation but
often, she notices, his eyes stray to her as she ties off
Copper to a branch.

"And who do you join?" asks Father.

"I am with the 19th Indiana Volunteers under
Captain Meredith and am off to Camp Morton on
the morrow to take up my duties."

"Your father must be very proud," says Aunt
Jenny, her eyes glazed with admiration.

Ernest is self-depreciating, "Like any Hoosier, I
must do what is needed at this time."

"So true," Mother agrees.

"And what of you, James?" Ernest asks. "Will
you serve, I would be pleased to have your company
on the march."

James is surprised at this request as so often
during their schooling, Ernest had bullied and
mocked him for his artistic trend.

"I think I am better served here to attend my
mother and father," he answers a touch coldly.

"Sweet boy," minces his mother. "So loyal."

"But how are you here?" asks Father. "Is this a
last merry ride before you depart."

"Not quite," admits Ernest. He is striking the
expected pose, standing stiffly erect with one foot
before the other. A hand rests on the hilt of his saber
and the other with its thumb tucked in the sash.

"You have other reasons?" Mother asks slyly.

"Your maid there was seen at my father's store

buying goods for this picnic and it seemed to me I should ride out and wish you all farewell before I left."

"So thoughtful," says Mother.

"So pleasant here," says Ernest, looking around. "You have chosen well."

Ellen studies his profile. She sees him in a wholly different light. Her earlier childhood memory is unraveling and now Ernest takes on the appearance of some kind of martial god. A neat, firm-jawed, and mustachioed handsome warrior that brings the breath faster in her nostrils.

"Yes," agrees Father. "We are not for noise and turbulence, the peace of countryside is our true family home."

"May it remain so," muses Ernest and yet a doubtful flicker plays in the back of his mind, for he has seen the massed ranks of the volunteer army and feels that if they are unleashed then there will be little peace for such families as these.

"Tell me, Mr. Lyons, would you object if I might have a few words with your daughter?"

Father twists his lip and lowers his brow; he turns to his wife. "Mother?"

Mother reads the request and her face brightens and becomes enervated and for a moment is in disarray. "Why, no, no. Certainly not, dear Ernest." She turns to Ellen. "Daughter, pray come here. Mr. Haywood would have a word with you."

A coy Ellen arrives at Ernest's elbow and she licks her lips and looks up at him in consternation. For once, words freeze in her mouth and she is in awe at his tall mature figure standing beside her.

"Might we walk, Miss Ellen?" he asks.

Ellen swallows and nods briefly in affirmation.

"Will you take my arm?"

She fits her small hand in the crook of his arm and under her fingers feels the stiff freshness of the new material and the narrow gold curlicues of his rank on the sleeve. At an easy pace, Ernest leads her away toward the tree with the forked limb.

"What do you think, husband?" breathes Mother in a whisper. "Does she have herself a beau?"

Father who is now thinking more of indulging in another glass of brandy, shrugs noncommittally.

"Oh, dearie me," says a flushed Aunt Jenny. "How romantic."

"Let us sit again," says a pleased Mother. "Pay them no heed, let nature take its course."

———

"I hope you will not object to my sudden arrival during your holiday?" Ernest asks.

Gently, Ellen clears her throat then shakes her head negatively.

"I have so little time now and must perforce press these final moments."

"I'm sure you have little time," Ellen agrees.

"Might I say that you look splendid today, Miss Ellen."

Ellen lowers her head, unsure of how to respond but secretly pleased at the praise. He likes her but she has no understanding of such a thing and until now has only considered herself as an attractive female in the most abstracted of ways.

Expecting an answer he is concerned with her silence, "I trust I am not too forward."

"Not at all," she manages.

"It is just that you are truly a vision to me and have been so a long, long time. I would be bereft if you would dismiss me but, of course, if that is your preference, then I shall take my leave."

"Oh, no," she bursts. "Please don't do that."

He smiles and she is pleased to see he has even teeth with only a single missing tooth along one side.

"I would ask a favor, if you will?"

"Anything."

"Will you permit me to write while I am away?"

A small smile stilts her lips. "Assuredly, it would be a pleasure to receive your news."

"Oh, thank you, thank you, dear lady." He allows a ragged breath to escape and then she realizes that he too has been nervous and unsure and this knowledge reasserts her old self to a degree.

"Why this attention, Ernest?" She lifts her shoulders in curiosity. "I had thought myself of little interest."

"Ah! No, indeed no. You are the fairest, sweetest creature in all the country. I am lost in your image of femininity and have long thought so. Perhaps it has not seemed so but I would admire you from afar and not trust myself to express my concern until now."

"Really?"

"Really," he accedes. "It is true."

Thoughts are now running through Ellen's mind

as fast as a racing horse, all of them different and confused. The hidden meaning behind his words are implying all kinds of possibilities that have never concerned her before. She thinks of behavior, of how far she is allowed, how will she kiss? Will it be chastely or with some demonstration of passion? Then her thinking runs far ahead to marriage and all that that implies.

Wordless she stares up into his eyes, they are an intense blue and she sees them as crystalline and clear as running water. She is at a loss and must rely on him to take the lead, which, she decides, is what society expects of her. Yet the thrill of the close proximity of a man, the smell of him and his bold desire for her leaves her breathless.

"It will give me great pleasure to advise you of our deeds," he says. "For I shall think of you often while suffering the vicissitudes of campaign."

"You must take care, Ernest. Promise me you will."

He lowers his head and lets his hand cover hers at his elbow. "How kind you are."

The touch is magic to Ellen. She notes the soft warmth of his broad hand and the trimmed finger-nails, and she cannot doubt this attention that melts the last traces of her youthful tomboy resolve.

Her eyelids flutter. "We should go back."

"Of course." He nods. "And I too must be away to pack my final belongings."

His hand leaves hers and rests a moment on the tree as he looks down at her, "I am much pleased," he says.

She does a thing she has never done before,

cocks her head to one side in girlish manner and portrays a bashful pose as she has seen other girls do at dances and until now has thought them stupid.

"But what is this?" asks Ernest, his fingers touching the trapped paper in the tree's fork.

"Let me see."

Ernest unfolds the paper and reads, "It is a note, perhaps a poem."

"Ach!" spits Ellen. "It is my stupid brother, he thinks to commune with nature with his rhymes. Give it here. I shall return it to him."

Ernest chuckles. "He writes to trees, how unique."

Ellen shakes her head. "He is mad, quite mad. Sometimes I do despair."

"My letters will hold no such flights of fancy, I fear."

"I sincerely hope not," says Ellen forcibly.

CHAPTER FOUR

In a forest clearing, gloomy where the dim sunlight cannot reach, slowly the rest of the men leave the dense forest to stand beside Jubal.

"Anybody?" asks Jubal.

"Nary a sign," says Brack. "Not ours or theirs. Nobody just damned trees."

"You Linus?"

Linus shakes his head negatively.

Jubal pushes his cap aside and scratches his head. "Mighty strange."

He sees that Linus still carries his spade and Brack the Enfield rifle. "You got any shot for that rifle?"

"No, Sergeant. I left the ammunition pouch on my belt hanging over the cannon limber, wherever that might be now."

"This is hellish weird. There should be a whole battery out there, let alone a battalion."

"Something ain't right," complained Linus.

"Say that again," agreed Brack. "What's happening here, Sergeant?"

"Let's think," ponders Jubal. "What do we last remember before we found ourselves here?"

"I recall digging earth," says Linus dumbly. "It were mighty hard, full of rocks."

"You Brack?"

"Me, let's see? I do recall standing with my hand on the wagon, I was sent to guard her."

"And I—" said Jubal thoughtfully. "I was near to the captain and Caesar; they were stood not ten yards away. I can still feel the warm bronze of that Napoleon cannon, it was hot from the firing."

"Well, a twelve-pound cannon c'ain't just up and disappear, can it?" asked Brack.

"No, sir." Jubal frowned. "What was in that wagon you was guarding?"

"It was gunpowder and shells, fully loaded and just arrived."

"I had a dream, you know," interrupts Linus, with a thoughtful look and lowered eyebrows.

"A dream, you dummy," spits Brack. "What the hell use is that?"

"I was flying," Linus continues, unperturbed. "Me, like a bird high up over them emplacements. I was looking down on y'all and I could see this great big hole. Huge, it were an' all smoking."

"You mean like an explosion kind of hole—a crater?" Jubal grimaces.

"That's it, like that. Then I was standing with the rest of you on that hill out there. I guess I just floated down."

"Hot damn!" Chuckles Brack, amused by the

simplicity. "You is something else, Linus, you really is. I dunno how you come up with it, I surely don't."

"Not so fast," muses Jubal. "Maybe Linus has something. Suppose—now I know this is going to sound crazy—but just suppose them Yankees sent over a few shells and one of them landed in that ammunition wagon."

Brack pulls a face. "That would certainly make one hell of a bang."

"But we were all that close, weren't we? We would have been obliterated by it, surely."

"Nah!" Brack barks a dismissive laugh. "I ain't seen no pearly gates, nor St. Peter checking on my sinning accounts."

Linus looked downcast. "You saying, Sergeant, that we is dead and gone?"

"Maybe that's the case, improbable as it sounds."

"But I ain't ready yet."

"Look here," presses Brack. "We still talking and I see y'all, so it c'ain't be. I ain't no ghost."

"Then how did we get here?"

"And why'd we be here?" asks Linus.

"Those people out them, those picnickers," Jubal continues. "You seen it, they pay us no heed; you got to have seen that. Maybe that's it, we're as spirits to them. They can't touch or hear or feel us."

Brack is watching him askance, "Get away, Jubal. This is nuts. If we was dead we couldn't even talk like this."

"How do you know that? Let's go see, we'll go try to have words with them folks."

Brack shakes his head but follows as Jubal leads

TONY MASERO

the way and they all troop back to the edge of the forest. The captain still sits sipping his wine with Caesar standing attentively behind him. Below, the Lyons family gathers about Ernest Haywood all of them wishing him well as he prepares to leave.

"Whoa!" cries Brack. "Look there a damned Yankee is with 'em. Hell, wish I had a ball for this gun, I'd take off his knobby head."

"They still don't see us," supplies Jubal.

"*Wha-hoo!*" hollers Linus loudly. "*Wha-hoo!* Y'all c'ain't see us, can you?"

"Hush," bursts out Brack. "What you doin', Linus?"

Nobody turns at the loud call except the captain and Caesar who gives them a curious look. Without any response from the picnickers Jubal and the others slowly move forward until they stand alongside the sitting captain.

"What y'all hollerin' for?" asks Caesar.

"It's weird," mumbles Brack, beginning to wonder if the Sergeant may be right after all.

"We is dead, that's all," supplied Linus, sure now of the solution.

"Dead?" snaps Caesar. "Holy Roller! What is you talkin' of, I was just down there. Took me this bottle for the captain."

"You talked to them?" asks Jubal.

"Sho'did, they didn't say nutting though. Then this Yankee soldier boy turns up an' they was busy with him."

"Captain," presses Jubal. "Beg to report that there's no sign of our troops anywhere."

"How can that be?" asks the captain blithely.

"Surely they have moved and are just beyond the ridgeline."

"No sir, we are all alone here," he pauses, doubtful of how to continue. "But there is another consideration."

The captain lifts the bottle to his lips and swallows, wipes his mouth with the back of his hand. "Speak."

"Well, sir, we have been thinking. It appears we was all standing in the vicinity of an ammunition wagon and that is the last thing we remember. Linus here thinks a stray round hit the wagon and it was blown sky high."

"And so?"

"It took us with it, Captain."

A deep frown penetrates the captain's brow. "Are you implying, Sergeant, that we are no longer amongst the living?"

"Yes, sir."

"Poppycock, boy! Look here, I am drinking this fine wine and sitting on this green grass. These are no Elysian Fields, fellow. See here, these people, they are all alive and well."

"So they are, Captain, but I fear we are not. With permission we aim to test the theory?"

"How so?"

"We shall approach said party and engage them in conversation, if we can, all well and good. But if they cannot see us or communicate then you must allow some credence to our belief."

The captain's face breaks into a bearded smile, the first he has given in many months, "This is a jape, surely, Sergeant. You are set to amuse the men with this nonsense, are you not?"

"No, sir, I am in deadly earnest."

"Then go ahead with this tomfoolery by all means. We all shall enjoy a jolly jest, by God, we all need one to be sure."

"I shall see it done," commits Jubal. He sees the Union officer is mounted and moving away down the hillside with the family all waving their farewells. Ellen follows at the run, gazing up at Ernest with her hand upon his stirrup. He gives her one small smile then slaps the reins and leaning forward brings Copper to the gallop, leaving Ellen standing alone on the slope.

Mother has a hand to her breast as she watches Ernest's stalwart departure. Father stands with hands behind his back and puffing on the remains of his cheroot while Aunt Jenny clasps both hands prayer-like before her and stares whimsically after the horseback rider. James still lying on the ground, his boredom all to obvious, thumbs his notebook impatiently. Grandpa still sleeps, his dreams full of boyhood ramblings and Misty bites her bottom lip as she watches Ellen and wonders, with some hint of jealousy, at the arrow that Cupid has cast into her young mistress's heart.

Jubal strides purposefully across the green to stand before the family.

He salutes politely. "Excuse me, I wonder if I might have a word with you people?"

They stand as a chorus watching Ernest's departure and ignoring the Sergeant totally.

Jubal starts again, "We are men of the 2nd

Alabama, Coultry Battery and must ask what yonder federal is doing here?"

Grandpa awakes and ruffles his feathers as he tries to capture reality from his dreams, "What do you want, fellow?" he asks the blurred figure before him.

"Who?" asks Father, turning to the old man. "Who is it you speak of, Grandfather?"

Sleepily, the old man mistakes dark shadows from the overcast sky sliding across the forest line, "I thought I saw men in buckskin are they amongst the trees?"

"No, Grandpa," says Ellen as she climbs back up the hill. "That was Ernest Haywood. He is a lieutenant of infantry and no militiaman."

"Can I have something to eat?" whines the old man, taking on a pathetic tone.

"Of course, Papa," says Mother. "Here, let me prepare you a plate. Misty, will you help?"

Jubal moves forward and catches Father firmly by the arm. "Sir! I must trouble you."

Father shivers.

"Are you all right, Edward?" asks Aunt Jenny.

"Yes, yes, indeed, quite all right, just a slight chill in the air. A breeze perhaps."

Jubal steps back astounded that he has no impact at all on these living souls. Accidentally he steps on James and stumbles but it has no effect at all on the lounging youth.

"Oh, dear, it is so," sighs Jubal as he realizes his worst fears. Unsteadily, he turns away and heads back up toward his companions. As he climbs the rise, his thoughts are bereft, an image of his wife and child flash through his mind, his young brother, widowed mother and stepfather. No more, they are gone and their images flutter on the edge of his consciousness as flicked pages turned in a book.

"Well?" asks Brack.

Jubal hangs his head. "It is true; we are no more than vapor. My words and my touch meant nothing. We are creatures of the shades."

"A fine joke," slurs the captain, more than a little drunk and sipping from the bottleneck again. "You are to be commended for your humor."

"Don' you be talkin' like that," bursts Caesar, his black face full of horror and dread. "You be setting duppy on us. Sergeant, you don' play with dat dead man talk. I tell you dat ting is fearful."

"You must all face the fact," says Jubal solemnly. "We are no more and must make our peace with it."

Linus wrinkles his nose. "But if it so, I should be in heaven, seeing the Good Lord Jesus on His throne. We all had that promised us, didn't we?"

"Well, maybe *you* did. Personal, I never gave it much credence," says Brack.

"The thing that troubles me," says a worried Jubal. "Is why we are here. If we are gone, we should be committed to paradise or perdition, as that is the assured end to it all."

"Instead we're sitting in some damned field watching folks eat their fill," observes Brack. "Don't make a lot of sense, do it?"

"Not at first," ponders Jubal. "But perhaps there is a meaning to it."

"I don' want nutting to do wid dis," says Caesar, turning his back on them and fiddling with a small sack hidden inside his shirt that is tied by a leather thong around his neck.

"You playing with them bones and grave dirt, you black savage?" sneers Brack. "I seen you toying with that magic bundle before, you think you can save yourself with all that hocus-pocus. You're crazy."

"Tings you don' understand," Caesar mumbles over his shoulder. "I ain't crossing over, not my time right now; I had it off'n Ole Miss Julie, the conjure woman on de plantation. She got the hoodoo an' say I be set for a silver chariot when it be my time."

"*Silver chariot!*" guffaws Brack. "The only place you be going is to hell, you heathen and that'll be in the back of a tumbril cart."

"My mojo bag say it ain't so."

"Leave it be," cuts in Jubal. "He believes that, so let it go. We got more important things to consider."

"What you think, Captain?" presses Brack, turning to the officer. "You think this black heathen of yours ain't dead like the rest of us?"

The captain holds an imperious look behind his alcoholically glazed eyes. "I can only say, that if it be so, I am well pleased. I shall see my beloved Cora again and all my blessed children and I shall take pleasure in their company. But I do not see them anywhere yet awhile."

"Nor will you," mumbles Brack.

"That ain't it," snarls Jubal. "If it were so we would all be gone."

"Maybe not," adds a dour Linus. "Maybe we got to wander. You know, like spirits lost and forever cast into darkness."

"Lord love us," sighs Brack in exasperation. "Give me rest, will you?"

"It must be to do with these folks here," says Jubal. "Why else would be placed at this spot? There is something we have to do before we are released."

"What we gonna do?" asks Brack. "They c'ain't see us, c'ain't hear us an' sure as hell c'ain't touch us. What we gonna do for them?"

"There has to be something. Look there, Caesar picked up a bottle and in so doing he carried something away. Perhaps we can hold a thing as long as it ain't living."

"That's one thing you got right, Jubal and if that's the way of it I reckon I will just walk on down there and get meself a bottle. How about that?"

CHAPTER FIVE

Father now lays full spread on his back upon the ground. His fingers are laced over his stomach and he closes his eyes against the warmth imposed by brandy and cigars.

Standing again beneath the tree, Ellen is left alone with her thoughts and remembers the folded paper Ernest has found and opens it out to ready the lines.

> *The bruise that marks the heart*
> *Lies within my darkest flower*
> *Kept in this shuttered house apart*
> *With tasted sweetness yet so sour*
> *Behind a door I write for mine*
> *Alone and in this distant tower*
> *Holding your vision to my breast*
> *Where only fearful symptoms cower*
> *Awaiting for the surest sign*
> *Misted in love's eternal shower*

Her mood is changed after Ernest's departure and she sees the poem in a different light now. No longer full of ridicule her heart is softened by the discovery of her feelings for the young lieutenant. A new sensation and a sudden ache that she has never known before brings an inherent sadness to the written words.

To her surprise and for the first time, her brother's words no longer hold the ramblings of an insensate character who would rather drift in dreams than hold the bold characteristics she has found to admire in Ernest.

She wonders whom it is James alludes to. Is there some secret he holds, some female he admires from afar or does he speak in pure abstraction. Ellen can think of no one that would fit that bill, her brother rarely moves abroad and yet here he displays lovesick and sadly lost musings.

It is the final line that gives her the clue. Can this be, she frowns? Could it be that James holds the colored serving girl in admiration? How unlikely this appears and it is surely not a situation for one of his standing. To keep affection for an unsuitable person of such a lowly station is unthinkable.

And yet she recalls his glances, his watchful gaze as Misty goes about her day. At once Ellen's memory is of James's readiness to help when all other menial tasks he avoids as if they are beneath his pride. She sees him now, laid out on his side with a bowl of apple pie before him that he picks at with a spoon as he slides appreciative looks toward the serving girl.

Misty for her part is unaware Ellen is convinced of this. She sees the maid sitting with hands cupped patiently in her apron lap and staring unseeing off beyond the treetops. She is prepared in sentinel fashion and ready to answer any call and spring into subservience in an instant but Mother is still sitting steady and oblivious with the umbrella above her like a tent and a dozing Aunt Jenny resting her head in her older sister's lap.

Ellen replaces the poem in the cleft of the tree and catches Misty's eye and beckons her across.

"Tell me, what think you of love, Misty?" she asks.

"I dunno, missy."

Ellen shrugs. "You have no beau of your own?"

"No, ma'am, but I seen you and that soldier boy. I think you is keen there, ain't you?"

Ellen draws a breath. "He cuts a fine figure, doesn't he?"

"He sho' do, you be lost, ain't you?"

"Oh, I don't know. Can such a thing happen in so short a time?"

"It be like a thunderbolt, they say. Come quick an' catch you up all sudden like, that's what the old folks say."

"Do you wish it were so for you like that?"

"I don' expect so, I ain't seen no young mens since I was a child, 'cepting that old handyman Benjamin that Massa Lyons keeps about the house."

"And did you know of any when you were little?"

"Yes 'm but we's just playing, you know?"

Ellen is suddenly interested, it is an area she has no knowledge of and yet now she finds that maybe she should be giving it consideration. "What did you do, Misty?"

"Why, we's playing like chillen do," says Misty evasively.

"You played at what?"

"Aw, mommas and poppas, that kinda thing. I had me a rag doll was made for me and this were my baby child. So this boy, Rastus was his name, he be husband and I be wife and we have a place back of the shed we call our quarters."

"How was that? What did you do there?"

Misty was embarrassed and a blush came to her round cheeks. "He be going to work in the fields and then come home and he kiss me on the mouth like we seen big people do. So I makes him pretend beans and rice and then we lays down together as to sleep."

"Was that nice?"

"I dunno." Misty shrugs. "Weren't nothing but wet with the kissin' as I recall."

"And you were content with this?"

Misty pouted with her lower lip. "Sho' it were just playing."

"What if I were to tell you that you have an admirer now?"

Misty's eyes go round. "You mean like a regular fella?"

"I surely do, a full-grown man at that."

"Then I don' believes you, Miss Ellen. You be funning with me, ain't you?"

Ellen looks away, knowledgeably smug; a slow smile spreads across her lips.

"Who that be?" Misty frowns. "There ain't no Black fellas about here."

With tongue in cheek, Ellen teases, "Maybe he isn't a darkie."

Misty drops her eyes, saddened by what she considers playacting. She knows only too well that White people enjoy the occasional joke at a colored soul's expense and she must keep her place and remain silent in response.

"I best be going back, missy," she murmurs.

"You watch out," admonishes Ellen. "Keep your eyes sharp and you will see him."

"In a pig's ear," whispers Misty to herself as she leaves.

To Ellen the thrill of her own romance beats in her breast and she would fulfill another's joy even though the consideration of James and the girl is only a fantasy. She is enamored of the notion and plays it through her mind as if it were the pages in a novel, a thing without significance except as a pleasant distraction.

———

Brack strolls in amongst the dozing group and unnoticed steals a bottle of wine from the hamper. Misty whose troubled thoughts are still distracted by Ellen's words sits again at the fringes unseeing as Brack strides away up the hillside.

"He's right, goddamn it," says Brack, proudly holding aloft the wine. "They don't notice nothing. Man, can you imagine, we can walk into any house and help ourselves there'll be no outcry of thief and robber. I like this notion, if this be dead then there's some miles to cover here."

The captain frowns at him from under hoary eyebrows. "You are still a soldier, best you don't forget that, trooper."

Brack grins, showing uneven and brown teeth. "No I ain't. No siree, I ain't in the army no more."

"You wear the uniform and you will obey command," says the captain sternly. "Don't forget what we are about here, we are still at war."

"But we's all dead, you fool. What you going to do, have me shot?" sneers Brack.

"No need for disrespect," barks Jubal. "Who knows how long we shall be here? Why every minute maybe completion draws nearer and we shall be sent our various ways."

"Yes, sir," intones Linus with solemn religious fervor. "I be waiting for my place in the heavenly choir. There's many palaces in the Lord's Kingdom so they say and I want me one of them."

Brack forbids himself any sly remark as he struggles to pop the cork on his bottle.

The captain turns to Jubal. "So, Sergeant you believe there is a plan to all this?"

"I believe so, sir. Is there not God's plan to all of life? There is reason to this I am sure of it."

"But what is it then if you are so convinced?"

Jubal shakes his head. "As yet I do not know but I think we are held here in reserve for some reason and it is to do with these good people here."

The captain casts an eye over the sleeping picnickers. "They seem most content already, to be sure."

"T'ain't none of our concern," growls Caesar somberly. "We's shouldn't be fiddlin' with dis."

"What of that federal soldier?" asks Linus. "You think he will call up others and place us at risk."

"Risk of what?" spits Brack, at last relieving the bottle of its cork. "We ain't got a weapon between us and as we's being so-called dead is unseen by all." He raises the wine to his lips and glugs down half the bottle. "Ah, yes," he sighs, licking his lips. "That cuts the dust, it surely do."

"Something's at play with that billet-doux," says Jubal, rubbing his chin thoughtfully. "They pass it around and keep it hidden in that tree for some reason."

"Weren't nothing but some tish-tosh is all, I reckon," sniffs Brack.

"You think it's intended for one of these?" asks the captain.

"Perhaps so," agrees Jubal.

"Well then, what is there?" muses the captain. "The old woman is too old and married to the older man anyway, I've no doubt of it. The young flighty girl has her federal lieutenant. That leaves the younger fellow and the biddy asleep on the old woman's lap and I doubt if there is any significance there."

"What about the Black gal?" asks Brack.

The captain shakes his head. "No White will be interested in the slave child, I'm sure."

Brack swallows another mouthful. "Oh, I don't know."

The captain looks down his nose at him. "I fear

not many are of your consideration in regard of the Negro sort."

"Go on, Captain, you ran a heap of them on your plantation of yours, didn't you? You ain't telling me you never paid no late-night visits to them slave quarters, are you?"

The captain draws himself up, his beard bristling in offense. "You are impertinent, soldier. If we were alive I would have you beaten clear to the picket line."

"Well we ain't is we? So you can forget about that. I bet there was plenty half-an-half pickaninny's running around the back of your house back then."

"Certainly not," bursts out a now angry and red-faced captain. "Sergeant, take this impudent man into custody at once. It will be the stockade for him."

"You tell us, Caesar," presses Brack. "It were like that, weren't it?"

Caesar who has been studiously ignoring them, removes his battered stovepipe hat and holds it his chest. "I never did see none of dat by de captain."

"There you have it," says the captain. "From the mouth of one who knows."

"Were plenty of others though," admits Caesar.

"Who?" Frowns the captain. "Who, goddammit, I'll have them thrashed."

Caesar ticks off the guilty respondents on his fingers. "That one who was foreman, Mistah Stallenby-Jones. His assistant, the German, Hoffman and the young Mastah Clive, they was all down theyah regular."

The captain's face is ashen. "Clive, you mean my boy, my son? Surely no, this is not true."

"Oh, yessah, yo' boy he was real keen, like to run hisself dry he was so eager."

"That cannot be," mutters the captain sullenly.

"He like a high yella gal called Rosemary Jane particular," Caesar confirms. "They all like her jus' fine."

"I cannot credit this," moans the captain.

Brack is pleased with himself. "See there, I told you so. So when you say that Black serving girl don't count, now you know it ain't so."

"So is you saying, Jubal," cuts in Linus. "That this note is intended for one or the other?"

"Maybe," answers Jubal. "That could be the key, to see it gets into the right hands."

"But surely this is a love note?" advises the captain. "Are we to play as the sons of Venus now? That does seem most unlikely."

"It leaves the old aunty," observes Linus. "She surely is in need."

Brack is dismissive. "What that sour face, who's gonna be joining her on the primrose path?"

"Are you sure about my son, Caesar?" asks the captain, who is still pondering on his boy's act of perversity.

"I seen it wid my own eyes," promises Caesar.

"My word!" whispers the captain. "Boy needs a horse whipping, to be sure. Abusing the help is not to be considered."

"Oh, it ain't unusual, massah. Don' you fret none, thet be done all over."

"Not in my house," barks the captain. "Not under my roof."

"Well for sure you c'ain't do nothing about it now." Smiles Brack.

"Perhaps you might haunt them," suggests Linus. "You know, kinda payback."

"*Whoo-oo!*" teases Brack, rolling his eyes and waving his hands in the air. "Real scary."

They all freeze suddenly as they hear the distant rattling sound carried on the still air from far away beyond the lower forest.

"What's that?" asks Linus.

"That'd be firearms," says Brack. "Small arms, maybe some rifle fire."

"Heavens!" bursts out the captain. "A battle is started and we are far from our proper place."

"That is no force of arms," supplies Jubal. "I'd say an ambuscade or small raiding party."

"Is it ours or theirs?" wonders Linus.

CHAPTER SIX

There is a collective cry from the picnickers as a copper-colored horse bursts from the tree line and races up the hill toward them.

"Oh, dear Lord!" cries Ellen. "It is Ernest's horse."

"How fearful," sobs Aunt Jenny. "Oh, how fearful."

They gather waving arms to still the animal and Ellen stands before the restless horse, collects the trailing reins and holding the bridle she steadies the horse.

"He is so frightened," says Mother. "See how his eyes roll."

Ellen falls into a natural role of calming the beast, her hands slide gently over its flanks. Then startled, she pulls her hand away and it is stained red.

"That is blood," cries Father.

"What will have happened?" bursts Aunt Jenny, her nervous features ravaged with terror.

Ellen does not hesitate; she is grim-faced as she swings herself into the saddle. Her hooped dress billows behind her and is crushed under her seat on the saddle.

"What do you do, daughter?" asks Father.

But Ellen is not listening, she turns the horse's head and drums her heels into the ribs, for the stirrups are set too long for her, then she sets off down the hill at the gallop.

"Daddy," cries Mother. "Where does she go?"

Father compresses his lips and watches his daughter as she dashes back down the hill, "She goes to find out what has happened to Ernest."

"Oh, no, the dear girl will be in danger. Some ill has befallen Ernest, I know it. Those were guns we heard but there are no troops nearby, how can this be?"

"Be calm now," says Father. "Perhaps they were only hunters. It might be Ernest has just taken a tumble."

"But the blood, Father. The blood."

"I have read in the newspaper of a great battle at Perryville in the south," mutters James.

"But that is many miles from here," says Mother, rubbing her hands together in dismay.

James bites his lower lip. "It may be there are troops loose from that fray. Perhaps a patrol or skirmishers."

"Oh, woe," cries Aunt Jenny, now openly tearful. "We are undone, the enemy is near."

Frowning, Father rubs his chin thoughtfully between finger and thumb. "It is best, I think, if we repair home."

"But Ellen…" says Mother.

"You must attend Jenny and Grandpa," advises Father. "I shall stay and wait for her."

"No, Father," interrupts James. "You go, Mother and the others will need you, leave me the saddle pony and I will wait for her here and bring her home."

Father dithers a moment, biting his lips as he sees the distressed women and the old man who is now barely awake.

"Very well, I shall harness the horses and fetch the carriage. Bring us word the minute you hear."

"I shall."

"*The minute*, James," Mother stresses. "Misty will collect the picnic things."

"Are we leaving?" wails Grandpa. "So soon?"

"We are indeed, Father. Now come, stand you up, Jenny will you help?"

Father takes James aside, out of earshot. "If help is needed, come to us immediately. You understand, James?" His lowered brows mean that he is indicating that he fears the worst.

"I understand." James nods abrupt agreement. Strangely, he is enervated by the whole unfortunate situation. The movement and the action fires some hidden part of him and the old lackadaisical attitude is falling away. It is not his normal attitude and yet for the first time in all his somber years he feels keen and eager to take part.

Father is looking off to the forest edge below where Ellen has disappeared from sight, "I should go after her," he mutters.

"No," presses James. "You must care for the

others they are in such distress, get them home safely."

———

"What you think?" asks a wry Brack, watching the ensuing panic as they struggle to help Grandpa into the carriage and Father pushes the nervous horse into the traces. Misty hurries from place to place, unsure of what to do and thereby being of little help. A weeping Aunt Jenny struggles to mount the gig with one hand clasping a handkerchief to her nose and wailing in despair. Mother, irritated now shoves Jenny irritably as she too pushes her way inside the carriage. Misty has closed the umbrella and waves it at the seated trio.

"What are you doing, girl?" bursts out Mother. "I told you collect the picnic things. Will you do that?"

"Yes ma'am," murmurs Misty, turning away with the unclaimed rolled umbrella still in her hand.

"Come, Father, hurry up," cries Mother. "We must away, just think if the enemy is near."

At that, Aunt Jenny offers a long and tearful sobbing cry that racks her whole body. Grandpa, crammed up tight against her, gives the woman a bemused look. "What's afoot, dear Jenny?" he asks. "Is it some insect that troubles you? You must know you must not fear the bees; they are creatures of God and give us sweet honey. All is well, my child."

"But, but," sobs Jenny. "It is dearest Ellen and her soldier beau, I fear something dreadful, we are undone, all undone."

"No, no," says Grandpa, patting her knee. "All is well, look at the beautiful flowers, they are everywhere."

———

"You think that soldier boy has met with some gunplay?" asks Linus.

"Well somebody sure has," supplies Brack. "If it's that Yankee, then all to the well and good."

The Confederates stand numbly, all watching the hurried anxiety as Father takes the reins and directs the carriage away.

"They ain't never seen no war, that's for sure," nods Caesar knowledgeably.

"No," agrees Jubal. "The poor people."

———

Left alone, James saddles the remaining two ponies, his and his father's while Misty collects the picnic things together. The basket is sealed and the left-overs collected in a bundle made from the tablecloth.

"What do I do wid dis, Mastah James?"

Away now from his family's watching eyes James mellows as he sees his opportunity.

"Here," he says, taking one handle of the large wicker basket. "We'll take it across to that tree, Benjamin can pick it all up on the morrow."

They drag the heavy basket across and fetch Grandpa's chair and the bundle of foodstuffs. James sits down and Misty stands alongside.

"You want I should go back now, suh?"

"No need, Misty. I will take you on my horse when Miss Ellen returns, come sit with me a moment."

Awkwardly Misty does as she is told and sits with downcast eyes on the grass alongside. James opens up the hamper and takes out a bottle of wine and a glass.

"You will have a glass, Misty? We are alone, no one will know."

"No, suh, thank you, suh, I don' take no strong liquors."

"Well then, something else, there is plenty here?"

Misty pauses, surprised by this overture. "Maybe a apple, might I hev a apple?"

"Of course." Smiles James. "Here, take two."

He sits on top of the closed hamper and pours himself a glass of wine. For once in his life he feels complete, here he is with the object of his desires and there is no one to object. In a burst of joy he swallows the full glass then quickly pours himself another.

Misty sits cross-legged and bites into the apple, she holds it in her left hand and the other in her right. It is as if she balances each as a scale.

Now James finds himself at a loss for words, in solitary writing he is master but the spoken word in company eludes him. So they sit silently, he sipping wine and Misty crunching her apple and both staring out to the forest down below.

"You think she be okay, Mistah James?"

"Who, Ellen? Oh, she will be fine, it would take a full-blown tornado to bother Miss Ellen."

"But that soldier boy she like, maybe he not so good."

"Perhaps," says James indifferently. "I would rather talk of you, Misty."

Misty is taken by surprise. "Me, suh? What's to say of me?"

James studies the roundness of her features, the softness of her brown arms and the swell of her unfettered breasts that show above the low neckline of her bodice.

"Will you take off that turban, Misty?"

"Yessuh," she says, obediently unwrapping the cloth about her head. Her black hair of tight curls is cut short and covers the top of her head like a cap. James is entranced and smiles at her completeness.

"That is much better," he allows.

Misty is wondering what he is about, this behavior is most unlike the young man and she is concerned he has other activities in mind. So thinking, she looks away in embarrassment and concentrates on eating her apple.

James clears his throat and attempts to take his long held feeling by the horns, "You really are a most fetching creature, Misty."

"Thank you, suh," she mutters.

"You know it is such an unfortunate matter that station should play so important a factor in our relationship, I would that it were other."

Still looking down, Misty does not understand him fully, "Is it rumpty-tumpty, suh?"

James frowns, "*Rumpty-tumpty?*"

"Yes, suh, I don' mind." She spreads her knees

apart beneath her skirt and drops the free apple into her lap. "I ain't got no man an' I be young."

"What do you mean, Misty?" James catches the drift but cannot quite believe it, he sees her spread legs and understands two aspects of his nature, one that with trickles with lust and the other that has imagined this moment in a totally other way. It was meant to be full of vows and promises, of soft words that are veiled in obscure terms and flower in secret understanding.

"I ain't never done that," confesses Misty.

Just then it seems some errant breeze has plucked the folded paper from the tree fork and dropped in Misty's open lap.

"What be that?" she squeaks and turns to look up at the tree but sees nothing there. "Where'd that come from?"

James, who recognizes it at once, says, "Why that is for you, it is a poem that I wrote for you."

He is a little distressed by Misty's overt advance and had not thought her capable of such a thing. There is something about it that unnerves him given his previous adoration of her imagined self.

Misty clutches the folded paper in her fist, the forgotten apple rolling on the ground. "Yo' wrote this for me?" she asks in wonder. "Jus' for Misty."

James swallows nervously. "That I did, it expresses my feelings. I hope you will not think it too outrageous."

"No, suh. I never had me no letter befo'."

Jubal who has picked up the note and dropped it in Misty's lap, backs away silently a knowing smile playing on his lips.

For the first time Misty raises her eyes to James and he looks into the mellow brown of them, he is about to speak when the thud of horse's hooves comes to them. Turning they both see Ellen part from the tree line and ride slowly up the hill toward them. She pulls to a halt on the old picnic site and attempts to dismount but only slides awkwardly from the saddle. Clutching at the stirrup she falls away with one forearm thrown across her brow and tumbles in a heap to the ground.

James and Misty leap to their feet, Misty thrusts the scrap of paper into her apron pocket and they both run across to Ellen. James crouches down by her side. "Sister, is all well. How are you?"

She turns red-rimmed and tearful eyes toward him, her once cheerful and lively face is sunken and pale.

"He is no more," she sobs weakly. "Poor Ernest is no more."

"What? What are you saying? What has happened to Ernest?"

"An accident they say. He was to his brigade, riding they say and some pickets. Young sentinel recruits unpracticed as yet, challenged him. He did not hear or answer and they fearing that the Rebels were upon them opened fire on him and shot him in the breast, he is quite dead."

"Oh, no!" gasps James.

"Missy, my Missy!" cries Misty, already tear drops sheening her eyes. "That be too bad."

James, most unlike his previous self, is overcome with pity and clutches his sister to him, cradling her head and trembling body in his arms.

The Confederates, standing in a group above and grimly watching the sad threesome, are restless and say little.

"They done kill him with friendly fire," breathes Linus. "Now don't that beat all?"

"One less to worry about," grunts a bitter Brack.

Jubal turns on him. "That poor girl don't know nothing about the hate, she only knows that love is gone from her."

"Well," says Brack awkwardly. "She shouldn't fall for no soldier then."

Jubal shakes his head in despair. "How can crippling a heart give you cause to give her blame?"

The captain clears his throat and gives out suddenly with an unlikely prescient thought. "Well, men, a sad affair most certainly but it seems to me our time here is done and now we must rejoin our own."

At his words and in silent agreement they all back away and move into the darkness of the forest and are soon as insubstantial as wisps of smoke sliding between the trees. Rising in unison as a soft mist into the air and drifting high into the upper atmosphere they move freely across wide skies and deep oceans. There, inhabiting clouds of forgetfulness that are heavyset with the rain of clemency, they slide down again unknowing into the ground and fall to nourish soil and become again the salt of the earth.

Of that crumpled note residing in Misty's pocket, little was known until years later, for the serving girl had never learned to read and write and so could not know its contents even though she treasured it for the rest of her days.

In time James became owner of the family home, he married an intelligent and well-read woman of a wealthy Boston family and had three children with her. His earlier infatuation with the serving girl was lost to him from that Easter picnic day and he wondered evermore why he had thought in such a fashion until the notion itself was lost to him and he thought of it, if at all, as a mere youthful fancy.

Ellen, bereft for what might have been, first took to nursing in aid centers throughout the war until the terrible scenes she witnessed there tore at her even more and drove her to escape her loss. She traveled far and had many reckless adventures along the way eventually ending her days in New Mexico where she found wild lovers and wealth in the cattle business.

Misty freed by Lincoln's decree had nowhere else to go and so stayed on with the Lyons family as a servant. Eventually, after some years a freed man in the carpentry trade married her and gave her a home and family. At her death the scrap of worn paper was discovered still in her possession but the penciled words had faded over time and their meaning was all but lost to her surviving children.

MOURNING GLORY

CHAPTER ONE

T he track up to the house was ill-maintained and only visible through curtains of Spanish moss hanging from the cypresses that bordered the path. It was hot, a misty steam rising from the nearby swamp blown in from the sea in this part of Virginia where loblolly pines were plentiful and grew on all sides in an untidy profusion that kept the place hidden or at least so it seemed. But there was evidence of an earlier occupation on the level dry land extending beyond the swamp.

The overgrown gardens on the approach were laden with weeds and bonfires had been lit amongst the trees and the earth beneath was scarred and burned in black rings that were raw with the cloying stink of charcoal and ash. Remnants of a tented camp were left in the shape of poles cut and left bound in broken pyramids, scraps of torn canvas flapped or lay in moldering heaps. Broken casks and forgotten tin mugs were scattered amongst other detritus and half buried by dead leaves in the brush.

It must have been a fine place in the old days but now one end of the building was lost to fire. Blackened beams rose skywards from where the roof had once been and scorch marks rode over the white paint remaining on the main front of the property. It was a plain-style antebellum building built from wood on two stories with narrow windows and a tall brick chimney at one end. There had been another matching chimney at the opposite end but now all that remained of it was a jagged stump of broken masonry.

In the shade of a long porch and behind a simple fenced railing that made up most of the frontage she waited, looking as solitary as a sea captain on the deck of a ship or more properly a lone woman on a widow's walk.

She wore mourning black and looked quite severe inside it.

A slender woman, one might say thin, tight under her corset and small, not more than five feet tall. Puffed at the shoulders and with bustle at the back gave her some breadth but the black clothes made her appear slimmer than she already was. In all, the effect was of a woman trapped or held tightly within the morose and somber windings that bound her as tightly as a mummy.

At her throat there was a black choker and a glass fronted framed locket that hung to her chest on a thin gold chain and inside under the glass lay trapped the pale curl of a lock of human hair.

A chignon of dark hair rose above the back of her head and the face beneath was attractive enough despite the hard look and pale skin. She was about thirty years of age but life had already taken a toll on her and given her some strains of white in her hair.

When she spoke it was with a refined accent but a harsh sadness lay at the back of her voice, "My name is Mrs. Antonia Geraldine Lake and I have need of a working man."

————

Gale Doolie stood silently before her with his wide-brimmed plantation hat held before him in both hands. Any stiffness had long since departed that hat and it was ripped along the brim and stained with the darkness of sweat, dust, and black powder.

He knew he did not look attractive to her, his Confederate infantry jacket was split and threaded at the shoulder and several buttons were missing. The threadbare and dusty roll of blanket he carried was looped diagonally over his shoulder and tied at the waist like a pig meat sausage. The roll held all his worldly possessions inside it, which didn't amount to a whole lot, his cutthroat razor, folding knife, tin mug, and a spoon.

The yellow stripe down the outer edge of his faded blue pants was coming away at the seam and his boots, well, there was little to say about the boots. They had covered many miles on the march and showed wear with the loose soles coming apart from the uppers and scuffed leather at the toe.

"How long have you been out?" she asked, looking him up and down.

"Since the surrender, ma'am."

Antonia held pale hands by her side almost lost in the folds of her dress, small but work-worn they fidgeted and she rubbed thumb and forefinger together repeatedly as if nervous.

"And who did you serve with?"

"Fourth Brigade, second Alabama, ma'am."

"You should know that this household was a firm supporter of the Southern cause and defeat is not a thing easily accepted, at least not by me."

Gale nodded affirmation.

"I doubt it is so but should this trouble you in any manner," she continued. "Then say it now and we'll go our ways without malice."

"Don't bother me none, ma'am."

"My late husband was an officer with General Pickett and was lost to us at Gettysburg during that ill-conceived charge. Were you there?"

"No, ma'am, I wasn't."

She drew herself up and Gale saw the ring of house keys at her waist that would have been better suited to a housekeeper than a mistress.

"Very well, we shall give it a trial," said Antonia. "You will sleep in the old slave quarters and you may suit them how you like for your comfort. I shall prefer you clean and shaven and you will labor from first light until dark. You shall be fed and paid eleven dollars a month. I'm sure we might find some suitable clothing for you; I think that what you are wearing now is best suited to the fire. Is all that understood?"

"It is."

He stood a moment unsure if he should speak or not.

"You have a question?"

"Yes, ma'am, how many you got working here?"

She smiled with her lips but not her eyes. "We have *you*, Mr. Doolie."

"Just me?" he said in awe and turning to look at the destroyed property. "For all this?"

Antonia shrugged. "It's all I can afford. They have wiped me clean, Mr. Doolie, almost burned us out and I have little enough left as it is. It's the best I can do. If this is not to your preference then I suggest you move on."

"No, ma'am, I seen what it's like out there already. A whole country torn up by conflict, there ain't nothing left. Livestock and grain all taken, I ain't seen a single horse, mule or cow in the past month. People are starving."

She nodded her head emphatically. "That is why this place must live again," she said. "The darkies have all gone but soon enough they will be back, they need to eat just like the rest of us."

She led him to the rear of the house and showed him the old slave huts. There were four of them, simple rectangular wood built structures with hip roof and chimney.

"Take your pick," she offered with a wry smile. "They are all empty. Settle yourself and I shall bring you something to eat."

"Thank you, ma'am. That will be most welcome, I ain't eaten in a while."

"Well, I fear it's not much, Mr. Doolie, so don't be expecting great things."

She left him then and Gale entered the nearest hut. On a beaten earth floor, empty except for a slat

133

bucket with a rope handle and two wooden chairs, one with a broken back. In a corner a mattress that had seen better days lay on the bare earth. The large open brick fireplace took up one wall and the interior had been painted with white distemper at one time but now the planks were gray and etched with dirt. Above his head amongst the roof timbers dangled swathes of cobwebs, dank and ominous in the shadows.

She came back with a lit lantern as evening approached and handed him a small bundle of cloth with a large cut slice of bread inside spread with some dark matter. There was a mug of what looked like black coffee.

"I spread the bread with pickle," she explained. "That's all they left me, they broke all the jars of preserves we kept in the cellar, so this will have to do."

"Thank you, ma'am," Gale said, eyeing the bread hungrily and not caring a damn whether there was pickle on it or fresh butter and honey.

"This is a coffee I make from powdered acorns, it tastes terrible but is all we have here."

"I'm obliged," he mumbled.

"Very well," she said. "I see you have your own blanket so make yourself as comfortable as you can. I'll bring you some of my husband's clothes to wear, you seem of similar size. I shall see you on the morrow, Mr. Doolie."

"Yes, ma'am," wishing she would hurry and leave so he could devour the small portion and drink the coffee he was that desperate. It had been three days since he had eaten anything and then it had only been some dry crackers he had found in a deserted house.

"Go easy with the lámp oil," she warned as she left. "We have so little left."

When alone, he ate hungrily finishing the small meal in minutes and sucking down the hot drink uncaring what it tasted like.

Exhausted, he thought no more about his surroundings, he had slept in far worse over the past months and he settled quickly on the sorry mattress and wrapped in his blanket was soon asleep only too glad that providence had given him shelter.

CHAPTER TWO

T he next morning she arrived early with breakfast, carrying it on a tray covered by a napkin.

It was simple in extreme, no more than a hot dish of beans and biscuits with the same excuse for coffee. The bundle of clothes she left tied with string sported a fine frock coat, pants, underwear, a calico shirt, hat and best of all, leather gaiters and boots.

She stood watching him with the same slightly imperious but keen look in her eyes as he gobbled down the food without moving from his bed.

"I would like you to start on the destroyed part of the house," she said. "It would be best of we could seal it off before winter comes."

Sitting cross-legged on the mattress he was scraping the last of the beans with his spoon and looked up at her, a faint hint of embarrassment running through him at his display of starvation.

"I fear them clothes is too fine for that kind of

labor, ma'am," he said. "Best I work in what I have on and save them others, there'll be soot and a pretty mess I'm thinking."

She shrugged. "Whatever you think best."

"You have tools?" he asked.

"There is a box of things, hammer, saw and such."

"Timber?"

She shook her head. "That would be best but cut lumber and transport is too expensive right now if it's at all possible. I hear they burned down the lumber yard at Loughton fearing we might be making seagoing vessels with it."

"Then we shall bring down one of the slave huts, there's plenty wood there. How about nails?"

She shook her head again negatively.

"Then best we reuse what comes with the slave timbers and beat them straight. Failing that we must cut pegs."

"Good, good," she mumbled. "That is fine."

"Is there water nearby?"

"There is a creek beyond the house but what shall that be needed for?"

"To caulk the timbers, ma'am. Once built, we need to seal the joins with mud and straw against the weather and these old timbers will come in all shapes and sizes I'll warrant."

"You seem to know what you speak of, Mr. Doolie."

He snorted dismissively. "I've done my share of handiwork, ma'am."

"Glad to hear it. Is there anything else?"

He pouted thoughtfully, "I was thinking, you

don't have any fowling piece, do you, ma'am. Maybe I could fetch us something for the pot, a rabbit or pigeon perhaps."

She paused, worrying for the moment in allowing a stranger access to such things but then determining that her extremities were such there was little point in such doubts she said, "A fine idea, a change of diet would be most welcome. My husband had me bury weapons at the outbreak of conflict when he left to join the army, luckily the Federals never found them."

"What were the bluecoats doing here anyway?"

"A Union General and his staff made this his headquarters and he had a troop with him camped out in the woods. The officers were gentlemen and treated me well I must admit, but the soldiers I fear were of the more common sort."

"They left a fine mess."

"They did so, I advise best beware of the creek near the house, Mr. Doolie, it is foul as they used it as a latrine but upstream I assure you there is clean water."

"Might I ask what weapons you have then?"

"A Springfield rifle and two handguns, cap, and ball pistols."

"You have ammunition?"

"Some buried with them."

"Then we shall dig them up."

"Fine."

Within the hour, Gale was hard at work dismantling the destroyed section of the house. The timbers were indeed sorely damaged and of little use but he stacked them where he could away from the building. The broken bricks of the chimney made a huge pile that needed to be separated into usable and broken and these likewise stacked neatly. The longer distorted timbers that rose high above the roof and spiked with long nails were more difficult and he wished he had some means of their retrieval but without a working horse it was a risky business and he resorted to an axe and rope for this work. Soon he was blackened by the soot and charred wood.

Antonia came to him with water and another slice of bread for his lunch. She wore the same black dress but also a wide-brimmed straw hat against the sun and a stained apron about her middle.

"You are doing well, Mr. Doolie. I am pleased to see so much already done."

He sat on a pile of bricks and ate the bread while covered in black from head to toe and looking for all that like a regular chimney sweep.

"It will be some time yet," he admitted.

He was stripped to the waist, his body streaked with soot and channels of sweat ran through the black to show stripes of his white skin. She was pleased to see he was a firm-bodied man, slim and muscled under all the filth and felt she had judged him fairly as a hard worker.

"I am trying to revitalize my market garden," she explained. "Over there, beyond the house. It was a great resource at one time; of course we had many Negroes to maintain the vegetables back then.

Unfortunately, the Federals rode cannon and limber across it and destroyed much but I think maybe some potatoes are saved for planting. Perhaps some tomato plants and beans might also survive. There are apples in the orchard that will be ready later in the year."

"Quite a feast," he said, half joking.

"It is little but will be our priority come the winter," she allowed.

"Indeed so."

She looked at him for a long moment, then said, "So carry on," and turning away, she left him abruptly.

———

That night Gale paced out his cabin and found it was no more than fifteen feet long by seventeen wide. Exploring the other cabins showed him they were the same dimensions and enabled him to discover a rickety table in one and the last of the four had the look of better timbers being used in its structure.

With a long post taken from the burned house he worked at knocking away the sticky swags of cobwebs that haunted the hut. There was a scurrying in the roof at his assault and a steady rain of spiders that ran across the floor. Gale feared that rodents also inhabited the roof but as there was little he could do about it he settled to live in their company.

The weather and the breeze through the swamp brought warmth on the night air along with its fecund scent of decaying vegetation, it was a gentle draft that moved the trees and rustled the leaves about him peacefully. He heard the infantile scream of a fox along with the hum of bugs and the distant rumble of thunder somewhere far off to the east.

Once he had completed his clearance of the cobwebs, he sat outside with his back against the hut wall and stared up at a clear dark sky and the mesmeric disc of a moon as bright as a silver coin. He wondered about the woman and how she had survived alone in this place with no husband or help and surrounded by enemy. It must have taken a strong type of personality he decided and was not surprised by her stern disposition. Looking toward the rear of the house he saw one lighted window high on the upper floor. It appeared that Mrs. Lake could equally well not sleep and spent the night using her fragile supply of lamp oil instead of moonlight.

Of Mrs. Lake he had no clear thought. So much had happened over the past years during the war when faces and names had come and gone with such regularity around him that she made no more impression on him than that of this distant employer. He had learned to live in the moment and for now he had a place to rest his head and some food to sustain him. The misery and rapacious activities he had witnessed during his service had left him more drained of any desire for human contact than resentful of his fellow man. So he lived an insular existence best protected by the hardened shell developed for survival amid the angry sounds of destruction that had haunted the country for the best part of four years.

He had no dreams or if he had he did not remember them and awoke only to be reminded of his labor by the ache in his limbs, the ingrained dirt and the raw tightness of his fists.

CHAPTER THREE

Within a week Gale had begun work on dismantling the slave hut for its timber and it was an odious task. The filth of years had collected in the rafters and apart from the vermin, there were cottonmouth snakes that had found a nest there.

She came to him while he crouched upon the roof prizing boards free and tossing them down.

"Mr. Doolie!" she called.

He turned, propping himself against the angle of the roof with his boot.

"I intend to attend worship next Sunday and would be obliged if you would accompany me."

He chewed his lower lip. "Have to tell you, ma'am, I ain't much of a one for the prayer meetings," he allowed.

"That is quite all right, I just wish company on the road that is all. We will pass along the forest trail and undesirables dwell there, I would feel safer with your attendance but there is no need for you to enter the chapel."

"I see. What kind of undesirables do you mean?"

"They are men, once guerrillas under Colonel Mosby I believe and while I admire their reluctance to surrender I fear these bands are now no more than bandits and I believe they intend harm to passersby."

He nodded understanding. "Some of those old boys just can't give it up. You have run up against them before?"

"Yes, just once, with my husband's name in my defense I managed to escape without harm but I fear they will not be so kind the next time."

"Then I will come with you."

"Thank you, I think best that you bring a pistol with you for they are all well armed."

"Very well, ma'am."

"Thank you, Mr. Doolie."

———

That afternoon Gale took the Springfield rifle and determined to find them some meat for the table for by now he was becoming tired of their meager fare. The gun had been greased and wrapped in oilcloth before burial so was in good condition. An unusual weapon for the Confederacy it was a long gun and fired a .58 caliber minié ball from a paper cartridge using a percussion cap, the rifle was known to be accurate for at least four hundred yards or maybe more. Gale hoisted the nine-pound weight of the gun and with a sack of ammunition tied to his belt and a haversack over his shoulder set off into the woods to see what he could find.

There were white-tailed deer here and wild turkey he discovered seeing their tracks in soft ground. He knew small birds were out of the offing as the heavy gauge bullet would more than likely dismember them when struck but a turkey would be fine. Some rabbit if he was lucky with his shot and later he would check the creek for fish.

He moved through the thickly wooded forest quietly and with the ease that came from his military experience. After some time deep in the forest he came upon a wide pool in a deep gulley at the edge of the swampland. Here he hoped to find creatures coming down to the water, he knew it was the wrong time of day for such but he was hopeful nonetheless. Crouching down amongst brush, he waited patiently enjoying the calm flat water that reflected the sheen of blue sky above. Waders moved here and duck darted amongst the reeds. Feeling relaxed Gale recalled earlier times before the war and wished he had a fishing pole so he could sit as he had done as a youngster and while away the hours in peace and solitude while waiting for a catch.

Then he saw movement.

Three heavily bearded men moved along the far bank, it was the pale blue shirt of one of them he had noted and only that as they all moved in unison and with quiet stealth. Almost as if trained woods-men, they were separated from one another and tracking in the same direction, moving smoothly across his vision as they traveled with determination through the undergrowth. They wore a rough mix of shabby civilian clothing and shapeless slouch hats but all were armed and carried rifles. Not remarkable in itself as they could have been hunters as he was but their sense of purpose made them something different. There was an unsettling air of predator and intensity about the men. Vanishing from his sight amongst the trees Gale breathed a sigh of relief that he had not run up against them earlier for he felt that they were in all probability a dangerous breed.

Relaxing with their disappearance and returning to his brooding, he froze as he was suddenly surprised when a deer came out of the tree line near him and tentatively moved down to the water's edge. It was an easy shot for him, not more than eighty yards and yet with the nearness of the men across the water he deferred. With Antonia's warning of the type of men inhabiting the forest he thought it best to avoid the gunshot noise even though the promise of a two-hundred-pound buck would fill their larder for many a day.

Perhaps, he wondered, if they shared the forest with these types of men, and he had certainly seen enough of their capabilities during his latter days of travel through the crippled country, a more stealthy form of hunting was called for. He would prepare snares and lay them across the paths or burrows where there was greenery and that should fetch them some rabbit for the table.

As it was, as he made his way back he came across some wild turkeys in a clearing and risked a shot bringing down a large bird. Antonia said nothing at sight of the creature save giving him a slight smile at his presentation but Gale noticed how quickly she sat and eagerly began to pluck the feathers.

They dined that night on roasted turkey and were content with the change in diet although Gale thought it wise to make no mention of the men he had seen.

———

She called for him and stood waiting outside his hut in black cloak and bonnet with a prayer book in her hand and he thought her a solemn picture amongst the bright color of the day.

"It is Sunday," she said. "I must attend the chapel."

"Ah!" he sighed. "I had lost track of the days. Forgive me, I shall dress and come immediately."

He decided to put on the clothes she had brought him. They felt and smelled strange after being stored for so long but the fit was close enough to be comfortable. The frock coat was a little tight in the shoulders but the long tail hid the pistol that he pressed into his pants belt at the back. It was strange for him to be dressed so after the loose fit of his tired uniform and looking at himself in the broken slate of mirror he had found he was momentarily surprised by the ordinary fellow that appeared in the reflection. A normal person stared back at him and it left him with a strange sense of unease as if the likeness did not belong to him.

She still stood patiently waiting as he left the hut

and without a word turned and marched off. Gale followed on behind mildly irritated that she made no comment and he was expected to trail her as if a manservant. She set a fast step and strode on energetically into the forest with Gale some paces behind.

They came to a wide passage where the trees rose high above and hung over the broad path in an almost cathedral-like archway. Little sunlight barely penetrated the overhanging leaves and they moved through the hazy shadows of the pathway that seemed to dwarf them by its size. A breeze moved the treetops that swayed with a gentle susurration filling the silence of the forest and sending spots of sunlight jumping and dancing across their backs. Gale watched her small figure striding in front of him and thought that she moved much as she presented herself to him—almost as if he were not there.

She paused, listening for a moment, her footsteps faltering and then Gale too heard the metallic rattle of accoutrements and the steady tread of horse. Antonia gave him a quick glance over her shoulder and he saw the pale moment of fear that crossed her face. He drew up alongside her as a troop of Union cavalry rode around a bend and approached them at the walk. There were twenty men lead by a lieutenant and sergeant and the officer called a halt as he came up on them.

"Good day," said the officer, studying them from his mount. He was a young, fair-haired man with a mustache and small beard at his chin and struck a pose with one gauntleted hand on his hip in a gallant fashion.

Antonia took a tentative step back as if his words struck her and at sight of the blue uniforms Gale felt the old animosity rising up to raise the hairs on his neck.

"May I ask, where are you bound?" asked the lieutenant.

Both Antonia and Gale looked up at him without replying.

The sergeant, a burly fellow, dark-haired with a scar marking his cheek and with a broad unshaven chin urged his horse forward with a rattle of bridle and saber. Scowling, he leaned threateningly over the saddle toward Gale.

"You!" he barked. "Show some respect. Take off your hat when you talk to the officer."

Gale stared back coldly, "Who gave you that scar?" he asked.

"One of you wretched Johnny Rebs," spat the sergeant. "That's who."

"Be careful you don't receive another one the like."

"Why you—"

The lieutenant raised a gloved hand. "Be still, Sergeant."

"But, sir—" growled the sergeant.

"We are going to church as it is the Lord's Day," supplied Antonia in a strong clear voice.

At the sound of her accent, the lieutenant raised an eyebrow as he recognized her as a woman of standing and he gave a small bow and raised a finger to the peak of his kepi in salute.

"Forgive me, ma'am, we must ask. We are under Reconstruction orders and commissioned to be sure that all is in order on this route. There are, I fear, some malcontents reported nearby in these woods."

"As you can see, sir," replied Antonia. "We are hardly robbers or road agents."

The lieutenant jerked his head toward Gale. "This man is your husband?"

"More like a lousy secessionist," muttered the sergeant.

"No, Lieutenant, he works for me. My husband met his end at Gettysburg with the rest of his brave company."

The lieutenant swiveled his attention to Gale. "You are armed, sir?"

Gale spread the wings of his coat wide glad he had tucked the pistol at the rear. "As you see."

"Good, good. Ma'am, might I trouble you for your name?"

"I am Mrs. Antonia Geraldine Lake."

"Indeed, a pleasure, ma'am. I am Lieutenant Forby Sinclair, at your service."

"He's one of them, sir," growled the sergeant, glaring at Gale. "I'd swear to it."

"Sergeant Malone!" snapped Sinclair. "I beg you to watch your manners, these people are obviously of no interest to us." He gave another slight bow to Antonia. "Pray forgive the intrusion, Mrs. Lake. Please go on and attend your service."

Antonia inclined her head. "Thank you, Lieutenant."

Sinclair raised a hand and ordered the platoon on and with a jingle of harness they rode past. As they did so, each trooper looked down at the two figures standing in the path with disdainful and distant eyes. There was an air of arrogance about the men that portrayed them as conquerors and yet, as the bitterness of their glances implied, the attendant sadness of the recent conflict was still written all too clearly in their memories.

With a tight face and a hiss of breath from between clenched teeth Antonia turned swiftly away and continued her striding step toward her devotions.

CHAPTER FOUR

The two Negros arrived while Gale was still disassembling the burned timbers of the damaged wing.

The man was tall, well built and handsome featured, the woman with him was not so pretty, her bunched hair was in disarray and her flat features appeared haggard and worn. Both wore down-at-heel clothes and stood silent and still in the yard out front of the house.

It was Antonia who stepped onto the porch to speak with them and the sound of her voice drew Gale's attention from his position on the ladder.

"Can I help you?" she asked.

The man took a few steps nearer. "Scuse me, mistress. You spare us something to eat, if you please?"

"Stay where you are," replied Antonia sharply.

"Sorry, mistress," said the man stepping back. "Don' mean no offense."

"Who are you?"

"I be Samuel Porter and this be my wife Luella May."

He had the supplicant posture and demeanor of a petitioner but there was also a firmer quality evident in his character that was latently hidden by the lowered head and downcast eyes.

"And where are you from?"

"We be from the old Gascoigne place over yonder, m'um."

"Why did you leave there?"

"Ain't nothing there no more, they all done leave, white folks and darkies. Them tobacco and cotton fields is wrack and ruin now. One of them carpet bagging people done bought the place, they say he don' pay much."

Gale had left off his work and descended the ladder. Wiping his soot stained hands on a rag he walked over toward the pair.

"I can he'p you, suh," Sam said quickly, turning toward him. "I ready fo' work."

Gale looked questioningly across at the frowning figure of Antonia.

"I'm sorry," she said. "There's nothing here for you, we barely have enough for ourselves in these trying times."

Gale scratched his chin thoughtfully leaving a smudge of soot there. "I could do with the help, Mrs. Lake. We can make do, I reckon."

Antonia's face tightened and she looked at him ignoring the Negroes, "They are freed now; President Lincoln has given them emancipation. I cannot pay them wages and how can we feed them?"

"We be happy to work fo' found, ma'am," Sam

cut in. "And Luella May, she be trained in the house."

Antonia raised a critical eyebrow and eyed the Black woman's rounded belly. "She is with child if I am not much mistaken."

Luella May's face crumpled and she dropped her eyes to the ground, she made no sound but her sadness was all too evident.

"They can have one of them cabins," suggested Gale. "Won't hurt none to clean up the trash in that old camp site as well."

"Oh, yessuh," said Sam eagerly. "We do a good job o' work hard fo' yuh."

Biting her lower lip Antonia pondered, "You have anything with you or only what you wear, is that all you have?" she asked.

"We got some pieces from our old place."

"Very well," said Antonia. "You will have a week and we shall see. Use the slave quarters but don't expect much, times are hard all around."

"That is fo' sure. Mighty obliged, mistress."

"My name is Mrs. Antonia Lake and this is Mr. Gale Doolie, who will oversee. You will be respectful and I expect prompt attention and no lingering, are we clear?"

"Yessum, Missy Lake."

————

The couple trooped off back into the woods from where they came and Antonia beckoned Gale over.

"I am not sure of this, Mr. Doolie. Are we wise?"

157

"They're starving, ma'am, and the girl's pregnant. It ain't right to turn them away."

Her voice was suddenly sharp. "That's remarkably considerate of you, considering this is *my* home."

"T'ain't no part of that, we all seen our fair share of hardship, I'll be bound. Time for that is over now."

She took several deep quivering breaths and met his gaze. Her hand went to the locket at her throat and enclosed it in a firm grip. "You are right, off course. I am too much lost in all the terror. Even now I feel the fear that we are enclosed in it and dread is all around."

"You're a Christian woman, Mrs. Lake. You have the faith to sustain you."

Tears filled her eyes, her cheeks flushed and her small body began to tremble. The sudden flood of emotion seemed to remodel and leave her momentarily defenseless. "But there has been so much grief, it tears at me and I feel that my cup has run over and only despair remains."

"No, no, it ain't never going to do that. This here kindness is a step in the right direction."

She frowned and shook her head, a single tear ran slowly over the roundness of her cheek. "How can you consider that? Surely, you must have seen many more terrible things than I on the battlefield."

They were close now and he watched as the tear spilled its trail across the curve of her skin and something moved in him and quite naturally he reached out a soot stained hand and with one finger gently brushed the tear away. In doing so he left a watery trail of black across her cheek.

"I never went to war over that slavery thing," he admitted. "I went to be with my people. I weren't no more than nineteen years old and straight from the farm, what did I know? But my friends were there and their fathers were there too, we all went together."

"Such foolishness." Her voice broke and she gasped a sob. "My dear John, a loving husband, he was not made to be one for shot and shell."

"None of us were, lady."

Gale was seeing another side of her; the outer shell of harshness was put aside and vulnerability showed through. It was in his mind to take her in his arms to comfort her but some reserve held him back. It was not a proper behavior and society forbade such actions that would be considered forward in the extreme. For a man of his class and one of hers it was a thing never to be considered however unlikely the circumstances.

"It will be well," he said softly. "Have no fear."

Sam and his wife were returning, pulling a small two-wheel handcart loaded with their few possessions. Two chairs and a small table, a trunk and bulging canvas sack.

Antonia turned away, hiding her face from them, "You had best show them the cabin."

———

Gale led the way and the two blacks followed him

around the rear of the house to where the slave quarters stood.

"What's in the sack you got there?" he asked as they approached the cabins.

"That be peanuts, suh. We been living on dem all dis week, ain't much else to forage fo'."

"I got this first one," Gale said, pointing out his hut. "The last one we take apart for the timber but you can have either of the others."

"Thank you, suh," said Sam, ushering Luella May forward. "Take yo' pick, gal."

"I shall return to my labor," said Gale and while Luella May was engaged in exploring the huts, Sam stepped forward.

"I he'p you now, suh?"

"Surely you will settle in first."

"No, suh. Luella May be fine, I come along wid you."

"Very well."

"You be master heyah?" asked Sam for clarity.

"No, Sam, I'm just a soldier fallen on hard times like so many others."

"I hear dat, de roads be full of dem."

"Going home if they have one to return to."

"Yes, suh. Lord! There c'ain't be many of dem left, that's fo' sure."

———

Gale was pleased to find that Sam worked well with him. He took direction easily and did not argue as if he knew better as so often is the case when some men work together. Sam would see what needed doing and had a quiet understanding that went beyond the normal prescribed instruction. His only suggestion being that they forge the used nails and straighten them out under heat as they would a horseshoe.

The renovation moved along well with the two of them at work and before many months had passed the repairs to the house were well under way and completion before winter seemed assured.

————

Gale for his part needed to hunt more regularly now that there were four mouths to feed. He had laid aside his need for silence and moved amongst the trees shooting his prey without consideration for the noise and the wild men he knew inhabited the forest.

There was no avoiding them though and one day he came upon them as they waited for him.

Gale parted the foliage and stepped into a small, almost circular clearing of beech trees; there was water nearby and the pale cautious movement of egrets visible as they picked their way through the tall grasses. An oppressive silence filled the forest even the birds seemed to have temporarily stopped their calls and it was there that Gale found the two patient men quietly confronting him. Both were shabbily dressed with long beards and tattered hats cocked on the backs of their heads.

One lay full-length, casually stretched out on the ground and resting his head against the trunk of a tree. He toyed with an unlit clay pipe in his mouth and a rifle lay on the ground next to him. In his belt was a revolver and in his hand another pistol held casually across his middle with the barrel pointing toward Gale. The man looked slyly across at Gale from the corner of his eye, apparently untroubled by his presence and ruminating over the pipe he rolled between his lips.

His companion, a short solidly built fellow with battered features and a nut-brown complexion had a dense beard that reached down to his chest and stood facing Gale with his legs apart and a long rifle couched in the crook of his arm.

"How do?" said the man, effectively blocking Gale's path. "Knew you'd pass this way so thought we'd say howdy. Us being neighbors an' all."

Gale nodded silent greeting and waited to see what both men wanted.

"Name's Jethro Bales and this here is Simon Endicott. Late of the Army of Northern Virginia serving under General Lee."

The seated Simon lifted the pipe from his mouth and gave Gale a faintly mocking wave.

"Good day to you boys. I'm Gale Doolie."

"Yeah," said Jethro. "We heard you often enough in these here woods, saw you when you first passed through. You was wearing the uniform so know you is one of us."

"Not no more," Gale allowed.

Jethro clicked his tongue in agreement. "Thought you might be advised as to who you was sharing a roof with."

"That so?"

"Indeed that woman is a collaborator, didn't know that did you? She been playing footloose with them Yankees stationed at her place. Can't say we approve and we aim to call on her sometime soon."

"Why's that?"

"Well." Shrugged Jethro. "We got a particular way of dealing with them that keeps company with the enemy."

"The lady was just getting by; she had no call on them invading her house, t'weren't her that invited them in."

"Not the way we see it," perked up the lounging Simon, waving his pistol loosely. "Best way with this sort is to make example, to cut off her hair and strip her naked, let the world see what she's truly made of."

Gale found the statement crude and offensive but he did not show it only shook his head negatively. "I fear you fellows have it wrong. Mrs. Lake is a God fearing Christian woman. Her husband fought and died in battle, I never met no firmer supporter of the cause, she swears by it."

"That why she was courting them Yankee officers and set up a welcome for all the other federal dogs in her backyard?"

"Come on, you men must see she had no choice in that."

"Look," said Jethro taking a different tack. "We come to ask you something else; we come to ask if you'll join us, that's our purpose here. We still fight the good fight and take out the occasional bluebelly when he's dumb enough to wander into the woods. We plan on raiding their depot and would be glad to have you along; there'll be rich findings in there. They got liquor and cigars, all kinds of pretty food-stuffs, them lousy invaders live high on the hog, believe me."

Simon was dragging himself into a sitting posi-tion and stuffing tobacco from a leather pouch into his pipe, his narrow eyes were still held fixed on Gale. There was something unsettling that glittered in the man's eyes and Gale feared that he was perhaps unhinged and held a touch of madness about him.

"Way I hear it," said Gale. "You fellows take to stopping folk on the road and robbing them of their possessions."

"Ach!" said Jethro dismissively. "We has to levy a righteous tax, we're still fighting men at war and have good cause to take a portion."

"The war's been over for a while now."

"Not for some of us," said Jethro. "We ain't giving up that easy."

"What do you care anyway," spat Simon. "You met that peckerwood bluecoat Forby Sinclair, ain't you?" Gale recalled the young officer that had stopped them on the way to church. "That's the sort we're up agin, sitting up there like some kind of lord coming down on us poor folk with no good cause. Him and his kind need taking down a peg or two. Always has, always will."

"Well, look here," said Gale, drawing a long breath. "Thing is I'm vouching for the Lake woman and I stand by her. She ain't no collaborator, not by any means, she's just a woman fell on hard times and trying to make do, like we all is. Lost her man and had her home half destroyed, I'd certain sure I'd take it as a mean affront if anything should happen to her."

"You're one of us, Gale," offered a more conciliatory Jethro. "We wouldn't like to give you any call for offense."

"I sincerely hope not as that would cause me grievous displeasure."

"Okay, okay." Nodded Jethro. "We'll leave her be but you think on what I said. You get sick of waiting on her ladyship and digging like them darkies, when you want to do some real work then come along of us, we're easy to find."

"I'll think on it," promised Gale, although in his mind he was far from considering it.

"She kind of sweet, is she?" Simon offered with a sneer.

"No call for talk like that," snapped Gale.

Simon lifted himself and stood up, sliding his back against the tree trunk and rising from his sitting position with a slow oiled ease like a snake unrolling itself.

"You just remember, we be watching you," he said through parted lips cast in a smile where the tips of his teeth showed in the darkness of his mouth. "Can't abide no Johnny come lately appeasing the Yankee rendering of the law."

"Leave the man be," growled Jethro with a tired air of disapproval. "He ain't like that. Trouble with you, Simon, is that the fighting bitterness took hold on you and won't let go. Don't you mind him Gale, Simon is a good old boy most of the time."

Simon gave a hollow-sounding snort. "Yeah, I'm

good all right, I just hate the fact we's driven to live like groundhogs in our own country, that's all. But maybe I's just a tad mean tempered today, you go your way in peace, old fella, and don't mind me none."

CHAPTER FIVE

It was late in the year and the nights were drawing in early when Gale returned to his cabin. He found that Sam and Luella May had lit a fire outside and were cooking their evening meal over the flames.

Sam strolled across. "Mister Doolie, suh," he called.

"Yes, what is it, Sam?"

"Well, we'd be obliged if'n you would join us dis evenin'."

Gale looked from him to the fire. "That's mighty kind of you," he answered. "That sure smells good, I just reckon I will if it's no trouble."

"Come you over and welcome, suh. T'ain't nothing more than a broth Luella May made from turkey bones and some mushroom and dandelion greens she found but we's be glad of your company."

Gale laid aside his rifle and crossed over to the fire. "Evening to you, Luella May."

The woman looked up from stirring the pot and nodded greeting. She very rarely spoke and went about her business with silence. Meanwhile the child inside her was beginning to show in her ponderous walk and swollen belly.

"A word to you, Sam," said Gale taking a seat on the ground beside the fire.

"Yes, suh."

"You should be aware that there are men out there in the woods."

Sam nodded.

"Could be they will leave us alone but they are lost souls and still committed to the old ways. I tell you this." He looked cautiously across at Luella May. "Not to bring fear into your lives but just to give you good warning."

"I know it, suh. We already been told by others what was lying in them woods. Lot of Black folks on the road tryin' to make their way and dem white boys done treat dem mean."

"If they trouble you or Mrs. Lake then you come tell me."

Sam nodded his head in understanding.

"How goes it with you, Luella May?" asked Gale as he accepted a steaming dish from the woman's hand.

"I be fine, suh," she said. "Missy Lake been havin' me he'p in her garden. We growin' tings."

"You like that?"

"I does, suh. There be tatties and peas growin', soon be plenty."

"And the baby?"

She stopped her ladling for a moment and

glanced down laying a hand over the ball of her round stomach. "He be kickin' and fussin' like a lusty young 'un."

"That's good, huh?"

"Yessah,"

"You hab any youngsters, Mistah Doolie, suh?" asked Sam.

"No, I don't, I left home to join up before I found me any wife."

"Yo' still got time, I reckon."

Gale smiled and looked up at Luella May and raised the dish, "This is mighty fine, Mrs. Porter, mighty fine."

Luella May supplied him with a small curtsy. "Thank yo', suh."

Later Luella May brought them coffee made from ground chicory roots and Gale delighted in the taste that was far better than the acorn grinds that Antonia supplied. That sat around the fire content with each other's company until Sam began to sing. He had a fine bass tone to his voice and his soft rendering filled the night air with a mellowness that Gale found fitting on this evening.

> *Wade in de water,*
> *Yo'gotta wade in de water,*
> *God's gonna trouble de water*
> *God's gonna trouble de water*

After some badgering Sam also convinced his wife to bring out her fiddle, which she did from the basket they had brought with them. After tuning she began to play and did so well, as Gale was surprised to discover. She had learned the instrument from her master on the plantation and gave a lively rendition that pleased them all.

When the evening was done, Gale strolled back to his cabin full and contented. He paused at his doorway and looked over to the house and the lonely lit window of Antonia's room. It brought a sadness to him that the woman should keep herself so secluded and he felt the isolation she must endure to be so. There was something rooted in the depths of her, he was sure of it, some deep and impenetrable sorrow that was beyond her husband's death and that still governed her existence and kept any kind of joy from her.

He wondered then at what the man Jethro had told him and how it had truly been with the quartered troops and how their presence had marked her.

It was to become clearer to him within days.

———

With winter coming a great deal of firewood had to be prepared, enough for the house and the cabins and Gale set Sam to felling and chopping the wood. Luella May he sent into the old campsite to clear up the rubbish as best she could and with a sack she began to pick up the trash. His task was the interior wall they had created in the house and to fill the spaces between the beams on that side with the moist mix that would set and harden before the colder months.

The inside of the house was large enough and

composed of mainly bare rooms with only the large and heavy furniture, dressers and wardrobes remaining, the rest had been stripped from the place. There were no pictures on the walls or tasteful drapes over the windows. Where there had been elegantly patterned wallpaper it had been ripped away and only the ragged vestiges remained showing the lathe beneath. The scratches of indifferently dragged spurs marked the wooden floor and poor lighting was from lanterns or candles wedged in empty wine bottles. It was a poor-looking place and Gale despaired over what it must have been like in earlier days. A few traces remained, some fine door furniture and one or two small items of china that had survived and these held pride of place on the wide stone ledge of the old fireplace.

He was working in such a way with the bucket of straw and mud mix when he heard a crash. Wiping his hands on the edge of the bucket and down his now well-worn infantry pants he went to discover.

"Are you okay, Mrs. Lake?" he called, moving toward the sound.

There was no reply and he pushed his way across the hallway and into what had once been a comfortable parlor.

Antonia was standing in the center of the almost bare room transfixed and shaking, she stood rigidly upright and at her feet lay the large pieces of a broken ceramic dish.

"What is wrong?" he asked, looking at her staring eyes and drawn features. "Is it some ague that affects you?"

Her mouth worked but no words came out and her whole body quivered as if in some terrible kind of fit. Gale went to her quickly and took her arms in his hands to still her shaking.

"Tell me," he said. "What is it?"

Still she said nothing and Gale despaired, he could think of nothing to calm her and despite all the social restrictions he pulled her body to him held her close.

"There, there," he muttered. "I have you."

She was so small in his arms, her body light and frail and he was overcome with the desire to steady her. She pressed her head into his neck and clung to him and Gale smelled her hair and the scent of her skin. Antonia's shaking body melded into him and he could hear the gasps that quickly turned to sobs. He would kiss her then and his mouth brushed her damp cheek and she turned her head and he felt her parted lips fasten on his. Antonia's eyes were closed and her breath coming fast as she pulled him tightly against her. A frantic kind of desire was in her, a desperation that threw aside all the previous restrictions she had displayed.

Gale, for his part, felt as if a sealed door had been opened and light thrown into a darkened room, he kissed her passionately, overcome by the willing frailty he held between his hands. He grasped her around her narrow waist and she flung her arms around his neck, the upward turned face beneath his chin seemed peaceful and the lids of her closed eyes held a passive serenity.

Then she bunched her fists and violently pushed at his chest.

"*No!*" she cried and with sudden determination backed away from him. "No, no, I will not."

"But—" he began.

"It will not be, no, no. I cannot."

She lowered her head and stared at him from under lowered eyebrows, "Forgive me, sir, if I have misled you but, no, I am forbidden."

"I will not harm you," said Gale, unsure of what had made this change. "Antonia," he said, using her name for the first time. "What is it that ails you?"

She hung her head and held her arms tight by her side. "This cannot be."

"But why ever not?"

Her voice was ragged and raw. "Because I have sinned. My guilt is great and I must pay the price in full."

"Never," he said softly. "There is no sin that is so great."

Gale reached out a hand to her but she stepped back away, her shoes crunching over the broken dish.

"It is unforgivable." Her hand rose and clasped the locket in one hand as she often seemed to do in moments of stress. "I must make atonement."

"Tell me then, how someone as fair as you can have committed such a heinous crime to cause you this distress."

She sagged bodily, her whole figure going limp and she drew jagged breaths as she tried to recover herself.

"Here, sit," he said softly as he gently urged her to the single chair left in the room. "Rest easy and tell me. I am here and I will listen, for it is surely something you have held too long locked in your breast."

She snorted a laugh but sat down on the chair and clasped both hands on her lap. "How can you hear me?" she asked. "What will a man like you know of such things?"

"There is much I have seen, so many terrible things and also shameful acts I loath to say I have taken part in, I am sure nothing you can say will shock or disturb me. I am for you, dear lady, can you not tell?"

"Why?" she asked. "What am I to you?"

"A great deal," Gale admitted. "I believe you have found a place in my heart."

She relented then and reached out, her head hung down avoiding his gaze and gingerly she touched his arm with her trembling fingers, "I am not worthy, believe me."

"Speak and let me be the one to decide."

Antonia drew a deep breath and began, "I will tell you then. When the Union army came, as I have said, the General and his staff were perfect gentlemen. There was no lack of consideration only the imposition of the officers taking over my house. I was asked to dine with them and partake in conversation as any normal assembly and there was no intemperate talk or political condemnation as to my support for Southern views.

"My son Peter, yes there was a son, he was five years old and a more bonny young boy you could not expect to meet. Curious, you know and always scurrying about. With all the horse and body of men he was excited each day and only too willing to explore. Even the troops camped in the woods took to him; they would play with hoop and ball and entertain him. Some even carved him small toys in wood, a horse or fish, charming things like that.

"The men had some women with them, wives and camp followers but not creatures of a very pleasant sort. I believe some were no more than prostitutes or women of low character. They kept to themselves mainly, cooking and mending for the men although on occasion I would spy them looking at Peter with a disagreeable eye that I took to construe as some form of jealousy.

"I believed we were safe with the soldiers and it was not at all what I had expected after the things I had read in the newspapers. Stories of rape and pillage and the general distress that war will bring. So, I admit to a feeling of security, the officers were quite friendly, not forward I hasten to add, but no more than if they were at home in the company of their families which I would guess they sorely missed.

"I was politely invited one day by a captain to accompany him on a horse ride. He had acquired a new animal and was keen to try it and hoped I might go with him on his regular horse. It had been many years since I had been in the saddle and I used to enjoy it so readily agreed.

"We rode out on a bright day and the man was a diverting conversationalist so we spoke of many things, of nature and philosophy. All subjects I enjoyed and a level of conversation I missed without the company of husband or agreeable neighbors.

"It was on our return that the horror struck."

Here Antonia stopped and her gaze wandered to the window and a veil fell over her features.

"I remember that day so well." Her breath caught and she drew in sharply. "He was dead; my poor little boy was gone. They said he had wandered into the camp and with his adventurous ways may have fallen and struck his head. I saw him." She winced at the memory. "His head was all broken and his soft curls congealed with blood, it was a terrible sight."

Gale reached out and enclosed her clenched fist in his hand and waited for her to collect herself.

"They said it was an accident but I have my doubts, I believe some evil overtook one or more of the women and they thought to destroy my boy. He was too beautiful for them to have around them, it might be they saw his advantage in this house or felt it unfair the benefits he might have. Whatever it was, the General commanded that he be buried with due ceremony and they took his body to the church graveyard where he lies now."

Gale shook his head in sympathy, he felt her anguish and held some understanding of his own against the pain she felt.

"Here," said Antonia, holding up the locket. "This is all I have of him now."

Gale looked at the small curl of pale hair, he had known death of course, many battlefield deaths and yet this was a departure shared with a woman that he had come to admire and it touched his heart.

"Soon after," she continued. "The general received an urgent courier and the army was sent on the march toward Piedmont. He ordered the camp struck and all the men to take their arms and follow him for the Confederate forces were gathering there. So in the space of a week they departed except for a squad of ten men he ordered to clear the camp and follow on afterward.

"It was then that things changed so radically I still find it hard to believe. Without officers the men left behind behaved in the most outrageous fashion, they came in this house unannounced and proceeded to loot or destroy everything they could lay their hands. I complained bitterly but they thrust me aside.

"They found drink and imbibed excessively and were soon drunk and caused more uproar and it was then I began to fear for my safety. There were lecherous exclamations aimed at me saying that I had pleasured the officers and now it was their turn, I was a Rebel whore and should be treated as such. It was then that the house caught fire through one imprudent drunken soldier breaking of a lamp, awful though it was, I thanked the Good Lord they were distracted for then I could flee. I ran into the forest and hid, my dress was torn from me in my escape through thorny briars and I was so frightened I could do nothing but quake and hope that I was undiscovered.

"Again the Lord came to my assistance and a great storm broke out, you will know they are often occurrences here in the season. It was a heavy downpour lasting three days but I dared not move, I was soaked and cold, hungry and full of terror. When at last I crept out from the forest I found that they had all gone and the rain had subdued the fire leaving the place as you have seen. But I was feverish and became sick, I do not know how long I lay like that in my empty house but gradually I recovered."

"My dear lady," said Gale. "I am truly sorry that you suffered so."

Antonia considered him now with more gentleness thanks to his consideration and perhaps for the opportunity to at last unburden her heavy heart. She sat, not forbidding his holding of her hand and gradually raised her eyes to his.

"You are most kind," she said. "If you will allow I shall call you by your first name now?"

"It will be an honor."

The moment was broken as a rapid knocking sounded on the front door and Sam crying out, "Mistah Doolie, oh, Mistah Doolie, will yo' come quick."

Gale leaped to his feet and opened the door, "What is it, Sam?"

"It is my Luella May, suh. The chile is set to come an' I am lost."

"You wish my help?"

"I do, suh. I do indeed so."

Gale turned to Antonia; he could see her through the open door still seated on the chair.

"Wait," Gale ordered and quickly returned to the parlor. "You have heard?" he asked Antonia.

"The baby comes," she said.

"Yes, will you help?"

She looked at him plaintively. "But what do I know of such things?"

"Most certain you know more than us men," he

replied. "You have born a son, so you say, now is your chance to let another live."

"I had a midwife with me back then and servants too."

"No matter," Gale pressed. "We shall be your servants, tell us what you need. Please, dear lady, let us help these people."

A sudden flow of resolve ran through Antonia and she rose from her seat with a glint of determination showing in her eyes.

"Very well," she said, striding to the door. "Sam, a fire first, we must have hot water. Gale, you will bring linen from my bedroom and you will tear it into usable sizes. A shawl also, I have a woolen one in my cupboard."

With that, she was gone, marching across toward the slave quarters and leaving Sam and Gale to carry out her orders.

When Gale arrived carrying his pile of sheeting he found Antonia, crouched over Luella May, who lay writhing on her mattress on the floor.

"I a-feared Mistress," cried Luella May. "It do hurt so."

"As it will," supplied Antonia. "There is little relief I am afraid. We have no laudanum to ease your suffering, best you consider the happy outcome above all else."

"The baby do come?"

"He is on his way," supplied Antonia. "Try to control the rate of breath, Luella May. I found it helped some in my own case."

"You hab a baby, ma'am?"

"I did, indeed I did and was my happiest day when he was born."

"Where be he now den?"

A sudden burst of contractual pain interrupted and Antonia avoided replying to the query. She turned to Gale. "It is best you leave now, it will be some time."

Their eyes met and a silent world of conversation was shared between them and Gale felt the glad response in his chest.

"Go," she said, ushering him out with a gentle smile. "Keep Sam occupied, he will be concerned but there is nothing he can do, it is best you tell him so."

CHAPTER SIX

Sam sat by the fireside a cauldron of water hanging over the fire and Gale could see he was a worried man so he settled down beside him.

"Any more to be done, suh?" Sam asked, his eyes round and worried as he looked through the firelight at Gale.

"No, Sam, we just wait now. Mrs. Lane has it all in hand."

"How she be, how be Luella May. I hear her cryin'."

Gale allowed him a slight smile. "It's a painful process so that ain't surprising but she'll be fine, it's nature's way to bring a newborn into the world with a little uproar."

They heard the boom of distant thunder and a glow of lightning filled the inside of pillared clouds.

Unexpected darkness had swept in from the east and gathered in a giant rolling wall of black cloud that covered the forest in sudden gloom. A rumble of thunder came to them again and on the horizon a bright flash of tree lightning seared the sky. The air was filling with heat and an electric smell of ozone filled their nostrils and pressed against their bodies.

"I don' like that," said Sam, looking off toward the approaching weather. "Maybe something bad be comin'."

"Just a storm, don't fret so. That water hot yet?"

Sam leaned over the cauldron and tested with a finger. "It be fine. Oh, Mistah Doolie, I do pray she be okay."

"You saw babies born before, ain't you, Sam. This 'un will be the same."

"But I seen dem born dead an' I seen the wimens lost as well."

"This one will be different, you see if it ain't."

"I want to thank you, suh. You an' the mistress been real kind to us, us being Black folk an' all."

"You pulled your weight around here, Sam, just like me. It's been a good thing that you're both here."

"I sho' hope so, I's appreciate it, we both does."

An instant of sheet of lightning flashed across the sky and was followed by a resounding crash so loud that it seemed to send a physical quiver through the air. The momentary glare set the surrounding trees into sharp contrast and sent dark shadows speeding across the ground.

"Oh, Lord," sighed Sam.

"You thought of a name yet?" asked Gale, thinking to distract him.

"I do if he be boy; I name him after my pa. He

be called Abiyo, that be his name when they brung him across here in de slave ship. De master call him Thomas over in dat Gascoigne place but that ain't his real name."

A long scream came from inside the hut and Sam visibly jumped, his anguished face turning toward the sound.

"There'll be rain coming soon," said Gale. "It's still a-ways off but it'll be here."

Sam shivered and clasped his hands around his arms. "Is dat what dat chill is I kin feel?"

"No." Gale smiled. "That's just you being afraid for your wife, that's all that is."

"I'm just hopes it ain't evil, dey say de Debil ride on nights like dis. Dat's what de ole witch woman tole us on the plantation."

Another cry came from the hut and then Antonia's call for the hot water.

Sam jumped to his feet ready to grasp the cauldron.

"No, old man," said Gale. "Best I do it, might be you is so jangled you will drop the thing."

He took a bunched rag in his hand and lifted the boiled water from where it hung on the iron tree over the fire.

"Sit there, Sam and say a prayer for your wife and baby," said Gale as he hurried over to the cabin.

"Oh, I be praying, don' you worry 'bout dat," Sam called after him.

Gale entered the hut to find Antonia with her sleeves rolled up and a whimpering Luella May with her shining face screwed up as she lay sweating on the bed. There was only a lantern light and it cast the two figures in a circle of orange glow that set their shadows leaping across the walls.

"Leave it there," ordered Antonia, too busy with her work to pay him any attention.

Backing away unsure of what to do, Gale stood in the doorway as a resounding tremble of thunder pounded the sky outside.

"Calm now," he heard Antonia say as she wiped sweat from Luella May's forehead. "Just take those breaths like I told you."

As he left Luella May let forth with a terrible scream that rang in Gale's ears.

"Yes, yes," said Antonia. "You have to push now. He's coming Luella May, push hard, my dear."

Sam was on his feet, watching Gale's approach. "She be all right, Mistah Doolie?"

Gale laid a hand on Sam's shoulder. "I believe so, rest easy, it's nearly time."

They both stood by the fireside, restless and not knowing what to do or be as the continuing rumble trundled over the heavens above them like cannon balls rolling down a wooden gallery.

Then they heard a long hiccuping wail as the infant drew its first breath.

"That's it, Sam." Gale grinned. "You got yourself a baby child."

"Oh, sweet Jesus, I praise de Lord."

Antonia appeared at the cabin door, "Sam, you want to come see your new son?"

"I do," said Sam as he hurried over. "I surely do."

"Be gentle," warned Antonia as Sam pushed his

way inside. "Luella May will need rest but be assured that all is well."

With a last look after Sam, a glowing Antonia turned and walked across to where Gale stood at the fireside.

He looked at her with a nod of approval. "You did well," he said.

"It is a wonder, I had forgotten so." A pleased Antonia sighed. "It really is a wonder."

Rain started to patter on the leaves and earth around them with a heavy tapping sound.

"We shall be soaked," said Gale.

"I do not mind, I really don't," said a happy Antonia.

"Come, my hut is here we can shelter there."

"No, no," she said, grasping his hand. "Come with me."

They ran, then as the sky let loose its downpour and rain sheeted heavily over them as hand-in-hand, they raced across the yard.

"Where, where are we going?" gasped Gale.

"To the house, you are coming with me to the house."

———

That night Gale lay for the first time with Antonia Lake and they were both content with the outcome.

The next day the rain continued its heavy downpour. On the fourth day it finally ceased leaving the ground pooled and sodden. There was little that could be done in such terrible weather and Gale splashed through the yard to see if Sam and Luella

May and the baby were well. They had survived with only a few leaks through the cabin roof and Sam had brought in sufficient firewood to keep them dry and warm.

Gale strolled back through ankle deep water toward the house, the rain freshened air smelled clean and the forest trees around him still hung heavy and dripped a steady fall. It was a bleak overcast day and Gale guessed that more rain might be on the way. He found that the creek had overflowed by luckily the slight rise that the house occupied had kept it clear of any flooding.

He was at the porch when he heard the splattering sound of horses coming across the soggy yard.

A cloak-covered troop of Union cavalry led by Lieutenant Forby Sinclair rode up. The men's capes gleamed wetly and they appeared miserable and soaked through as they spread across the yard and tactically covered all angles of the house.

Sinclair nodded at Gale. "Is Mrs. Lake to home?"

"I am here," said Antonia, stepping out onto the porch.

Sinclair bowed his head in salute, "I won't say good day, ma'am, as it is hardly that. I hope you survived the deluge?"

"We are still here, thank you," Antonia replied. "Damp but alive."

"I fear I have some troubling news, Mrs. Lake," continued Sinclair. "Our depot was raided during the last evening, we apprehended many of the rascals and the scoundrels will surely hang for it but some have escaped us. I must search these premises, ma'am. It may be they are hiding nearby."

"There is no one here but us, sir."

"Nonetheless, we must be sure."

"Very well, be about your business then."

Sinclair turned to Sergeant Malone and ordered half the platoon to dismount and search the grounds with the rest to remain mounted with rifles in hand.

"You will take coffee, Lieutenant?" asked Antonia.

"Obliged, ma'am," said Sinclair dismounting and crossing to the porch with Gale following behind him.

Staring after them, Malone asked Gale bluntly, "Where d'you think you're going?"

"Anywhere you ain't," Gale came back sharply.

"You stay here," said Malone. "I want you under my eye. I reckon you'll be a Reb sympathizer if you ain't one of them dogs already."

"Sergeant," called Antonia from the porch. "Mr. Doolie is in my employ and not yours. I would be obliged if you kept your notions to yourself. He will go wherever he pleases on my property."

Malone rubbed at the scar on his cheek and flushed angrily, "You are under military rule now, woman. Best you remember that."

"Guard your tongue, Malone," barked Sinclair. "Get on with the search and be sure there is no unnecessary damage done here in the doing of it."

Muttering barely heard imprecations, Malone turned away obediently and Gale followed Antonia and Sinclair into the house.

Sinclair took off his cap and cloak, shaking them

free of rainwater on the porch before entering. He frisked his damp and bedraggled mustache with a forefinger and spent an uneasy moment at the doorway looking around at the poor investiture of the house, and then stamping the mud from his boots he followed Gale into the parlor.

"You will forgive us, Lieutenant," Antonia explained. "Unfortunately the house was rampaged when last the camp soldiers left. We have only chicory and no coffee so I hope this will not offend your taste."

"That is too bad," frowned Sinclair, looking around the bare room. "I had not realized you were in such dire straits. I shall be sure that a pound of coffee beans are sent across directly I return to our base."

"You are most kind." Smiled Antonia, pouring him a cup.

"What happened last night?" asked Gale.

Sinclair looked at him momentarily with a mild show of surprise, not expecting that a workman would address him but when Antonia made no complaint, he accepted Gale's presence and answered, "A gang of ten or fifteen, in the early hours. A sentry spotted them though and a merry battle commenced. Many of them were brought down and one of my men wounded but the rest surrendered soon enough. Poor beggars were thin and starving."

"They are ill-advised and desperate," said Gale.

"Indeed so and unnecessary too, it defeats me, I'm sure you'll agree. The war is done let us get on with making the peace."

"For you the war is over, sir," said Antonia. "But then, you were successful while we must survive with only what remains."

Outside the noisy sounds of men overturning the stacked lumber and poking amongst the wood-pile came to them.

"I suppose it is so," sighed Sinclair, waving his cup toward the window. "My sergeant, Malone out there is good example that there are still many discontented with the outcome on both sides."

"It is enough that we are civil to each other," supplied Antonia.

"Indeed so," agreed Sinclair. "Well, I must thank you for your hospitality and we shall be on our way." He set down his unfinished cup and made for the door.

Watching them leave through the rain patterned window, Antonia came to Gale and wrapped her arm around his waist and he held her close.

"It begins again," he said as the first mist of driving rain covered the patrol and they disappeared into the gusting haze.

"Do you think?" she asked. "That Sam and Luella May might be more comfortable in here with us?"

Gale looked down at her and saw the first hopeful release of her old attitudes taking place and a newer and lighter Antonia free of despair and guilt beginning.

"I think that would be a very fine thing," he said.

"Then let them come, surely one fire blazing in the hearth is better than two. Besides I miss the child and would see how he fares."

"I shall fetch them over."

———

That evening, Sam and Luella May having gladly accepted the invitation, sat with Gale and Antonia huddled around a blazing fire in the hearth. A lantern lit the room and some candles that wavered in the draughts yet gave a warm light along with the fire's flames. The baby Abiyo lay coddled in a crib made of a blanket-lined drawer from Antonia's chest, the small body sleeping peacefully. They had just cleared the supper things and Gale was pleased to see Antonia leaning across and fussing over the baby with a show of motherly concern as Luella May watched them with a contented smile on her face.

Outside a wind howled and intermittent rain spattered against the windows with the sound of shot peppering the glass and all were glad to be inside.

"What be that?" asked Luella May, looking up nervously.

It was then they heard the cry, weak and wailing over the sound of the wind, "Hello, the house. Give us aid."

Gale crossed quickly to the door and looked out; he saw the drenched body of Simon supporting the sagging figure of Jethro with one arm while in the other he carried his rifle.

"I seen your light," called Simon. "Will you help, Jethro be shot through and we are in sore need with the Yankees on our tail."

There was a pause as Gale considered the implications and then he saw that the desperate measures could not be ignored.

"Sam!" he called. "Come help here."

Soon Sam was by his side and the two lunged from the porch and through the rain to help bring both distressed men inside.

CHAPTER SEVEN

Simon was a jaded man, he stood hunched and dripping water in the firelight his eyes glittering wildly as he looked at the two blacks sitting before the fire. The breath rasped in his throat and he dropped Jethro who slumped to the floor with a groan.

Antonia was on her feet instantly and running over to the wounded man. She kneeled beside him and studied the blood-soaked jacket, then glanced up at Gale with a troubled look and a small negative shake of the head.

"Best get that coat off," Gale said to Simon. "You're wet through, man."

Simon swiveled his head and stared at Gale. "What you got them Blacks in here for. They don't belong in a white man's house."

"They need shelter just like you," Gale answered calmly. "Give me your coat and warm yourself."

Sam climbed to his feet to give the man his place and Simon glared at him without a word.

"What happened to you out there?" asked Gale. "I know you attacked the depot, that Lieutenant Sinclair was here earlier looking for you."

"They're all over," grated Simon. "Every damned place we run, they keep coming. They was here already, you say? Then they won't be back just yet. You got a drink?" He laughed wildly. "You'd think I'd had enough water, wouldn't you?"

"Sure," said Gale, pouring him a glass and Simon swallowed it down greedily.

"How's Jethro?" he asked, peering over his shoulder at his companion. "Po' boy, he got a hole in him bigger than a wagon wheel."

Antonia looked up at him. "He's bad I'm afraid, very bad. Gale, Sam, we need to get him to a bed and get these wet clothes off him. Can you carry him upstairs, I'll see if I can bandage him."

"What do we do if them Yankees come back here?" asked Simon.

"We can hide you in the cellar or you run for the woods."

"I ain't going out there again."

He stood with his fists clenched and shivering before the warmth of the fire. Luella May swept up the baby and moved away silently to stand well away from the men.

"Is there any of you that got away?" asked Gale.

Simon shook his head and pulled a face. "Nah, they's all either shot or taken. Them Union boys caught us by surprise, it was a bloody slaughter."

"Well you put us in a pretty pickle here, ain't you? They come catch you and we'll be charged with harboring."

"You're for the South, ain't you?" asked Simon angrily. "Where the hell else we supposed to be except with our own?"

"We're not outlaws or irregulars in this place, you chose your road Simon, no need to bring your particular brand of hell down on us."

Simon raised the rifle threateningly and Gale noticed under the wet coat he still kept the two pistols in his belt.

"Well, you got us now," Simon sneered. "You'll do as I say, or maybe you want to argue with this here rifle."

Antonia interrupted from where she kneeled by Jethro's side. "We need to give this man some treatment, can we discuss the rest of it later."

"Here I kin he'p," said Sam, stepping forward.

"You leave him be," ranted Simon. "He ain't having none of your black hands on him."

Antonia looked at him steadily and said coldly, "He's a dying man and you have no say about it in this house. Here, Sam, take his legs and Gale his shoulders, we'll carry him up."

Antonia followed as both men went to the task and carried Jethro awkwardly from the room with him moaning vaguely in a muted tone.

Simon, left alone in the room with Luella May and the baby, laid aside the rifle and ignoring her he threw off his wet coat and stood glowering with clenched teeth working his jaw and both hands reaching out to the heat. Steam rose from his clothes and his staring eyes fixed on the flames with a manic intensity that mirrored a glow of resilient red light deep inside them. There was an unpleasant smell of funk emanating from him as his body heated, of testosterone, sweat, and unwashed body mingled with fear. It filled the room with a strong pervasive odor that was akin to the rotting stench of decaying matter.

Gale and Sam came back in the room and Gale said, "I'm afraid he's gone, passed over without a word we never even got him on the bed. Antonia's arranging the body best she can if you want to go see him."

Without turning, Simon flexed his shoulders dismissively. "If he gone then he's gone, c'ain't do no more."

"Der be something out there," said Sam, looking out through the night dark window, where torch light shone in star patterns on the rain-spattered glass. The lights jumped like fireflies as they moved between the trees in the woods.

"Aw, no!" wailed Simon. "They're coming for me."

"You leave a trail, they follow you here?"

"I don't know," moaned Simon. "I was running so fast and carrying Jethro and with him already half dead it were hard to move."

"You can't be here," Gale said grimly. "They'll either hang us or put us in jail. You have to go, Simon, take your chance in the forest. I won't have Antonia put at risk."

"You'll do like I say," snarled Simon.

"Wait!" cried Antonia from the doorway. She stood with sleeves rolled to her elbow and her hands stained with the wounded man's blood. "There is a way."

There came the sound of a resounding knock battering the front door.

"Quick," said Antonia. "The rest of you sit at the fire. Simon, follow me."

Rapidly, she and Simon fled the room as another knock came with a cry from outside. "Open up in there and give us entry or we'll be forced to break in this door."

"His rifle, he done lef" it," hissed Sam, quickly throwing his jacket over the forgotten weapon.

Gale made his way across and opened the door. "What is it?"

Outside stood a glowering Sergeant Malone, rain dripping from his peaked cap and behind him holding lanterns stood three other armed soldiers.

"Stand aside," growled Malone, pushing Gale out of his way. "We tracked them here, we know you have runaways in this house."

The men brushed noisily past Gale, their woolen capes smelling of wet and cold and their muddy boots making tracks across the floor. Malone blundered into the parlor and saw Sam and Luella May sitting at the fire, the baby was awake and beginning to make wailing noises at all the disturbance.

"You people seen these outlaws?" Malone bellowed at them. "Where are they?"

"You are too late, Sergeant," called Antonia from the bottom of the stairway.

"Late! Late? What do you mean, woman?"

The caped soldiers stood gathered around her in the hallway, their rifles held at the ready. The front door was left open and with a cold draft, thin rain blew in from outside.

"He is upstairs in the bedroom the poor soul has died of his wounds. He appeared at our door no more than minutes since in a state of terrible distress."

Malone turned to the men. "You two get up there and see to it."

Without answer, the men ran to the stairway and their heavy tread sounded throughout the house as they charged up the stairs.

"That it?" asked Malone. "You only got one of them up there?"

"Are there more?" Antonia asked innocently.

"A whole parcel of them," blurted Malone with angry relish. "Attacked us at the depot we've got most of them but a few got away."

"How terrible. Tell me, Sergeant, you and your men look wet through and exhausted. Can we get you something hot to drink."

The remaining soldier stepped forward. "Would real appreciate it, ma'am. It's a cold night out there."

"Of course, I shall see to it right away. Luella May," she called out. "Will you come help me, please?"

"Now wait a moment. Stand down, trooper," barked Malone. "We're on official business here. This is no tea party."

"Surely, Sergeant," Antonia said in kindly fashion. "On such a night you can rest a minute and accept our hospitality, you must be chilled through."

A trooper called down from the head of the stairs, "There's a dead man up here right enough,

Sergeant, looks like one of them Rebs. Been shot through and he ain't going nowhere."

Malone stood a moment unsure of what to do, he turned this way and that as the baby continued to raise an incessant howl from the parlor.

"Search the place," Malone ordered. "Turn it over, see if any more been given shelter here."

The men clattered off to follow his order and both Antonia and Gale stood to one side as they ran by them.

"I fear you are wasting your time, Sergeant," said Antonia. "The sorely wounded man upstairs was alone and fell on the porch at our door. There was little else we could do."

"We'll see about that," snarled Malone, looking across at Luella May as she tried to comfort the sobbing baby. "Can't you quiet that child?"

"He is distressed with all the noise and furor. Little babies need calm, as I'm sure you will appreciate. Do you have children yourself, Sergeant?"

Malone ignored Antonia and began spitting irritated expletives as the other soldiers came back to him all shaking their heads negatively.

Antonia looked at him winningly. "Perhaps you would like us to take care of the burial?"

"Do what you want with the dog," barked Malone. "Come on, boys, there might be others but we've done what we can."

"What about that hot coffee?" asked one of the troopers tentatively.

"No, come away now you'll get your coffee when we get back to the depot," snapped Malone as he headed for the door. "I have to make report of this, at least we got the runaway and that'll keep the officers happy." He turned at the doorway. "You people ain't heard the last of this, aiding and abetting albeit he's stone dead. Maybe there'll be a charge for that."

"We would have done the same if it had been you or one of your men," said Antonia, with a show of calm dignity.

"We'll just see on that," promised Malone.

Sullenly the other men followed him out into the driving rain and when they had left the porch Gale closed the door after them.

In the silence after they had left, a relieved Antonia sagged back against the wall.

"Where is he?" asked a grinning Gale.

"I put him under the dead man's bed, I guessed that would not look there."

"So they didn't." Chuckled Gale. "Well done, Antonia."

———

Simon's presence in the house caused a great deal of unrest; his animosity toward the Negroes and general crude demeanor upset the usually tranquil atmosphere. At first Sam and Luella May moved back to their cabin to create some space between them and the unpleasant man. But aggression came as naturally to Simon as the storms that racked the country at that time of year and he continued his belligerence whenever he saw them.

Repeated attempts by Gale to get Simon to leave

had no effect and using a perverse blackmail he promised that if he were taken he would bear witness and involve them all as participants. For Simon it was an easy life at the farm and far more comfortable than his days spent in the outlaw camp and he intended to keep it so. Ever watchful and sly he spied on their every move to be sure that they made no move against him.

Then Sam brought them some news, he and Luella May and the baby were to visit her sister Misty, a housemaid in North Indiana. She was to marry a local carpenter and they wished to attend the wedding, as Luella May had not seen her sister for many years. It was a reasonable excuse for them to escape the strained atmosphere that now invaded the place and despite obvious regrets they planned what was to be a long journey.

Gale was saddened to lose the companionship of Sam but much of the hardest labor had been accomplished with his help and all that remained was maintenance and general improvement to the house and land.

On the day they were to leave, Sam and Luella May came to the house to bid their farewells. The baby Abiyo had grown into a lusty young child and his bright eyes gladdened them all, except that was for Simon, who stood outside the group, leaning against the wall in a corner of the parlor and watching the departure with narrowed eyes.

Gale took Sam's hand and wished him well on their journey.

"T'ank you, suh, it been a pleasure here wid you."

"Did I say you could leave?" Simon interrupted suddenly, his voice hollow and unnaturally loud.

"No, suh," said Sam cautiously. "We done plan for the wedding is all."

"And maybe you will tip off the Federals on your way up there, is that it? Get some kind of reward for turning me in."

"No, suh. We don' pull down no grief on Mistah Gale or Missy Lane, no, suh."

Simon pushed himself away from the wall and glowered at them, "I reckon y'all better stay right here."

He stepped ominously toward the couple, pushing his face forward so it was only inches from Sam, who backed away at the unpleasant breath the man carried with him as if physical foulness were a part of his whole body.

"I c'ain't do that," frowned Sam. "We is going."

"You'll do as I say," barked Simon, pulling the revolver from his belt.

Luella May gasped and clutched her baby close.

"Put that away," snapped Gale.

"You be quiet," growled Simon, swinging on Gale with the gun pointed at him.

"I fear you are overextending yourself, sir," interrupted Antonia who spoke with a harsh coldness. "You are a guest here and an unwelcome one at that. You command nobody, sir."

Simon curled his lip in a sneer. "And what you going to do about it, huh? I say the darkies stay here and they stay here. You damned peckerwoods forgot all about how things is supposed to be. We tell and they obey or, as God is my witness, I'll blow them into the black hell where they belong."

Before anyone could do anything he swung back around and snatched Abiyo from Luella May's grip and held the child up high. Luella May screamed and the baby cried loudly but Simon had his pistol barrel held up against the baby's soft belly.

"See here," he shouted, cocking the pistol. "You do as I say or I'll plug this scrap, he ain't worth nothing no how."

"Leave him go," growled Sam, lowering his head with every intention of lunging at the man.

Simon swung the crying baby by the ankles hanging it upside down with the pistol held close against its body.

"Ain't a thing you can do, is there? Not a one of you."

Antonia moved across to boldly face him, "If you threaten anyone," she said. "It should be me. Lay the child aside and return him to his mother. You may hold me hostage in the stead."

Simon cackled a laugh, "Boy, this is it, I got you all where I want you, ain't I? Y'all way too fond of the black sort for my taste, they's just animals and should be treated as such."

"Give me the gun," said Antonia, holding out her hand.

"You think so?" grinned Simon, one side of his upper lip lifted to expose his crooked teeth as he swung the terrified baby from side to side. "You is one high and mighty lady, you know that? I do believe it's about time you got what's coming to you."

Unseen in the shadows of the hall, Gale raised the Springfield rifle to his shoulder and quietly levered back the hammer. His aim had to be true and he knew it, Antonia stood before him and he intended to shoot over her shoulder. The hanging baby and crouching parents were to one side but Sam might make a desperate move at any moment. Demented Simon, raging and angry with his finger tense on the trigger could let loose with the pistol at any second. There was no time to hesitate; it had to be now or never.

EPILOGUE

I t was four years later that Antonia had their twin sons born to her and Gale, two boys that they named Abel and Gabriel. A happy outcome for the parents and a bond that cemented their relationship for the rest of their days, although as they grew the two boys were as unalike as chalk and cheese. Abel it proved was more a homeboy and enjoyed the land and working on it. Gabriel was the restless sort, a wild kid always getting into fixes and fights and eventually leaving home to go step out on his own. They say he was reckless in his choice and as a young man had many adventures before going down to South America in search of gold but disappeared in that vast land and was never heard of again.

Sam and Luella May found that North Indiana was to their liking and decided to stay there and raise young Abiyo in a more temperate political climate.

Antonia lived for fifteen more years before she

passed when Gale was surprised to discover she had left him the entire property. He continued to stay on at the place with Abel for the rest of his days and survived until 1918, long enough to enjoy his grand-children.

Little was said of those final days at the farm, with most folk about then trying to forget as best they could the upheaval of war and all the desperate days that followed, although it was rumored within the family that two unknown graves were planted somewhere at the rear of the house. They had no markers and the earth was pressed flat and weeds and wildflowers grew over them and they were soon lost to sight. It gave flight to local stories that abounded about the place. It was told that some mysterious figures in the dress of raiders were often seen walking the woods on nights when the moon was high and that they were in all likelihood the ghosts of lost souls left from the last days of the Civil War.

...But then folks will believe anything if it makes a good story.

THE PATH LESS TAKEN

CHAPTER ONE

L ooking down the road at sunset where streaked scarlet and orange clouds trace a boundary line before the darkness of approaching night. A mellow evening is settling in with the air off the desert still warm from the heat of the day. The road is a long chalk-white marker stark in the dimming light and it disappears out of town beyond the empty stockyards to eventually be lost in the evening haze of coming night.

The last locomotive in the station at that end of town is hissing and shunting, throwing halos of steam that brighten uncannily like luminous clouds under the harsh brightness of the station arc light.

Across the way where the road rises slightly the desk clerk at the Loughborough Hotel is lighting the lamps along its portico ready to welcome any stopover guests from the train. That hotel used to be called Mullings Saloon until the owner developed what can only be described as a severe headache. Built like a beer barrel, Mullings was a heck of a guy and the only saloonkeeper I ever knew who waxed his mustache and his hair, parted it down the middle and always wore a clean apron over his neatly pressed pants. Pure white and ironed, that was the state of his apron and somehow it always seemed out of place as the saloon he owned was a gloomy hole favored pretty much by drunken deadbeats and low-life marginals.

Mullings was a big man and invariably put paid to any trouble by clambering across the bar top with a wooden bung hammer in his hand. On the day of his demise he got one large thigh across that counter, catching his breath he was balanced there when a stray round from a couple of fighting miners stopped him in his tracks. Poor Mullings was stuck halfway across with one leg over, a bullet hole above his left eye and his pristine apron dragging in all the beer and whiskey slops.

After that, the more entrepreneurial Evan Loughborough came along and bought out the widow Mullings and ran the saloon as a hotel but when the cattle drives starting coming in and the stockyards were built a half mile down the road he found his hotel was too far away from the railhead. Passengers had to hike a-ways with all their baggage if they wanted a bed for the night. But being an enterprising soul Evan had a twenty-seat tram built and with a driver and two-horse team it carried folks and their baggage to and from the train station comfortably. The damned thing became such a novelty amongst the locals that folks would ride it just for fun, so Evan started charging two bits a ride and I can tell you he did very nicely out of that.

Three Mexican tannery workers are coming down the road on their way home, one of them is singing softly the other two talking quietly together. The Spanish song is sad, "*La Llorona*," it tells of a ghostly mother searching for her lost children. Somehow it is a fitting hymn to the night, where the shadows are adrift with wraith-like strands of mist as the day's air cools.

The smell of supper cooking is filling the street and oil lamps are being lit in the houses along the roadside.

It is a placid evening and I enjoy the softness as I sit on my old rocking chair in the space between houses where the heat of the day is still trapped.

The far end of the road is lost in darkness now and I cannot see anything up there, at least nothing beyond my memories, because if you did not know the place back then you would not recognize it now.

Let me tell you....

Back in the day, us, the whole family of Boyds, were busted, broke and living downright poor in a drying shack on the St. Louis riverbank but even so everybody in the family did their best. My big brother Cyril, the eldest and whom I adored, was a tall and handsome smart young man with broad shoulders and a ready smile, he was working in the meat market humping sides of beef around on his back.

Of the two younger brothers Petey was selling newspapers and dime novels on a street corner kiosk. Teddy, being swift on his legs was working as runner for the foreman at the cannery and my ma and two sisters, Mary and Emmeline, spent the day sewing on buttons for the shirt factory.

James Boyd, that's me, well I was too little to do much else but play in the dirt of our doorstep with the little pony Cyril had whittled for me from a hunk of wood.

If truth were told, my folks were a grim couple and I only ever saw Ma smile once but that was down the line a-ways and I'll get to that, most of the time the pair of them were a dour-looking pair who said little. They seemed to think they had done their duty by bearing us and after that their responsibility toward us was restricted to vittles and patched pants.

Pa was always something of a chancer, not a big man but he was wiry and strong with a hard acquisitive gleam in his eye. The story goes that one day he noted a poster that interested him and he saw advantage in, so he determined to get the job to pay the way for all of us. It was described on the advertisement as a risky affair and only bold veterans need apply.

Pa was surprised and a little mystified when he arrived at the near-empty interview rooms to find there were so few applicants and momentarily he wondered just what the dire dangers involved were exactly but not deterred he continued with his application.

He certainly did raise eyebrows when he stepped into The Drovers Hall that day and stood before the Fast Overland Mail and Transport Interview Board. Pa was not at all what they had expected.

Back in 1862, Pa had been fighting with Burnside's troops in the Battle of Fredericksburg and taking part in the deadly assault on Marye's Heights. He had suffered the steel spike of a Confederate bayonet piercing his right thigh; it went in one side and out the other. The story goes he put his left foot in the Rebel opponent's face, drew out the bayonet and used it on the Confederate owner before struggling on up the hill until his leg finally gave out just short of the famed stone wall.

It left Pa with a leg as stiff as a wooden gate and to watch him walk was a miracle indeed. He would swing the offending limb around in a half-arc to meet his left foot, step forward and repeat the swinging motion and in such a continuing manner make his way.

The frowning chairman studied him from under bushy eyebrows as Pa came into the hall, "I know we asked for veterans and men of valor, Mr. Boyd and I see by those medals on your breast you are indeed a bold fellow but I fear we did not ask for *wounded* veterans."

"Do not be deceived, sir," said Pa, swinging confidently forward in that weird gait of his. "I am in no way impeded by this limb. In fact far from it."

The Committee was making mumbling noises of critical dissent into their beards but the chairman having drawn mention of the medals on Pa's chest and being an ex-military man himself was patient.

"How so, Mr. Boyd?"

"If the Committee will be so kind," said Pa, moving into the room. "Allow me to demonstrate."

The chairman was mildly amused by his forward manner. "Pray do so."

TONY MASERO

Without further ado, Pa moved to the applicant's chair placed before the Committee's long table. He laid both hands on the backrest and then proceeded with the most complex and effective series of gymnastics. He swung that stiff leg in circles at shoulder height, pirouetted and cartwheeled over the seat using his leg as a counterbalance. He rotated, spun and flipped around and with dexterous ease he pinpointed balance on the rigid member while spinning the chair above his head only to drop it down and sit himself cross-legged upon it.

There was laughter and gasps of impressed surprise from the Committee and the chairman himself chuckled with astonishment.

"Gentlemen," he said. "I like this man."

Pa, ever the po-faced gentleman, stood up, offered a small bow and promised, "If I am chosen for this task you will not be disappointed."

Little did they know that Pa had been entertaining street corners with the very same performance all over St. Louis so that we might eat for the past two months.

"To be clear, Mr. Boyd," said the chairman, suddenly serious. "This is no easy undertaking; we as a company are stepping into unusual waters that are not without risk. We intend to forge a new stagecoach route through Indian Territory. It will be frowned on by the government. There's no doubt of that but we expect their interest to be limited. The tribes shall certainly detest us; Station No. 3 will be a dangerous place to be. Do you think that you could manage such a place?"

CHAPTER TWO

I remember well that day six months later.

A clear bright sky washed of blue and so hot it beat your head like a hammer. All of us were windswept and sunburnt riding atop a high-sided wagon with all our possessions. My three brothers, two sisters and me balanced awkwardly on beds and chairs and trunks.

It was a bleak country white with alkali dust, wide and empty without any redeeming topographical features to rest the eye.

Ma and Pa sat up front on the driving seat, saying nothing and looking as sour as usual. Maybe even *they* were wondering what they had taken on. Then Pa drew the wagon to a halt and turned to us. One side of his face was coated with the alkali dust cast up by the wagon team and as he spoke it crumbled away like a plaster mask.

"There it is, young 'uns, that's your new home."

There on a ridgeline before us stood the Old Spanish mission still being worked on by the

Mexican construction workers the Stagecoach Company had imported.

"That's mighty big walls all around, Pa," observed Cyril.

"The old courtyard's been extended," Pa supplied. "You wait, you'll see inside. There's stables for two teams and storerooms for tackle, even a blacksmiths forge. We got a well in there and those walls are two feet thick built of stone and adobe and will take a fair hammering. See that double gate?" Partway along the high wall a sweeping curved stone archway covered massive wooden double doors. "That's wide enough for a Concord coach and six-horse team to pass through and high enough for a loaded freight wagon and a team of thirty mules."

"Where're we going to live?" asked Petey, who was often worried about his comforts.

"There," said Pa, indicating with his pointing finger at a rising ziggurat of adobe structures within the walls and to one side of the courtyard. They were squat, ugly boxes piled one on top of the other, the sides peppered with narrow rifle slots. "It's a safe place," Pa added, but I caught Ma looking at him askance for a moment as if she was not so sure.

There was no doubt we were in a dangerous part of the country although us younger ones did not know that then. Station No.3 was intended as a swing station on a route forged through the heart of Indian Territory from Arkansas clear through to Texas. Thing is it ran straight across the red man's lands and we were in the middle of it.

Amongst the tribes forcibly relocated there by force of arms were warlike Cheyenne warriors and

Arapahoe, Comanche and Apache, Creek and Chickasaw and it would only be a matter of time before they objected violently to our presence. It was a daring move by the Stagecoach Company sending coaches through Indian Territory all in an effort to save traveling time normally spent by following the Red River route around the southern fringes of the Indian nations. They figured as long as they could hire people dumb enough to risk their lives in such a manner they could make a great deal of money from freight haulage and travelers eager to get across the state as quickly as possible.

We were unaware at the time but already settlers were nibbling away at the outer fringes of the Territory and soon enough under the Oklahoma Organic Act the western part of Indian Territory would become Oklahoma Territory and as the tribes were squeezed in further they would become even more restless.

"I shall call it Fort Azarel Longfellow after my commanding officer back in the army, he was a fine gentleman and is deserving of recognition," declared Pa. "Never mind Station No. 3, that is a tacky title if ever I heard one and gives no credibility to man nor beast."

So the place was called that originally.

We youngsters loved it as for the first time in our lives we had room to run around in. There were stairways between the rooms and a large dining room and kitchen. The living quarters were more of a redoubt as the Company expected some trouble from Indians and raiders. In truth later on it was attacked more than once, I can well remember as a youngster having to drag buckets of ammunition to the men at the rifle slots while the walls shuddered and dust fell with the impact of all the bullets and screaming ricochets sent our way.

In those times, Cyril was always there at his station by a high window, moving from side to side, his rifle hot from use. He took time to smile and wink at me and I could see the fearless excitement lighting his eyes. But Pa had been right and that redoubt was indeed a safe place and no one ever broke in, they did once get into the courtyard and set fire to the storerooms and stole away the horses but that was only the one time.

Come evening when the days tasks were done Cyril would get out his study books and begin his learning, he was a determined student and had taught himself to read and write and in those days this was no mean feat without a guiding teacher's hand. My sister Mary was the only other of us children in the least interested and so Cyril taught her too and as I grew able she eventually taught me.

Cyril petted me and we grew fond of each other, him as the eldest and me as the youngest. He would take me for rides in the wild country outside of the fort, me sitting behind him on the pony's rump with my arms around his waist as he recounted wonderful tales of antiquity from books he had read. Of gods that lived up in the clouds and heroes battling strange creature, like giants with only one eye in the center of their foreheads. They were wondrous tales and I was of an age to be duly impressed by them.

Often he would add a personal moral note in reference to the brave heroes he spoke of. It was some kind of muted appraisal and often was said more to himself than to me. The fine sentiments played in my mind for years to come and only added to the respect and love I held for Cyril.

"I think the best we can do, is be just like those fellows in olden times and that is to have courage and see service as the greatest attribute," he mused.

"Will you always like me, Cyril?" I asked in my curious childish fashion. For I loved my big brother with all his kindnesses to me, his patience and his talk as if I were an adult and not a child and in such a fashion I felt free and able to approach him in this manner.

"Don't worry," he tousled my hair and promised. "I'll always be your buddy."

Cyril always called me "Buddy" after that and the name stuck and I was Buddy Boyd for the rest of my life.

———

Pa kept on some of the Mexican stone workers when the fort was finished and they helped out in the stables and some proved to be adept at blacksmithing as well. Ma and the girls took over the kitchen and were ready when the first stagecoach arrived. It was big and black with a dark six-horse team and came riding in like thunder on the wind.

Only three passengers were inside and two guards on top beside the whipman.

There was shouting and the jingle of harness as the sweating teams were exchanged for fresh horses.

"Any trouble?" Pa asked the whipman.

"Naw," replied the grizzled driver. "We seen 'em keeping track of us riding the skyline but they never did nothing."

"Was they Indians, mister?" I piped up.

"Sure were, son. But they never troubled us, so we never troubled them. Now you ain't got any coffee brewing, I don't suppose."

"Buddy," ordered Pa. "You take these folks into your ma in the kitchen, they'll be a mite hungry after their journey I'm guessing."

"Obliged," said the whipman, following me along with the passengers and guards.

Of course, it wasn't always so easy. Sometimes that stagecoach would arrive peppered with shot and arrows sticking out like thorns on a prickly pear. Some never arrived at all and we only heard about their failure when a later coach passed by and saw the burned wreckage and tortured corpses of the occupants. But it was a journey some travelers seemed prepared to make, their urgent journey driving them to take this risky route despite the dangers.

————

Most of us kids were left to our own devices, which could be a dangerous thing as we grew. Teddy, my second older brother, was a reckless soul, always risking his neck and jumping from high places and running up and down the redoubt stairways and going nowhere in particular without any purpose as if he had endless energy to expend. Which I guess he did.

Pete was a quiet one and moved in the shadow of the older brothers, he said little and was content to watch or spend his time with Emmeline.

Emmeline was indeed a beautiful child, so pretty she shone like the sun and yet there was a darkness within her. Not an evil one I hasten to say but more in the nature of an abstract failure to develop. When Cyril bought her a china doll one time she took to it and petted over it as if it were a real child. The doll was a large one with shiny cheeks and big eyes and Emmeline went everywhere with it. She and Pete would play at families, a thing that made me feel a mite uncomfortable at times even though I was only around eleven years old by then.

Mary the older of my sisters, was a stolid-looking girl, not pretty but well built and steady of nature despite her plainness, she wore all the airs of reliability and Ma was pleased to have her in the kitchens. Mary took the work seriously and made up for the vagueness of Emmeline and her dreamy existence.

———

That's how we lived on this swing station island in the middle of an alkali sea cut off from most of civilization. It evoked a sense of freedom despite the dangers involved and as the years past each of us grew in our own particular ways.

CHAPTER THREE

One day a band of cowboys drifted in.
It seemed they were driving a herd of cattle upcountry west of us and heard of the station and came over hoping for some company and refreshment. They were nice enough young men and Pa obliged them and set them up a bottle in the dining room.

It was the start of a regular event as more herds were driven north. The drovers would take time out to ride across and get themselves some home cooking and something to drink.

Teddy became enamored of them from the start and began hanging around the dining rooms when they were in there. Most of the cattlemen were young bloods, maybe eighteen or twenty years old and full of youthful energy. They were pretty much a bunch of kindly souls and treated Teddy as if a younger brother and he doted on them, listening to their exaggerated adventures of life on the trail with rapt attention. He would fetch and carry for them, bringing extra glasses if they wanted or moving a spittoon a little nearer.

As young men do on occasion, the high testosterone levels meant that trouble would break out and be resolved by a bout of fisticuffs.

Pa countered this by keeping an old beat up chair in one corner of the dining hall and when the brawl started he would come out with a double-barreled shotgun loaded with no more than birdshot. He would let rip with the gun and blast that weathered chair until it was even more splintered.

The loud gunshot would bring the cowboys up short and when they saw Pa and his blasted chair they would invariably leave off fighting and start laughing and further trouble would be avoided.

I have to say that in truth it was not always this way though.

I recall there were two older men driving different herds. Jez Reed of the "Lazy Y" and Walloping Sam who ramrodded the "Crazy Eight," it appeared the two had a long-standing bone of contention with each other and things came to a head one time in our dining room. Shouting kicked it off, followed by curse words and resentment until finally pistols were drawn.

Now I have to say that despite views to the opposite handguns in those days were not that accurate. Nor quite often were the fellows handling them. The gunfire was loud in the enclosed space and everybody in the dining room and courtyard outside ran for cover as there was no telling where the stray bullets might fly. The Mexican workers hid behind barrels or if caught in the open lay face down on the ground with their hands over the heads, most everybody disappeared from view.

Jez and Sam blasted away, wildly missing each other until Jez stepped outside and stopped one in the ribs as he did so. He tumbled down the high porch steps and was kneeling in the dust below when Sam followed him out onto the porch above. Jez did not hesitate, he fired off a shot that went through Sam's chest and killed him instantly. Sam did a forward roll off the porch and landed in the dust next to the wounded Jez.

Once it was all over, both teams of cowboys came out and stood in a circle studying the two protagonists.

Pa stepped up being all business. "Right," he says. "Take that wounded fella back to your camp." Jez, who was now only semi-conscious and groaning was lifted by his companions and hauled off to fetch their ponies. "Now this other one," Pa went on. "You men can take his saddle pony back with you, but whatever else he has on him pays for his burial."

"Now hold on," cried one drover. "That's a fine pistol and gun belt Walloping Sam owned, seems an awful lot for a funeral."

"Well it didn't do him much good, did it?" Pa replied sharply. "Now I run this station and I don't like gunplay on the premises. What we're always left with is a body that the Mexicans have to wash and prepare for the last rites and then bury out back in the cemetery. Who pays for them gravediggers? Who stands over the grave and says the right words? Who makes the marker with the deceased's name and suitable words?"

Grudgingly, the drovers agreed that it was a fair exchange.

Once they were gone, Pa knelt awkwardly on his stiff leg and took Walloping Sam's gold pocket watch and chain, a few silver dollars for the Mexican burial party and a nice pair of rowel spurs leaving the rest of the clothing for those that wanted it.

Maybe brutal and indifferent but that's the way it was done back then.

———

After a fair bit of badgering, Teddy's desire to take up cowboying finally came to fruition when he was offered a work as a Little Mary chuck wagon helper. He asked Pa if he could go and Pa gave him that expressionless look of his and said that right enough he was old enough to make his own way now. Pa allowed him a spare saddle pony and we all stood and watched him go, a lone figure but contented that he was going to do what he wanted to do so much. He took little enough, a hat and blanket of course and saddlebags with a couple of sandwiches Ma had fixed and wrapped up in wax paper for him. She never came to see him off and that we considered a strange thing as she had always shown a particular shine toward Teddy.

After that a letter arrived once a year saying Teddy was doing okay and wishing us Christmas or Easter good wishes or for whatever season it was. There was very little other information except for the postmark. Teddy never did take up Cyril's offer of reading and writing so the letters were written by some companion or a paid advocate rather than by his own hand.

As the years passed and his letter arrived every year from all over the country it was obvious Teddy was still unsettled and drifting from job to job. Ma received each missive with a light in her eye and a tight smile on her lips as she clutched Teddy's letter to her breast and hurried off to read it in private and most likely before we could see her tears.

Eventually, a year was missed with no letter arriving.

Then another, and finally they stopped coming altogether.

CHAPTER FOUR

I guess seeing his brother go stirred similar thoughts in Petey's mind. Always the private and secretive one, he never did ask Pa's permission but one day quite covertly he joined one of the regular stagecoaches passing through and was gone. Where he went none of us had any idea. I tried asking Emmeline as the two of them had always been close but my sister lived in the clouds somewhere and could give me no clear answer. Unfortunate that such a pretty young woman could be so vague and dreamy; even as she approached her frail womanhood beset by many obscure ailments still she fancied her collection of dolls above all else. I would catch her sometimes speaking to them as if they were living creatures and more dear to her than her real family.

By now the station was expanding. As the threat of Indian or raider attack faded, settlers and shopkeepers moved in. A trading post was built and then a dry goods store all along the road outside the courtyard walls. Shacks and storerooms followed and gradually the station extended itself into a small center for business. Travelers would stock up here on supplies before they moved on.

One itinerant passing through was a lawyer called Jason Binder; he took one look at poor Emmeline and decided to stay. He hung up his shingle and began to operate out of a rented hut and all the meanwhile attempting to woo Emmeline. He brought her presents and was lost in his devoted attraction for her. There is no doubt that she certainly was a beautiful young woman with the kind of fair looks a poet might draw the best of conclusions from, but sorry to say, her brain was as empty as a pocket. However Jason never seemed to notice this and in time he proposed marriage. Of course she did not know whether she should or not so it was left to Pa to decide.

So they were wed, and Emmeline hardly seemed to notice the change in her personal circumstance she remained true to her relationship with the dolls that were the true objects of all her ardor. Those inanimate objects were not given to argument and would stay the same however they were treated, in such a way Emmeline filled her days with secure fantasy and avoided all the pitfalls and dangers of reality. Jason doted on her and barely appeared to recognize her distracted lack of intelligible conversation. My older sister Mary stepped in now and again to make the transition easier for Emmeline but it was an uphill task. Mary was a stalwart creature of substantial build, not pretty by any means but bright enough and a hard worker. I got on very well with

Mary and as I said it was she who passed on the ability to read and write that she had learned so well from Cyril.

Around this time we received some sad news about Petey.

A rider passing through, a man who had known Petey as a youngster, gave us word that he had died in a Mexican prison cell of dysentery. How the hell he got there or what he was doing across the border the fellow did not know. So Petey passed as quietly as he had lived and left no mark behind him, in some strange way it was almost as if he had never existed at all.

Cyril was also getting restless as he confided in me on our daily rides. I was bigger now and could ride my own pony so we would mosey along side by side and he would speak his mind. He had taken to training me to shoot with a pistol and rifle and promised me I had a good eye. He still shone like gold in my eye, a big bold man full of good will. He was more than a brother; he was a friend and mentor and almost a father as Pa took so little interest in other than managing the station.

Pa was so engaged in this task that when Ma passed away he barely seemed to take heed. She went in her sleep and it was then that we found that her pillowcase was stuffed with Teddy's letters, there was no doubt she had favored Teddy above the rest of us and treasured every word he had sent. We laid her out back in the cemetery and at the graveside stoic Pa, still kept his stony gaze much as he always had and offered no expression. No sign of grief crossed his features but from that day forward there were subtle changes that began to find a home in his behavior.

He took to sitting alone on the porch outside the dining hall with a bottle of brew by his side and smoking hand-rolled cigarettes which was a new venture for him. Pa would sit there staring at nothing and sip whiskey until he fell into a doze and the burning cigarette would smolder dangerously close to his calloused fingers and then Mary would have to come out from the kitchen and remove it.

Then life took a hold of us and shook as only it can on occasion.

Some enterprising cattlemen had convinced the Eastern Railroad to run tracks to Fort Azarel—by now everybody had dropped the "Longfellow" part of the title—and run the cattle north to the slaughter yards from a depot rather than the long drives across country. They invested in the building of stockyards and extended the whole town along the length of the stagecoach trail.

Cyril foretold it would be the eventual demise of the stagecoach line. Locomotive travel was taking a hold all over the country and not least of all in our isolated fort. It determined Cyril to find something else, he wanted to serve he told me, to do some good in the community before life passed him by.

Finally he showed me the letter he had received from Captain Ira Aten, commander of the Texas Rangers Company D. As Cyril had the ability to read and write they were able to look on his application favorably and willing to enlist him as corporal in their company. They even sent him one of their new badges neatly cut from a Mexican Five-Cinco coin.

A part of me felt the shock of his coming departure with great sadness and yet another part recognized that Cyril was fulfilling his destiny and for that reason I was pleased for him. It was dangerous times for the Texas Rangers though with organized bands of raiders coming up from across the border and hitting isolated farmhouses and smallholdings but this was where Cyril felt he could do the most good.

He rode out along that long familiar road one day and I watched him go as he went past the new stockyards and the gangers working on the track-laying for the coming railroad. I saw him turn in the saddle one last time and give me a wave of farewell and I have to say at that particular moment his loss came home to me and I felt suddenly empty and alone.

———

A second blow came one evening when I found a handwritten sheet pinned to my pillow.

It was from Mary. She explained how she and the lawyer Jason Binder had fallen in love and he planned to leave Emmeline and they intended to be free to go far away and live together as man and wife. She begged me to help Emmeline see past any resentment and to forgive her for such an act of infidelity.

I could not blame her; she was no longer young and had missed her chance at happiness in favor of her family and the hard work that had denied her any hope of a future. As for Emmeline she stared at me blankly when I told her the facts. It seemed as if the notion did not penetrate the dullness of her brain. A week passed before the news finally did sink in and she reacted, it was then she began to wail pitifully. She howled like a coyote day and night in a bed crowded with her collection of shiny faced china dolls, whose unfeeling expression was as fixed as our father's.

Pa paid it no mind, he still sat in his chair on the porch drinking and smoking but now nobody came to remove the burning cigarette from his sleeping fingers.

And we never did see Mary again.

It took eleven months for Emmeline to fade and die, she would take no food but continued to weep pitifully over Mary and her husband's betrayal. Always a frail creature, the sadness filled her to over-flowing and her distant mind was overcome by the loss of her partner no matter how distantly he had filled her trance-like life. She faded away as a vaporous ghost might pass through the solid walls of our station and with no more noise than a sad whimper in her passing. I had tried to comfort her, seated on her bed, her hand in mine but she paid it little heed and was surrounded only by the many glassy and impersonal stares of the dolls and finding no relief in their presence except the coldness of their china hearts.

I told Pa when she was gone and his wordless answer was to hold out a crumpled yellow sheet of telegraph paper. It was from the Fast Overland Stagecoach Company and told how they would be seriously restricting their service from now on. As Cyril had foretold it was no longer viable for them to maintain the station with the coming of the railroad.

How Pa felt about that I could not tell; it seemed his only redress for all the years of hard work he had put into the place was to be found in the bottom of his liquor bottle.

How I wished Cyril were still here. There was no one left to make decisions except me, as Pa's interest was only limited at best. As I considered the problem all that Cyril had taught me rang true, the memory rising up through my being and giving me purpose, I resolved to handle matters as he would have approved. I was old enough by now and I took the problems by the horns and did something to solve them.

First off I turned one of the courtyard storerooms into a post office so that the few company wagons still coming through could leave or pick up mail and parcels there for the residents. Next I changed the stagecoach team stables into a livery with hire gigs and ponies and finally I kept the dining hall open as a drinking parlor for passing trade.

It worked too.

The expanding town was pleased with the pragmatic result and both the older members, the dry goods store and trading post owners, offered me praise and partnership. But I kept my own council and when I found Pa slumped in his chair on the porch no longer drunk and unconscious but having passed over in his sleep I was left as the sole manager in Fort Azarel.

Now that the interest had shifted with the advent of great herds of cattle using the railroad, the country outside the fort gradually filled up with ranching settlers. The Indians were pacified and sent to unwelcome reservations, border raiders kept at a minimum by the stern law enacted by the Rangers so the fort faded into disinterest as a defensive redoubt and even its name as "fort" was dropped and the whole rambling town became known simply as Azarel.

Being the last of the original Boyds in town I found that people deferred to me with respect for some reason and was not surprised when they decided to offer me the position as police officer. I was assured that it was merely to give the town some credibility and standing in the modern age. I reckoned it was a nominal job and would not draw on my time too much so I accepted and became the town marshal for Azarel. At first, having no previous officer, the blacksmith beat out a poor-looking star in tin but eventually the hotel owner, Evan Loughborough sent back east for a genuine shining steel badge embossed with the correct heraldry and presented it to me with due pomp.

I used the empty buildings in the old fort for my offices and even had one room walled up as a jail with a barred doorway put in.

Once I was settled and seemed content it was then that more sad trouble came down that road.

It was a letter from Cyril's captain in the

Rangers and briefly told of his courage and sense of duty and his sad loss in the line of duty. All emotion drained from me as I read the words, it was if I had been struck by a thunderbolt. The man who had been my kindly counselor as well as brother, a man who had all my respect and devotion was suddenly dead. The demise and loss of all my previous family members had not made such an impact on me as this one. I was shaken to the core; it seemed impossible that such a lively and intelligent soul as my brother Cyril whose mission had solely been for the benefit of others could be taken from this life.

When I had recovered, I wrote to the Ranger captain asking for more details but I never received an answer. So I took to writing out flyers offering a reward if anyone could give me details of my Texas Ranger brother Cyril Boyd's passing. I distributed them with anyone who was passing through and even took some up to the locomotive agent to pass out along the train route.

CHAPTER FIVE

The town was growing all the time.

It was expanding beyond the boundaries of the fort, running down each side of the old stagecoach trail and spreading out into the surrounding countryside beyond the stockyards.

I began to regret taking on the role of policeman as the success of the growing town began to attract less desirable elements.

Crazy people began to hit town. Kid Salado was one of them and a particular pain with his excessively wild and drunken displays; he would strip down and ride naked except for his boots and then charge along Main Street shooting out window glass and streetlamps.

Until now I had little to do as town marshal, a few drunks and fistfights but nothing much to test my abilities as law officer.

The Kid however was different, he was a short, ugly little fellow with one wayward eye and hair chopped across his brow in a pudding bowl crop. He was totally demented and prone to explosive bouts of temper at anything and anybody without reason. He fueled his uncontrolled animosity with drink and did not mind whom he upset with his aggressive attitude. The city fathers tired of his behavior and begged me to do something about it.

I knew if I fronted the Kid it would become a gunfight that I would probably lose, as he was a renowned gunman. It called for some careful consideration and I wondered how Cyril would have handled the matter. I had no doubt he would have been fearless; the Kid was insane but that would not have stopped Cyril. In all probability he would have taken out his pistol and whacked the Kid good before sending him on his way.

The Kid had taken to holing up in Mama Mose's Dance Emporium, that being a high-class title for a house of ill repute that had been built on the other side of the tracks at the fringes of town. Yes, there was dance in there but not the kind you found on any ballroom floor.

I rode up there one night hoping to catch Kid Salado off guard. In the dark street outside, I saw a client with his pants around his ankles and his female companion with legs in the air as they both coupled against a wall in the shadows. They did not notice me they were so occupied but I despaired as I considered this is how low things were becoming in this town and a high-minded man like my brother Cyril would not have stood for two folks huffing and puffing in such a fashion and in plain view.

I found the Kid inside in his underwear, sitting on top of the stand-up piano with his bare feet trailing over the keys. He seemed morose and out of sorts with a gloomy stare that stayed fixed before him. There was a half empty bottle of whiskey beside him and he wore his six-gun belt over his long johns but nothing else.

Mama was a big, overheated fat woman dressed in a shoulder puffed bombazine dress and she bustled up to me smelling rather unpleasantly of a mix of sweat and cheap perfume.

"You gotta do something about him, Marshal," she whispered urgently. "He's upsetting my customers, glaring at them like that all the time."

"You got people out there screwing in the street," I admonished her.

"Really?" She looked momentarily shocked. "It won't be any of my girls, I don't allow any such free-lancing."

"You'd best be sure. I don't want any barnyard behavior in this town."

"What about him? You gonna do something about that?" she asked with a sidelong glance at the Kid.

"Sure," I said, sounding confident but not feeling it. "Hey, Kid?" I called. "You ready to go yet?"

He raised his sad eyes to look at me and it was like looking into a dry empty well.

"Come on, boy," I urged. "It's time to go. You had your fun. Now leave these folks some time on their own."

He slid forward on his seat and his bare feet stepped down onto the piano keys with a jarring crash.

"What do you want?" he grunted, but he seemed

to me that he was far away and operating in some kind of dream state.

"You're going to have to come sleep it off, cowboy."

"You want me to sleep it off?" he slurred. All the time he was strolling up and down the piano keyboard crashing and banging out disconsolate chords.

"Get down here, Kid, and stop playing the ass."

"I like playing the ass, law-dog."

I felt the strength of Cyril flowing through me then, almost as if he was there beside me. "Yeah," I said firmly. "Well it stops now, Kid. Get down and come along of me to the jailhouse."

He snorted amusement. "Like hell, you dummy. You're like all the rest of them in this town, always watching but too pissant scared of dying to do anything about it. Well, I ain't scared of nothing, not death nor perdition and I'd soon as blast you one in the head as look at you."

Then it happened. I can't say what motivated it. I was still thinking about Cyril and how he would have handled the situation when I found my six-gun revolver smoking in my hand.

The Kid was screeching a high-pitched whine, standing on tiptoe clutching at his neck with both hands while blood streamed from his throat and onto his chest. I did not remember even firing but as he fell rigidly forward from the piano and landed heavily on the whorehouse floor I knew it had been me and I had taken him by as much surprise as it had taken me.

Those whores and their clients, who had been in

parlor, withdrew in shock and horror and their noise was extraordinary as they squealed in a mix of surprise and admiration that I had shot down the dreaded Kid Salado.

Mama Mose, who had withdrawn a few paces, was looking at me with an air of wonder. "Well, ain't you the dog's whiskers, Marshal. I never thought you had it in you."

Me either—I thought.

"Get this cleared away," I muttered, trying to sound like I did this kind of thing all the time and looking down at the Kid lying face down in a spreading pool of dark blood. "And make sure none of your girls is making a little extra down the alleyway outside, you hear me, Mama?"

"Sure, Marshal, I'll look into it, don't you worry." There was an air of respect in her voice now and I realized right there that something had changed in my standing in the town.

The Kid's death gave me a sense of confidence and aligned me with all my thoughts about my upstanding brother, Cyril. He would be proud to see me now, I was a lawgiver and like him I was serving the community, it gave me some sense of pleasure to think I had achieved such a role at last.

———

Time passed and as some months flew by, an interesting letter arrived telling me that an ex-Ranger called Barney May had seen my flyer and had some information for me about Cyril's death. I was to bring the reward money and go visit him on his ranch outside of Buena Vista. I knew the town; it was a small place far south and almost on the border with Mexico.

I packed my saddlebags and took some time out from my duties in town. It was a long haul down there but to date it had been the best sounding information about Cyril's passing I had received.

When I arrived, Barney May turned out to be a muscular, cautious looking and round-shouldered fellow, who gave out with a great many sly sidelong glances as if he suspected someone nearby was about to attack him. Which may well have been the truth of it; the Rangers were not ones to mince words and were known to have committed some extreme acts in their tenure and even in retirement doubtless found themselves up against ruthless people who did not forget.

Barney said he had been a Texas Ranger for eight years and looking over his well-situated property I thought he had done very well out of it. There was a string of fine looking thoroughbreds in the corral and I wondered how he had afforded all that and the ranch on his pension. Obviously a man who counted every cent in his billfold he made sure I had the fifty-dollar reward money with me before he started on the information.

He told me he knew where Cyril was buried, he said it was he that had discovered the body on a routine patrol and buried it. He had found Cyril lying face down in brush alongside a dried-out creek bed, both hands had been roped up behind him and he had been shot in the back of the neck.

"Who could have done that?" I asked.

Barney shrugged. "Heck! We had a tough old war going on back then, plenty of raiding greasers and renegades coming across the border and causing mayhem. Could have been any one of them."

"You say you know where my brother's grave is, will you take me there?"

"Sure, you got my dues first. I can't afford the time to do all this from the goodness of my heart."

I shelled out the fifty dollars and he saddled a pony and mounted up without a word. Leading the way out from the ranch we traveled for a hot hour through an arid land that was covered solely with saguaro cactus and thorny chaparral. I was glad I had thought to wear my leather chaps for the thorns would have torn the clothes from my limbs without their protection. It was a bare desperate land, baked by the sun without respite and fit only for snakes and lizards.

Finally we came to a dip in the desert and a tumbledown shack stood there. The weather and time had done its work and the shack was in a poor state, the windows were empty except for some threadbare remnants of curtains and the front door missing showing that the dusty interior was empty.

"This here belonged to a Mex couple called Delgado back then," said Barney. "When I brought your brother in, I had the woman get him ready for burying. She did it right proper, washed the body and had him laid out with his hands like this," Barney folded his arms across his chest. "He looked real nice."

"Where's the grave?" I asked.

"Out back," Barney supplied.

"Let's go see."

The back of the property was a leveled field and somebody, Delgado probably, had cleared it of rocks. The discarded stones made a low wall along one side. You could see how nothing had ever grown there; the whole place was dry, rocky, and desolate.

"So where is it?" I asked.

Barney scratched his head; I could tell that now he had his money he was fast losing interest. "Hell if I can remember, it was a long time back." He began to walk across the field vaguely kicking up dust. "I had them put in a marker," he said. "It should be around here somewhere."

But the harsh weather and years had done their work and we found no trace of any marker.

Barney took his leave figuring he had done all he could to fulfill his part of the bargain, his parting shot made me wonder.

"I heard of him, you know?" he said, looking down at me from the saddle. "Your brother, Cyril Boyd. I never was in the same Company but we all knew his name. He was a damned good Ranger, you should be proud. Without him the Border War would have dragged on for years, he knew how to settle hash and took down some pretty nasty folk."

When he had gone, I sat on the broken porch steps of the ruined house and wondered what to do next. I would have liked to erect some kind of marker for Cyril; some way of remembering he existed. It occurred to me that the owners of the old house who had seen Cyril's body in the ground might well remember exactly where it was buried.

The village of Buena Vista was not far off and I determined to find if the Delgado family lived there and see if they could recall Cyril's last resting place.

I found him all right, Juan Delgado. He was a widower now, his wife having passed some time earlier. An amenable little figure willing to please and we sat together on the low wall outside his adobe house on the edge of town and I asked him about the Border War.

"Ah yes," he said. "That was bad, many peoples were killed. Such a sad affair. A bandit chief called Esmeraldo Pais, came up from over the border with many men and raided amongst the Anglos. The Texas Rangers were called and began to track them down and a big fight continued for many months."

"It was bad, huh?"

"A great bloodletting, senor. Many evil things were done. But if you wish to speak with Esmeraldo Pais, he is staying nearby and will perhaps tell you more. I will take you to him if you wish?"

I was surprised to hear the bandit chief was still alive and a free man but being so, I was sure I wanted to ask him if it was his men that had murdered Cyril.

"I will come," I said.

Delgado fetched his mule and I mounted up my pony and he led the way into wide desert land covered with thorny brush that fills the empty strip of land paralleling the border. There were no trees, not even of the Mesquite or Judas variety; everything was low and growing on nothing more than dust. It was a desert place and there were many flies that pestered us continually as if something had died in the vicinity.

We traveled some hours until Delgado pulled up.

"There, senor," he said, pointing to a shack roof visible over the taller brush. "There you will get your answers maybe."

"I see," I said. "You coming?"

"This is as far as I go; I do not wish to see this man, the old ones in our village say it is best to avert your eyes from him as if he looks on you he has the power to drink your soul. May God go with you, senor, although I think maybe you are about to meet the one who is perhaps the Devil himself."

CHAPTER SIX

With that gloomy pronouncement Delgado turned his mule and rode off without even a backward glance.

I shrugged it off and pressed on through the waist-high brush until I came to the clearing with the shack. It was fairly new built and in good condition and the sloping roof came down and shadowed the porch of a plank veranda outside.

Seated on the veranda was a strange apparition. A large, aging Anglo woman dressed entirely in black was rocking gently backward and forward on a rocking chair, and from her creased lips was the narrow stem of a smoking corncob pipe. Her fingers were busy though and she did not need to look at what she was doing the habit being so firmly ingrained, her hands nimbly worked with needle and thread on some obscure crochet design. Her hair was gray and bound up and her features lined with many creases and upon her head sat a small bonnet with black feathers decorating it. She was a large, statuesque woman and although elderly she held herself well and her eyes slid away from me temporarily as if my arrival held little interest for her and could not be an important interruption to her day.

I pulled up my pony at the porch step and only then did she deign to recognize my arrival. She cocked an eyebrow in my direction.

"He'p you?" she said in a voice surprisingly strong for her years.

"I'm looking for Esmeraldo Pais, I'm told he lives here."

"Inside," she said with a jerk of her head toward the dark open doorway.

With some trepidation I approached the doorway and kept my hand hovering over my pistol grip. I had no idea what to expect. There was the faint shuffle of movement from within but it was dark in there after the bright sun and I stood a moment at the doorway until my eyes adjusted.

The single room held a dense and ugly smell, a thick outhouse stink of feces and urine that made the bile rise in my throat. The gloomy room was almost empty, just plain wooden boards on the floor and bare of furniture except for a single bed with a figure lying on it. The shadowy figure was dressed in a loose-fitting filthy brown nightshirt and the few rumpled sheets on the bed were stained and dirty. Nothing about the man was clean and the smell was strong and revolting. Flies buzzed in lazy circles above his stinking body that had obviously fouled itself on more than one occasion.

It was a dark, curly-headed, hollow-cheeked and

bearded man with a pale face running with sweat that lay there. What had once been tanned skin was now pallid and almost yellow with the sickness and the flesh hung loose on his bones. He breathed throatily from deep in the chest and turned his head slowly toward me. There was a burning light in his eye that at first I took as a danger signal but then I realized it was just the fever. Above his head hanging from the bedstead was an ornate gun belt with shining silver Conchos embedded, a silver-plated revolver with a pearly grip rested in the well-used black leather holster.

I stood in the doorway my shadow falling across the distressed figure in the bed.

"You Pais?" I asked. "Esmeraldo Pais?"

"Who wants to know this?" he rasped, his accented voice no more than the sound of dry leaves on stone.

"My name's James Boyd, although some folks call me 'Buddy.'"

"You come to kill me?" asked Pais. "I seen that star on your vest."

"Depends."

"On what? Look *cabron*, I don' care what you do. I'm bound for the grave anyway; this damned sickness is sucking the life from me. I cannot walk and my arms so weak I don't pick anything up; I have to rely on that old bitch out there to feed me. And she does that only when she feels like it."

"You pay her to do that?" I asked curiously.

"Sure I pay her, why else would she do it? Listen, friend, if you've come to do me, do it now. Two slugs in the chest," he raised a shaking hand and weakly allowed the fingers to hover over his heart. "About here, because I am done and I don' think I can go on any longer."

"I need to ask you a question."

"Go on then, go on. Get it over with and then finish me off."

"You ever hear of a Texas Ranger called Cyril Boyd, he was my brother."

"Hah!" it was almost a laugh but came out more like a throaty cough. "I have not heard this name in a while. The Hanging Ranger, that's what we call him."

"The Hanging Ranger," I repeated. "You meant he brought a lot of bandits to the gallows?"

"The gallows!" snorted Pais. "They never get that far. No, *senor*, Cyril Boyd was a special kind of man."

"What do you mean?" I was troubled by his discriminatory tone.

"These Texas Rangers were all hard men, they had no charity, a cruel bunch, you understand? It was an all-out war we fought," rasped Pais in justification. "They did not give us a fair chance so we did the same. I mean, *por dios*! We just come here to take a few cattle, maybe steal away a good-looking girl or two but they come down hard on us like the demon from hell. I tell you, one time that brother of yours was with a small party of Rangers and they come across the camp of twenty of my men. Boyd disarmed them and shout that they don' deserve no trial and that he should hang them all right there but there wasn't no trees about. So you know what he did? Put a lasso necktie around their throats and dragged them one at a time behind his pony until they was dead. Strangled, or "hung" as he liked to say and he done this in front of all their wives and children. Oh, *senor*, that Boyd was a piece of work all right, the worst one of the whole rotten bunch."

I was stunned and wondered how much of what he was telling me I could believe because none of it sounded anything like Cyril.

"You trying to tell me my brother was a wanton murderer operating outside the law? I just don't believe you."

"Ach!" spat Pais. "What do you know? I have seen the bodies of the men he tortured with the hot iron."

I could not believe any of these acts were ones committed by my Cyril, it was all a fantasy concocted by this wretched creature.

"What happened to him?" I asked. "He was found hands tied behind him and murdered execution style."

Pais was evasive. "Hell if I know, Jesus! We kill so many back then. Look, you gonna help me on my way and not just stand there asking these damned foolish questions?"

"I think you're a liar," I said, turning to go out of the door. "That isn't my brother, Cyril."

I was outside and I breathed the fresh air deeply, glad to be free of the cloying stench of sickness and death that filled the tomb-like room I had just left. I was about to speak with the old lady who still sat rocking and smoking her pipe when I heard a hefty thump on the floorboards behind me. I turned to see the pathetic figure of Pais, dragging himself awkwardly across the floor, the silver six-gun held in both his shaking hands.

He was pointing the gun up at me and struggling to bring back back the hammer but there was no strength in him not even enough to cock the pistol.

"Damn it, damn it!" he cursed through gritted teeth. "Will you finish me, you dog?"

I leaned down and swept the gun easily from his weak grip and tossed it over and into the old lady's lap amongst her crochet threads. She furrowed her brow, looked down at the pistol and then across at Pais.

"Get him back inside," was all she said.

I took hold of the bandit's grubby nightshirt collar and dragged him over to the stained bed. "There you are," I said, looking down at him disdainfully. "Consider this your bed of sins, think on that."

He followed me out of the door with a string of invectives, mean words that meant little to me coming from the dying man who had probably killed my brother.

I jerked my chin at the old woman outside. "What're you doing this for? He's just suffering."

She looked at me with her eyes turning cold and hard as stone. "I'm here to make sure he *does* suffer right up to the end. I keep him alive so he can suffer more. It will not bring back my loved ones but it gives me relief to know that every day they can see revenge paid out in liberal doses for what that evil son-of-a-bitch did."

I didn't ask what Pais had done to her kin I just turned away and fetched my pony.

CHAPTER SEVEN

I am old now, sitting in the ruins of what was Fort Azarel as evening comes, the distant train whistle is blowing mournfully and I can hear the soft voices of ghosts calling, blowing like the wind through the dusty gun ports. The old stage-coach road lies alongside me where I sit and over it a tumble of adobe bricks from the broken courtyard wall are spread at my feet.

Teddy is there, I see him whirling in a dust cloud down the road; he is riding a lively cow pony that is perky and full of spirit. He pulls the pony around in a rearing pass through the dust of the road and grins at me, then with a wave of his hat he is racing away like a pale shadow and is soon lost to sight.

Here is Petey wandering by with his hands in his pockets, he is ignoring me and not really paying attention as if he is lost and does not want to be here anyway and then there is Mary. Mary standing tall, older and big breasted but content and holding a baby wrapped in her arms, she does not look at me, her attention is fixed lovingly on the child and I am happy for that. At a slower, more tentative pace, Emmeline shuffles in, looking diminished and sorrowful with dark-ringed eyes and a sickly pallor. The glossy shine of sweat that coats her skin is reminiscent of the many china dolls she favored and now it seems that their emptiness has finally filled her too.

And there down the road walking away from me is Cyril.

"*Cyril! Hey, Cyril!*" I call and he turns and in that moment I see it is not Cyril but just a young fellow from town on his way home.

"Howdy Mr. Boyd, you calling me?"

"Forgive me, I thought you were someone else."

"Okay." He is moving from the road and coming across toward me. "You need some help? You all right sitting there all alone?"

"No, I'm fine."

He stops his advance and turns back to the road. "Well then, if you're okay I'll say goodnight to you. Best not sit out here too long, Mr. Boyd, it will get chilly once the sun's gone."

The only chill is in my heart now and this emptiness is what I have based so much of my life on, the illusion that was Cyril and all the attitudes he advocated that I followed so willingly. What if they were in fact all distorted and I had deluded myself with his talk of service and honor? I think that maybe in all likelihood, the truth is that he had changed when he took on the Ranger's badge. Maybe it was that he saw horrors down there in Texas that shook him to the core and bent his heart out of shape.

But what was the true value of all those moral

principles if they could be lost to him so easily? I have no way of knowing, it was not my experience and maybe I should not be judging my brother. I had taken on his mantle easily enough without caring to forge my own path and in that, much to my distress, I found that there was only hollow emptiness once the mold was broken.

So now I sit and stare on down the long white road out of town, waiting for the last carriage that will surely eventually come and carry me on my way. Perhaps then I will see Cyril and my kin again but I can tell you in all truth, I really hope that I do not.

A BREAK IN THE CLOUDS

CHAPTER ONE

It was three weeks before they came to visit him.

He was occupying a single cubbyhole in a crumbling tenement block. It was a tall flat fronted building soot stained and stabbed by hundreds of tiny windows, at some time in the past it may have been a factory of sorts. Once he had tried to open the window in his room, a four-pane creation barely big enough to see through the glass was so filthy. The frame had stuck halfway and stayed there just open enough so he could look toward the distant Ellis Island where he had arrived those weeks earlier.

The building was teeming with immigrants of all nationalities and constantly buzzed with their noise and a whole variety of cooking smells that tainted the air. Screaming barefoot children played in the yard and women sung in their native tongue and hung acres of washing from their windows while the street below echoed with the sound of steel bound

TONY MASERO

freight wagon wheels and great horseshoe-shod dray
horses clashing across the cobbles at all hours.

The looming ornate buildings so close together
awed him on arrival, the streets alive with carriages,
cabs, omnibuses and trams. The bustle of millions
of people, pushing, hurrying, running to God knows
where. All of it so far removed from the sleepy fields
and white painted thatched cottages of his
homeland.

Confronted with such city volatility Malone kept
his usual stony-faced disposition; his life was
different to be sure, he came from a cause where
commitment was total and danger and betrayal were
prevalent and it was ingrained into his personality. It
left him closed in and self-possessed, unmoving, like
a stone in the river with the waters rushing around
it. He stood a big man at over six feet tall with broad
shoulders and hair cropped close to his skull. His
expressionless features told little but the clenching
and unclenching of his jaw muscles spoke of an
underlying tension that troubled his waiting.

———

Malone passed the waiting days penning poetry in a
small notebook, an unlikely aptitude in one such as
he but it was his secret want. All he had known in
the land of his father's was waxed with songs and it
ran in his blood. In this way he shaped his hidden
thoughts and brought to mind the trip across and his
meeting with the woman.

He had left Queenstown in June 1880 on the
ship Etna, although being a patriot he preferred to

call the port by its old Gaelic name—An Cóbh—and on that fair and windy day, where the choppy sea slapped gray against the hull of the ship he had bid farewell to his native Ireland. Taking passage on the steamship has been a luxurious choice, not his, of course, but the stateroom cabin was paid for by others to the exorbitant tune of fifteen guineas. Not the largest of cabins to be sure but better by far than the seven English pound payment for the cram of steerage, where they packed them in like boxed fish.

Two weeks or a mite more to cross the ocean they had promised him. He used the time patrolling the deck, as he preferred the briny scent of sea and the wide sky and to be in the open rather than the cabin after the life he had grown used to in the rural country of his youth.

He first noted her on the third day, there was nothing remarkable about the woman he had to admit and yet she caught his eye. A wafer thin figure, she had the same drawn features as many others aboard and a small sickly looking pale-faced boy of maybe eight or nine years that clung to her attentively. She held him tight too, her hand in the youngster's as the ship rolled on the open sea. Unused to the waves and the vastness of the ocean was written on her concerned face as the paddle wheel pounded loudly and sails whipped above. A great channel of black smoke poured from the ship's funnel that sent a trail far back to the shores they had departed and with it went all the trials and tribulations they and all the other hopefuls had left there.

Malone eavesdropped to the chatter of the immi-

TONY MASERO

grants as he wandered amongst them relenting his priv-
ilege of a better paying customer. He was one of them
after all and it was a relationship he treasured. He overheard how some had left to avoid the burden of English
values imposed upon them, others amongst the many
young women aboard embarking with the hope of the
earnings they might send back to their poor families.
There was gold, some said, nuggets to be picked up
effortlessly from streams or hillsides while others
promised themselves military service, easy money they
thought, fighting the primitive Indians with firearms
while the red men had only bows and arrows.

Such were the dreams of simple folk, Malone
thought, for he guessed that life across the water,
although different, would be as hard as anywhere
else.

There had been sickness aboard he discovered
after a week at sea, mostly amongst the teeming
steerage hold where either typhus or cholera was
taking a toll. That was when he saw her again,
standing alone in a narrow galley with her back to
him. The wind whipping at her dress and a shawl
tightly wrapped about her shoulders. Her dark hair
was tied up but some strands had fallen loose and
danced about her head in the raw wind.

Before her two sailors stood, a plank between
them and on it a small wrapped bundle tied in sail-
cloth. One of the men looked at her questioningly
and with a brief nod of the head she gave them way
and they lifted one end of the plank. The small,
wrapped figure slid from the plank and fell into the
turbulent sea to disappear swiftly in their wake.

There was no priest aboard and the captain chose not to attend, nor fellow travelers with their fear of sickness, so the sad moment was enacted in isolation. In that instant, Malone's heart went out to the lonely figure and he stepped forward, his hat in his hand.

"If you will forgive me, ma'am," he said at her elbow. "I would offer a prayer of passing for your child."

She looked around quickly at him, the terrible grief and emptiness written in the open grayness of her eyes. She nodded quick agreement and uttered words of thanks that were whipped away by the wind.

He laid a hand on her arm and felt for a moment her gracious melt as she leaned against him, it was a small pleasure at someone offering comfort and then she hardened just as quickly and turned away, her features mortifying as clay might meld into stone. She hurried away then, down the narrow galley and back toward the steerage, the wind thrashing at her skirts as she hunched bony shoulders against the chill wind and the coldness in her heart.

Malone saw her once more before they landed, she stood at the bulwark with all the others as they crowded to watch the great Statue of Liberty floating past while the ship entered New York harbor.

"I pray you are feeling better now, ma'am?" he asked, coming up beside her.

She glanced at him swiftly. "I don't think I ever

will be again," she admitted. "But I would give my thanks to you for your kindness, sir."

He nodded his head toward the statue. "Well perhaps there is a new promise that awaits us all."

She drew a deep breath. "I think mine is spent out there on the ocean."

"I trust not," he said.

To his eye she must have about thirty years although the stress of past days were worn on her features. Yet there was something about her he could not resist. Some show of hardy character that she wore about her and it rang a resonance in Malone's being.

"Might I have your name, ma'am?"

"Bridget, sir, Mrs. Bridget Riley, and you?"

"I am Malone."

"Just that?" she asked.

"That will serve, I am a man best kept simple."

A faint smile played on her lips. "And you go to the Americas for work?"

"It will be so, I'm thinking."

"Well, I wish you good fortune, Mr. Malone."

"And I you, ma'am."

Once in his tawdry New York room whiling away the waiting time he recalled that moment on the ship and in the strange anomaly that made up the man he scribbled in poetic form the memory for his notebook.

> *Did I wear rich and golden cloth,*
> *My hand I might offer in simple troth*
> *But I cannot give this reeling girl*
> *The pleasure of a single pearl*

And while away we all will cast
The memories of our lost past
Not one of us can ere deny
That loss is more than just goodbye.

CHAPTER TWO

W hen it came, the knock on his door was loud and persistent.

Three men stood on the landing outside. One, the talker and smaller of the three, was dressed in a Derby hat cocked on one side and with a tied scarf at his neck over a thick wool jacket and under one arm he carried a cudgel of sorts. It was a long narrow stick with a heavy bludgeon at one end and he kept it military fashion under one arm.

His two companions were solemn bodies, huge fellows with blank expressions and wearing long dark coats down to their heavy boots. Their faces bore signs of past violence in the shape of a scar here and there, with broken noses and crumpled ears.

"Good day, sir," said the talker. "Might you be Mr. Patrick Aloysius Malone?"

Malone studied them suspiciously. "I am that."

"Then may we have a word. My name in

Damon Fogarty and we have word of you from a mutual friend."

"Is that so and who might that be?"

"That will be Captain Damian Carruthers of the Irish Republican Brotherhood. Perhaps we might step inside and discuss this in private?"

At his words Malone peered into the darkness of the stairwell and recesses of the landing—one did not discuss such things so openly in his own country.

He eyed the two monoliths cautiously. "There's barely room for me and the bed in there, these boys here won't fit well."

"No matter, they'll stay outside, won't you boys?"

They nodded agreement in unison but said nothing.

"Now then, Mr. Malone let's talk," said Fogarty, brushing past Malone.

"Help yourself."

Fogarty looked around the small room briefly and crossed over to peer out of the grubby window. He was a small nervy character, sharp faced and energetic, moving in sudden dashes and bursts of conversation.

"Captain Carruthers tells us you do good work."

"If knocking off a couple of peelers is good work then that's what I do."

Fogarty chuckled. "And why you're here leaving such difficulties behind you, no doubt?"

"No doubt."

Fogarty nodded knowledgeably. "Well I have word for you. Orders. You are to appear before a mighty man and he will give you instruction."

"That so?"

"It is, we call him 'Boss' here, might be that you have heard of him back home?"

Malone shook his head negatively.

"We have here in New York a setup called Tammany Hall," Fogarty explained patiently. "It is a brotherly society with charitable and social principles." He chuckled slyly at this as if it was to say no such thing at all, "Now the Boss Croker runs things and he makes sure to have a finger in everything in this town. Everyone makes payment to Tammany Hall, if you get my meaning. The Boss is a Cork man and wily as they come, came up hard so he knows his way around. He wants a meeting with you, are you up for that?"

"I presume that's why I was sent over."

Fogarty cocked his head to one side. "You'll meet him at his favorite bar, 'The Old House at Home' at seven of the clock. Can you find your way there?"

"I'll take a cab if it's a well-known place."

"Oh, it is that."

"Then tell your man I will be there."

The Hansom cab charged Malone thirty cents, which he considered an excessive expenditure on his limited funds but it carried him promptly outside the paneled windows of "The Old House at Home" at five minutes to seven. Inside it was a large and lively pub-like place, hot and ripe with tobacco smoke and the vinegar smell of spilled beer. Dark wooden walls encased the room and brass spittoons shone with oily gleam on the sawdust-covered floorboards. The place was dimly lit with a bar counter to one side and a separated restaurant room at the rear. The bar was crowded with drinkers, jostling one with the other and Malone heard many Irish accents amongst the talkers.

He made his way to the dividing doorway of the dining rooms and was stopped before entry by a burly fellow dressed in a briskly waxed mustache and long white apron.

"I suppose you'll be wanting supper?" asked the waiter in a broad Irish accent. His tone was glib and a little imperious as if he had better things to do.

"I'm here to see someone," answered Malone.

"And just who might that be?" said the fellow, looking him up and down in a derogatory fashion.

Malone did not like the attitude but he answered calmly enough, "His name is Croker."

The attitude changed instantly to a more obsequies one. "Oh, Boss Croker, very well, sir. In that case come right this way, may I have the name if you please?"

Malone met his gaze and said his name.

The waiter led him past a few occupied tables in the quiet dining room, all of them set with starched white tablecloths and silver cutlery, to a place at the rear where a single man sat. Richard Croker was a round-faced thickset fellow with thinning center parted hair and sporting a beard and sagging mustache whiskers, small-shouldered and dressed in a wing-collared shirt and tie. His jacket was open and showed a waistcoat and gold watch chain and he was sawing his way through a plate of pork chops.

"Mr. Malone to see you, sir," introduced the waiter and Croker looked up. His face was expressionless and unmoving and he poked his fork in direction of the seat opposite without saying a word.

"You wanted to see me?" Malone asked.

Croker kept his head down and said nothing, concentrating on his meal.

The hovering waiter whispered to Croker, "Is there anything else you need, sir?"

Croker lifted his eyes and stared at the man a long silent moment, who bowed nervously and scurried away.

When he was gone, Malone said, "Will you speak or should I come back later?"

Croker twisted his lip irritably and stole a quick minute look at Malone. "Sit for a blessed minute, will you? Let me finish here."

"You take your time, that looks like a fair portion of pig, you have there."

Croker scratched stubby fingers through his beard, "So you have a mouth on you, do you, Mr. Malone?"

"I'm no servant of yours, sir. So don't treat me like one."

Croker smiled thinly and nodded his head in small appreciation, then ducked down to continue eviscerating his chops.

"I have a job for you," he said when a dice of pork hovered at his fork's end. "Are you interested?"

"I've been ordered to come and see you so I guess there is a mission involved."

"Aye, the boys back home know I take care of them but still I appreciate the gesture." He wiped his mustache with his napkin. "I love that country, you know. Been raised here since a nipper but still I ache for Ballyva and County Cork. But know I'm no bogtrotter, Mister Malone. My people had land in the old country but they came here to make their way, my daddy was a vet and served his time in the Civil War under General Sickles. Put me into public school for my sins but I've certainly made mine despite it all, that's for sure."

"So your man tells me."

"Ah, yes, Fogarty. A snotty wee whelp but he has his purposes. Myself I started on the Harlem Railroad as a lowly mechanical but left that off to run a gang around the teamsters and now look at me. I own this town, Mister Malone. Everybody answers to me, from senators to seamstresses, they all pay me heed and make their contributions as I command."

"I understand," Malone said, bored with such self-appraisal. "I have your message, you're a powerful man."

"So I am, sir, but don't think it rested there will you, I was a fighting man on the streets and with bare-knuckle fisticuffs I always boxed my opponents to a pulp. So I know the bottom as well as the top and if you work for me it's best to remember that."

"You have a fine opinion of yourself as well it seems."

Croker rested back in his chair and lifted a schooner of beer to take a sip. "And so you come straight off the boat and are not about to be overwhelmed by this resume?"

"I'll know a man by what he does not what he says."

"You will, will you?" Croker chuckled. "Not a

bad tenet to live by but ask around, boyo, you will hear that what I say is true."

"So, I am dutifully impressed," sighed Malone, tiring of the bragging. "What is it you wish of me?"

Croker stroked his mustache between finger and thumb, stroking it downward as he considered, "Listen, I like your cut, Malone. You will come dine with me at my house, I am just moved here to Harrison up in Westchester. It is a small place but we might talk there in private, there's too many ears in this place. I'll have Fogarty bring you out."

"Is it impossible to discuss this here and now?" asked Malone, thinking he had already had enough of this fellow.

Croker lowered his head and looked at Malone from under his eyebrows and said softly, "Look here, your Brotherhood has need of many things that I can supply." He hushed his voice and looked around to see if he could be overheard. "They need weapons and ammunition, explosives and such like, so where do you think they will get all that?"

Malone shrugged even though he well knew the answer.

"That's right," Croker said coldly, demonstrating his low anger. "From me, so as their representative over here I'd take it as a great kindness if you'd oblige me with your presence at my house. Not much to ask, is it, Mr. Malone. Unless, of course, you consider yourself too elevated a personality to even considering crossing my doorstep."

"Of course not," Malone said with enforced politeness. "Be only too glad to come, thank you for the invite, Mr. Croker."

Croker gave a sharp nod of acceptance and also of dismissal as he dived back into his supper plate again.

> *So I come with begging bowl*
> *To hear a hollow vessel toll*
> *And then accept on bended knee*
> *This gift from out across the sea*
> *Sworn promise of intended aid*
> *Yet priced in blood that must be paid.*

CHAPTER THREE

T he Hansom cab clattered over the cobbled street and its well-worn nag plodded along with an air of finality as the listless driver urged it on with a casual slap across the withers with the reins.

Malone did not like being pressed in close to Fogarty but there was little room to avoid him inside the two-seater. He wore some cloying oil that tampered down his hair and once his hat was off it filled the cab with its intrusive scent.

"So, Malone, how are you finding this fair land?" Fogarty asked.

"I barely know it, so cannot say."

"And did you find the Boss an awesome fellow?"

"He certainly knows how to make a noise."

Fogarty chuckled. "He does that all right. A brawny man if you did but know it, I have seen him knock the teeth from a fellow's head, and that's the truth?"

"You know, I think he might have mentioned that."

"But he has his sights set on a more political goal now I believe."

"So how far is this place of his?"

"Some twenty miles out from Manhattan, a half hour unless this sorry horse drops in the shafts."

Fogarty fussed with his coat and pulled the sleeves down over his shirt cuffs as if the mention of their destination reminded him of his attire and how he looked. He fumbled with the tie and diamond stickpin, lifting his chin to run a crooked finger around inside the collar as he did so.

Here is one nervous man—thought Malone.

"You yourself came across from Ireland?" he asked.

"I did indeed, set sail from Galway," Fogarty paused and glanced away at the gas-lighted street outside alive with passing carriages and pedestrians. "Must have been nigh on six years gone by now."

"And you don't miss it?"

"What's to miss? The starvation and oppressive British, I should say not. This is a fine land with a living to be made if you've a mind."

"You have done nicely then?"

"I have indeed, sir, with the Boss's firm hand on the tiller we all advance." Leaning forward, Fogarty touched him gently on the sleeve. "Pardon me asking but what is it exactly that you did in the old country?"

"I served the Fenian cause as I expect you well know."

"So it was said," Fogarty mused. "Yes indeed, so

it was said." He let the silence hang between them for a moment. "And now you bring your special services to our Boss Croker, is that it?"

"You've a mighty long nose, Mr. Fogarty, did you know that?"

"Oh, sir, I meant nothing by it, merely making conversation."

"In the old country that kind of *conversation* would earn you a bullet in a muddy ditch, I'm thinking."

"Land sakes, Malone! Don't take on so, there is little enough I am not apprised of."

"Would Mr. Croker be advised of that if it were so mentioned then?"

"Now, now," huffed Fogarty. "There's no need for such a thing. I am a loyal servant that is all I meant to say."

"Then keep your trap shut and your curiosity to yourself, you little gobshite."

At the harsh words, Fogarty had drawn himself away from Malone and pressed himself into a corner of the cab as a disturbed spider might hide from a heavy tread.

They traveled in silence that way for the rest of the journey.

The air smelled sweet after the city and quiet too without all the noise in the streets. It was night but some light still shone in the sky even though the sun had set. A silvery glow tilted the sky and was striated by lines of cloud that rode across the skyline and left Malone with the enclosed sensation of rural emptiness. It felt like the evenings of his home and all that was missing was the lowing of cattle and a single farmhouse lighted window in the blackness.

The "small" house when they reached it was nothing of the sort.

It was an immense, elaborate, twenty-room Victorian mansion built in Tudor style and lying at the end of a winding tree-lined driveway set in a landscaped acreage. The dark brickwork towered over the Hansom as they crunched over the white gravel and pulled up before an arched entranceway of large timber double doors set with black painted hinges and golden lion's head knockers.

A fitting estate, thought Malone, for a medieval lord like Boss Croker.

The door opened at their approach as if their knock was expected and Malone saw a manservant waiting in the light spilling out from inside.

"Gentlemen," he said in greeting. "Mr. Croker awaits you in the library."

A serving girl stood to one side behind the manservant ready to take their hats and overcoats and Malone started at the sight of her.

"Why, Mrs. Riley—Bridget," he burst out. "This is a surprise."

"Indeed, sir," she said, bobbing her head in curtsy. Beneath her lowered head he saw her eyes sneaking a look that seemed to be telling him to say no more.

"You know this girl?" Frowned Fogarty.

"We have met," Malone answered evasively.

"Aye, well," snorted Fogarty. "There's enough of these chippies about to be sure but it seems you're a fast worker, Mister Malone."

Bridget took their hats and coats and backed away out of sight into the shadows of the hallway.

"This way, gentlemen," said the manservant, ushering them forward across the checkerboard-tiled hallway.

"You go on," Malone said. "I have a thing left in my pocket."

As the other two moved off, Malone moved into the shadows after Bridget and found her hanging coats in an alcove. "Hello, to you," he said.

"Mr. Malone." She bobbed her head.

At least she has remembered my name, thought Malone. Her beauty struck him again though not the physical kind but there was some sort of indefinable quality that attracted him. It was an unspoken thing that he could not quite get his mind to understand but in his eyes she wore its subtle meaning as if a fine gown.

"What are you doing here?"

"Mr. Croker heard of my loss at the docks, he has been very kind. Taken me on as a domestic."

"He has?" There was an element of surprise for Malone in that charitable act, knowing the man as he did.

"Yes, indeed, a fine gentleman."

"Well," said Malone doubtfully. "They are expecting me, I suppose I should be getting on."

He turned to leave.

"Something troubles you, sir?"

Malone paused a moment teetering on his toes. "When are you free?"

"I get a half day Thursday and all of Sunday."

Malone faced her and asked almost coyly, "Will

you allow me to take you somewhere, a walk or dinner perhaps?"

She smiled then, a secretive grin that gave her faintly elfin features. "That would be pleasant."

He noted that she longer wore the gaunt and stony look she had held aboard ship and that there was a warmth to her now that had not been there before. Malone supposed that finding work so easily had been a relief and mellowed her.

"On Sunday then?"

"Thank you, Mr. Malone, you are most kind."

"Malone, just Malone."

"Very well—Malone, and thank you."

"No, lady," he muttered. "It is I who am grateful."

The library as was to be expected was as grand as the rest of the house, leather-bound books stood racked on shelves that reached from floor to ceiling. Croker sat on a deep armchair with a balloon of brandy beside him on a side table and Fogarty fidgeted in front of the great white marble fireplace it grate blackened and empty, as the weather was warm.

"There you are, Malone," said Croker. "Will you have a glass?"

"I will, sir, thank you."

Croker turned to the manservant and nodded and the man hurried off.

"With your permission?" asked Fogarty, taking a slender cigar case from inside his jacket.

Croker nodded his allowance and indicated the opposite armchair. "Take a seat, Malone."

Malone seated himself and they waited while

Fogarty lit his cheroot and the servant returned with Malone's brandy.

"I'd offer you one, Damon, but I know you must be on your way."

"Oh! Yes, sir," said Fogarty taken by surprise.

"Indeed, the matter I spoke of is urgent."

"You wish me to go now, Boss?"

"That would be best."

"Very well," fumbled Fogarty, obviously having expected to be invited to join them. "I shall take my leave then. Goodnight to all."

"Good night, Damon, you're a good lad and thank you for all your fine work in bringing our man here to us," praised Croker as Fogarty took his leave.

Croker lowered his brow that was a sign to Malone that he was about to get serious.

"So, Mr. Malone, let's discuss the matter in hand."

Malone laid aside his glass and leaned forward attentively.

"I am involved in a struggle for high office," Croker continued. "'Honest' John Kelly, now there's a misnomer, if ever there was. You will not know but he has been a successful comptroller here and has just stood for governor. I have his word that within five years he will hand over control to me. But there is a fly in the ointment."

"That is where I come in, I take it?" said Malone.

"It is indeed, there is a faction, you see. They seek to oust Kelly and in doing so they will push me out as well."

"And who are they?"

"They're headed by a man called Sam Tilden and he is promoting a do-gooder called Alonzo Cornel in opposition to Kelly. Tilden's a sickly puppy so I do not give two figs for him but one Joseph E. Grady underpins him and this is where I want you active. Grady fancies himself as, of all things, some kind of a cowboy, he is a fool but is worth many millions of dollars and that funding is finding its way to his good friend Sam Tilden. If we can take him off the board I believe it will ease our way forward."

"Grady is here in New York?"

"No," said Croker, his face wrinkled in disgust. "He has a ranch in true cattleman style and insists on living on it like some bloody cowhand. Loves hunting and shooting, not a brain betwixt his ears but he has the money. His father invented a patent medicine and the elixir made oodles of cash that he left to Grady so the wee snot now revels in that birthright and plays at frontiersman. I want him lost to us, if you get my meaning?"

"Let's be clear," said Malone, easing back in his chair. "You want me to assassinate this fellow Grady, is that correct?"

"Didn't I just say that?"

"No, sir, you obfuscate, work around it in best political parlance, I want it clear so we both understand. Say it, I know it hurts but plain speech is better."

"Very well, yes," spat Croker angrily. "Blow the dog's brains out. Jesus! Malone, you have more lip on you than I care to fancy."

"Well, best you understand one thing then. I do

this for the Fenian Brotherhood back home not for any Yankee political gain and I will be assured that they receive what they want or I shall be forced to come calling on you."

"You paddy's," muttered Croker in disgust.

"You were one once."

"I still am, goddamn you. Now look, Malone, it is best we don't fall out here. I know I am an irascible old bear sometimes but I mean you no ill will, you should know that."

"'Tis no skin off my nose, sir."

"Well then take my hand, we are agreed, are we not? I shall see that all relevant information is forwarded to you."

They ate in a large dining hall with a long narrow table set with candlesticks and fresh cut flowers, it was so long that further conversation between them was difficult as they sat at either end. The meal, Croker apologized, was a simple one of mutton broth followed by chicken sauté and mushrooms with grape and apple pie, cake, or custard pudding to follow. Quite as extravagant as Malone had expected and as far removed from the remembered meals of his childhood where potatoes and milk started the day, with herring for dinner and nothing for supper.

Afterward, when coffee was done and both of them puffing on cigars Croker took him across to his stables. There he kept fine thoroughbred horses that he treasured and raced.

Stroking the black silk neck of one fine stallion, Croker whispered affectionately to the animal that held its head high and turned away disdainfully.

"You see," said Croker. "How proud he is, he does not deign to converse with the likes of me. Are you like that, Malone?"

"I'll hold myself aloof from no man."

"I'll bet you don't," observed Croker astutely. "No man stands above another when laid out in the grave, is that not so?"

"The one place where we are all equal," archly Malone agreed. "Rich or poor."

> *Oh, to climb this rocky hill*
> *And look away to that far shore*
> *It seems that I am standing still*
> *With wounded heart that is so sore*
>
> *And yet within those soft gray eyes*
> *A voice that is a Siren's call*
> *Speaks promises wherein lies*
> *Some respite for this poor fool.*

CHAPTER FOUR

H e took her to Brooklyn and Prospect Park. There a verdant acreage is set between Flatbush Avenue and Ninth Avenue and laid aside for community leisure. There are walkways and meadows, arbors, picnic grounds and a great lake, with chestnut, poplar and oak trees flourishing all around. An impressive stone archway crowned with statuary and stamped "Defenders of the Union" marked the Grand Plaza entrance but once inside the park the rustic stillness and serenity of the place took over. They walked, a little awkwardly, side by side down past the old Quaker Cemetery and along the wide curving pathway to the banks of the lake. A few other New Yorkers were enjoying the park and walked or sat in leisurely fashion on grass banks beside the flat waters.

Malone noted that Bridget came dressed in the same black dress and shawl she had worn on the ship and he guessed that with little change of attire she was short of funds until she received her pay. It did not trouble him and in a way he enjoyed to see her the same as he had on their windswept crossing there was something simple and appealing about it.

"And how is your employ with Mr. Croker?" he asked as they made their way along the water's edge.

"As expected, a full day indeed."

"You were lucky to get the work so easily."

"I was, there were five of us picked up by his agent on the docks and he chose me. Strange as the others were all younger girls. I suspect that once he heard I was from Cork and for no other reason he decided."

"More likely he wanted someone with some experience and not a youngster to train, he is that kind of a practical man."

"Maybe," she hummed, taking a deep breath. "It is so good here, Malone. So fresh after the city."

"Indeed," he agreed.

They strolled on in silence both of them well-used to using their legs as a means of transport with the memory of miles to cover in such manner in their own land.

"You are working for Mr. Croker?" she asked.

"I have a task."

"Then not full employment?"

Malone bit his lip deciding on how much he should say, "He is a political animal," he said. "And has need of a layman's hand now and then."

She frowned and studied him a moment. "That is an evasive answer if ever I heard one, Malone."

"'Tis best these things are not spoken of," he said. "Your man likes his privacy."

"So he does," she agreed. "Already I have come

to see that in his house. A man of parts, he is, like some powerful lord we might find back home."

Malone nodded agreement. "Be careful there, won't you, Bridget."

"Why do you say that?"

"Ach!" He smiled. "Croker had his finger in many pies and not all of them are wholesome to my way of thinking."

"Indeed," she said. "Do you mean some kind of illegal activities, perhaps?"

Malone shrugged. "I cannot say and I only tell you to take heed as we are friends."

Bridget studied him with her gray eyes, the frown still playing gently on her brow, "So I shall and I thank you for your advice."

"Tell me?" he asked to change the subject. "About your son."

Her head dropped. "Aye, poor Dermot, my little boy, he was never a strong lad. But then the sickness on the boat…" She paused at a loss for words. "It was so sudden."

"A terrible thing, to be sure."

The same gaunt look flitted across her features as it had on the steamer and for a moment she was back there again on that windy deck with the two sailors and her dead son on a plank about to be dropped into the vast ocean. Swiftly she crossed herself. "It *was* terrible and still the ache fills my heart. The worst is knowing that he lies out there alone in deep water and that fills me with horror. There is no grave where I may visit, or flowers I may lay. No priest to bless the ground where he lies. There is no comfort for his little soul and my only hope is that the Blessed Virgin Mother has taken him to her bosom."

"And what of your husband, he never came across with you?"

"No, I am a widow woman. My husband was lost to me some years ago."

"A double loss then and I am sorry for that."

"And how about you, Malone? Do you have a wife?"

It was an abrupt and direct question and Malone felt that it was a thing that must have been preying on her mind.

He shook his head. "No, never."

"I find that hard to believe." She smiled teasingly. "You seem a bold young fellow I'm sure many bonny girls will have set their eye on you."

He chuckled. "Not me, I am not such a catch. Will you look at me, a big thuggish fellow lacking in any fancy style and ugly as a bucket."

Bridget wrinkled her lip. "You are most unkind to yourself."

This line of conversation made him think how strange they must look to onlookers with his bearish physique alongside her slender fragility.

She drew a breath and tensed herself and then said, "There is something I must tell you, Malone. I fear you will not like what I have to say but it must be told. I want no misconceptions between us."

They paused in their step and he looked at her steadily. "There is no need for confessions, Bridget. Not with me anyway."

"No, I shall say this. As perhaps you will hear it from another and wonder why I held it back from you. I was not married, you see, there was no husband. My boy was born to me out of wedlock and that is the true reason we left Ireland."

His smile seemed almost grim but it was there on his lips. "That is no great confidence, Bridget. You must know I think nonetheless of you for that."

"There is more," she admitted coldly. "The father, he was, you see, a soldier, a British soldier."

"Ah!" breathed Malone and his brow furrowed as he took the news in. Then he straightened his shoulders and pulled himself more erect. "You should know then that I am a soldier also but not for Britain."

She studied him closely. "You are a man of the Irish Brotherhood?"

"I am."

Bridget took a step back as if he had struck her, "Then you will despise me."

His hand reached out for her arm. "I will not," he said. "Maybe not approve but never despise."

Her trembling fingers went to her face as her eyes filled with tears and she turned away from him. "I'm sorry Malone, so sorry. You will think me a shamed traitor as so many others have."

"You have suffered then," he said, realizing all he knew about the treatment handed out to those caught fraternizing with the enemy.

"Yes," she gave answer with a muffled sob. "I understand, if you will take me home now, we may leave it there."

Malone was torn, his commitment to the cause was absolute and yet Bridget had walked into his heart and he found it hard, despite his dedicated self, to shed her so easily.

"I cannot," he admitted finally.

She looked at him, her gray eyes welling over with a gloss of tears. There were questions there and a single frown that marked her brow.

Behind them a breeze rippled the waters on the lake and a duck took off with a clatter of wings and a cascading spray of drops.

Malone was studying his boots unsure of what to say.

"You *cannot?*" she repeated.

Malone shook his head negatively. "No, Bridget. You have become a light in my life, and I will not turn my back on you."

"How so?" she said, a little forcibly as if spelling out the deed in detail would force his hand. "I have been with another and one of the invaders at that. Think on it, Malone. One of the enemy to our country." She said it almost spitefully as if there were a latent urge to drive him away.

"Don't ask me to explain," he mumbled into his chest. "For I cannot."

"Are you here on a mission now?" she asked with sudden certain knowledge.

"That does not matter," he said icily, lifting his eyes to glare at her. "Do not ask me that. We are not speaking of that now."

"Oh, but we are. This is the very thing we speak of for I am considered outsider now. A risk to the cause, they would have me done away with if I posed a threat."

"That will never be," he said with stern determination in his voice.

"Ah, man," she sighed. "Do not tell me you come here to America with blood on your mind, I pray that is not so."

"Believe me, Bridget. My duty here is of no concern, it should play no part in this."

"*This*! What is *this*? We have met and talked. I had thought you a fine man. Tell me what is your concern for me. Am I to you a lone woman that you befriend for something other than friendship and then, duty done you walk away. Tell me, for I will know?"

"No, there is more and you know it, do not dismiss me so. I have…I have only affection for you. Forgive me if the right words will not come, I am not trained in such."

Suddenly her hand patted the front of his jacket, playing along the lapels as she glanced into up his face, "You are very kind, I cannot believe ill of you," she allowed, her voice warming as she studied him.

"I fear I cannot help myself, it is how I am." Malone knew he was answering wanly and yet he felt defeated and drawn out, there was nothing he could do and he knew it and the knowing left him helpless.

Bridget tilted her face to him, reaching on tiptoe to bring her lips near to his.

Malone closed his eyes and leaned to kiss her softly and with that kiss a silent bell rang in his head that echoed through his whole being. Despite the public place and that they might be observed he forgot the social proprieties and swept her into his arms and they kissed passionately.

"Oh, dear God!" he breathed into her tear-stained cheek. "What have you done to me, girl."

She kissed his cheek, his jaw, his ear and neck and laughed joyously holding his stern face between her two small hands.

They continued to walk but now arm in arm. Out from the park and into the outlying farms and roads along Flatbush Avenue. Here, neat single-story houses stood with porches and picket fences along dirt tracks overhung by trees. The occasional wagon and carriage past them but there was little sign of life other than the few house owners working on their gardens and they gave a ready greeting as the two passed by. The rural scene was so different than the heavy movement of traffic and people in the city and both felt more at home in the countrified environment.

They were in a state of some numbness after their happy expressions of affection and said little content just to be in each other's company. Malone was bewildered, his mind in a state of whirl as he considered the mission he was tied to and the burgeoning outflow of emotion that he now expressed for Bridget.

For her part, Bridget knew only that for her a fresh start of companionship flooded over all the loneliness and despair of her lost son and past life. It was a thing she could not deny and despite the differences and past experiences the emotion over-rode them all and filled her to overflowing. In a strange subconscious manner, she did not notice it, but unrealized she was clinging to his arm now and held him tightly as if from some latent fear held in her mind, he would slip away and be lost to her.

"Are you hungry?" Malone asked.

"I could eat," she agreed.

"Then let us find a place in town."

A flatbed wagon approached down the road with a Negro driver and Malone waved him down and asked if they might travel with him. The somnolent Negro rolled eyes and said he had no seats for passengers but they could ride the flatbed if they so cared. Malone helped Bridget aboard and with legs dangling over the rear they rode into town smiling and as happy as a pair of children on a hay wagon at harvest time. The Negro carried them to a street market on the outskirts and from there they caught an omnibus that carried them into the city.

They found themselves a pleasant hotel dining room and chatted amicably as they waited for their meal. Malone chose lamb and Bridget duck, as she had never had it before. It all came with a wealth of vegetables that neither had ever seen in such quantity before. Malone ordered a bottle of sauterne and the complete meal cost him nigh on six dollars which emptied his purse but he thought it worth every cent as he saw the warm light in Bridget's eye over the candlelit supper table.

They were onto their Charlotte Russe dessert when a familiar face appeared.

"So here you are," said Fogarty, standing with a false grin spread across his face.

Malone frowned. "You are looking for me. How the devil did you find us?"

"I am indeed," said Fogarty. "There is not a crevice or crack in this city that Boss does not know of. Forgive me for interrupting your supper." He gave an oily tilt of the head in greeting toward Bridget. "I did not know you had company."

"Well now you are here, what do you want?"

Fogarty pulled up a chair from a neighboring table without permission from the other diners and seated himself. "Will you not introduce me to your lady friend, friend Malone?"

"I think you know who the lady is," Malone said coldly.

Fogarty nodded as if recalling a distant memory and turned to Bridget. "I believe I do, tell me, dear, are you not a girl who waits on the Boss himself?"

"I am," she said, with no show of emotion.

"Below stairs, is it? A housemaid or skivvy of sorts? I think I've seen your face there but of course I have little to do with the servants."

Malone felt the lash of his insults delivered as polite inquiry and he seemed to expand in his seat with the anger that boiled within.

"Guard your tongue," he warned before Bridget could answer.

"And what will you do in this public place?" sneered Fogarty. "I think you are above yourself, Malone. Remember you are only a visitor here and the Boss will be making report of your behavior back to your masters."

"What do you want? Get it done and get out of here."

"I'll be going in my own time," said Fogarty airily and then reaching inside his jacket he pulled out a thick envelope and tossed it on the table. "Here, this is for you. You have full instruction and cash money for expenses in there too, best you pay heed Malone, we have eyes on you." He swung around to stare at Bridget. "And you will say nothing of this, girl. Not a word or I shall come looking for you to be sure."

Angrily, Malone was about to rise from his chair but Fogarty beat him to it and pushed back his own seat and said with a strain of malice, "I'll be taking my leave now, so goodnight to you both and enjoy the rest of your meal, won't you?"

Fuming, Malone reseated himself and stared after Fogarty's disappearing back.

"I'll swing for that wretch," he hissed under his breath.

"I hope not," supplied Bridget calmly. "He is a wee guttersnipe, that is all."

Malone swallowed and recovered himself. "I do apologize, Bridget. It was unnecessary at such a time."

"No matter," she said, her eyes meeting his with a serious look. "But you must see now that you need a long spoon to dine with the devil."

> *Alas. The smallest wynd*
> *Still brings the shadows nearer*
> *Even though I find*
> *Her shelter far the dearer*

> *Ere with the sharpest razor*

TONY MASERO

To shear offense away
She'll walk inside my favor
And take me where she may.

CHAPTER FIVE

With a candle lit beside him, Malone scratched the words into his notebook. His private songs of anguish and love in rhyming sonnets to be seen by no others but himself. Even as he did so he recalled the hot night taverns back home with their bards and plain harpists, men that would ride a table top and sing their praises to the drunken sky or drown in cipher at the country's secret war. It was a tradition that lived within him and could not be denied and so he scribbled out the verses that arose from this natural legacy.

He laid aside his pen and picked up the unopened envelope and toyed with it between his fingers.

"Oh, Bridget," he whispered. "How I am unnerved by you."

Each breath he took now reverberated with that first kiss and the warmth of her hand in his. The intimate friendliness of their spoken words and how her slender body felt when it was close to his. Malone felt his purpose unraveling; he had come here with clear reason in his mind. A task set and one of which he had little doubt when first he arrived and now with the advent of this emotion the turbulence of his task seemed unworthy.

He knew other men in the Brotherhood who could set such things apart, could partition their lives with wife and children to one side and the struggle on the other. He knew that their commitment was such that they were able to do so but now for the first time ever he doubted that he could comply. The one did not fit well with the other it seemed. He was torn between the flag of independence and independence for himself.

Straightening himself and laying aside such thoughts, remembering the cause that he had sworn to uphold, he quickly ripped the envelope open. There were a small fortune of five fifty-dollar notes from The Central Bank (It seemed that Coker was no skinflint) and a sheaf of handwritten pages. Unfolding the notes he saw they were an appraisal of the targeted man known as Joseph Grady. A physical description outlined him as some fifty years old, tending to plump and a near simplicity of mind. It was his inheritance it appeared that kept him afloat in his meanderings as a frontiersman but the façade did not fit in any usual way with a gentleman of such wealth unless he were unhinged. It was rather politely pointed out that Grady was in fact somewhat mentally deficient.

He often appeared in the sort of clownish dress-style that he considered appropriate for his consuming passion as a Wild West character. A large, high-topped, wide-brimmed sombrero hat, fringed buckskin vest, checkered shirt and bandanna, and also woolly sheepskin chaps. He rode well by all accounts and loved firearms, always to be seen with pistol or long rifle while making frequent hunting trips into the wilderness.

He lived in Kansas near a newly developed town called Hutchinson. It was a growing concern apparently and Grady had built a grand ranch house nearby. The town was served by the Atchison, Topeka and Santa Fe railroad and the locals survived on a steady trade of wheat and salt.

Access for Malone was restrictive, to get to the town he would have to leave New York and cross five states before reaching Kansas, a conservative estimate of five to six weeks travel time including numerous train changes along the way. For Malone these vast distances were hard to conceive of, the equivalent to a trip to the moon after such similar assignments in his homeland where the whole of the three-hundred-mile-long island of Ireland could be dropped into New York State with room to spare. As a hit-and-run man, there was no way he could conceive of making a rapid escape over these distances.

There was one other alternative and it was included more as an afterthought to the notes and that was a small notification referring to the town house that Grady kept for his visits to New York. He held apartments in the city hall district but that lodging relied on his rare appearances in town. It would be a far better alternative if somehow they could attract Grady to make the trip. With over a million occupants of New York and that growing all the time escape would be far easier and efficient in such an environment compared to the mere thousand neighbors at Hutchinson.

Malone decided he needed an attractive lure to bring the fish to him rather than he going to it.

The next day he took himself to the impressive limestone walls of The Lennox Library on Fifth Avenue and used the newly opened reading rooms to begin scanning the newspapers for a likely source of interest. It took him some hours but at last he found what he wanted amongst the obituaries. It was the kind of preliminary detective work Malone enjoyed and after his successful research he crossed town to study the apartment block where Grady held his rooms.

Once this was done he sent a message via Boyd's City Dispatch to Croker asking for a meeting, the prompt reply received by return was that he should appear that night at the house in Harrison.

As Malone arrived that evening, he was met at the door by Bridget dressed in her neat black serving girl dress and full-length white apron with a little bonnet on her head and she took his hat and coat.

"No doorman to greet me, this time?"

"His night off," she replied.

"You are looking fine, girl, by God you are. Are you free this coming Thursday afternoon?" Malone asked her this quietly with a sly grin on his lips.

"I am," she whispered.

"Then I will come for you."

"Where do we go?" asked the intrigued Bridget.

"Wait and see," Malone said. "Now, where is his highness?"

"The library."

Croker sat in his favorite armchair with the inevitable glass beside him. He looked tired with dark rings under his eyes and a solemn gaze fixed on the empty fireplace. On the floor around him were spread loose papers and a cluttering of handwritten notes.

"Good evening, Mr. Croker," greeted Malone.

"And to you, sir. Will you take a seat."

Malone took the armchair opposite and Croker studied him keenly, "Well, what is it. You have news for me?"

"I will take your help," answered Malone.

"How so? If I can, I will."

"I have a plan to bring Grady to New York rather than some long journey to his home. He lives in a small place where many folk will know him on sight, not only for his bizarre mode of dress either. There, in that small place there will be too many witnesses aware of a stranger in town but here in New York amongst the droves the matter may be handled more adroitly it seems to me."

Croker lowered his brows and seemed deep in thought. "Go on."

"Recently there has been reported in the newspapers the sad passing of one Texas Jack Omohundro, who has recently died from pneumonia at an unfortunately early age. Do you know of him?"

Croker shrugged negatively.

"A most famous scout, a regular frontiersman of renown who gave shows all around the country."

"What use is that if he is in his grave?"

"There is no doubt that Grady will know of such a famous figure and my intention is to advertise a memorial in respect of the fellow. A grand Wild West entertainment, if you get my meaning. Feats of horsemanship, shooting, and lasso throwing, that kind of thing."

"That would cost a pretty penny although I have to say the horses will always interest me, I do so enjoy a race."

Malone shook his head, "No need for that, it will never take place. We will just advertise it as so and send a special invite to Grady to make an appearance and perhaps present prizes. Anything to get him here in town."

"That does seem most cunning, Mr. Malone. I approve, indeed I do."

"Then, with your permission, I will arrange flyers to such an event and see that one is posted off to Grady with his personal invitation."

"Yes, indeed, go ahead."

Croker paused as if something else was on his mind and he fiddled with the brandy glass at his elbow.

"It appears, Mr. Malone, that you are endeared to one of my staff here."

Malone pouted a lower lip and met his frowning gaze. "So you have a stool pigeon close by. Let me guess, is it that pipsqueak Fogarty?"

"I like to keep my ear to the ground," said

Croker. "He serves a purpose as I have already told you."

"Best beware, Mr. Croker, if he will be the rat with me then he might also be the same with you."

Croker smiled thinly. "I think not. You know, if I were to think on it at all I would consider that Fogarty is probably jealous, perhaps he has eyes for the lady himself. Even so he tells she is a woman wronged by British soldiery. By a certain lieutenant in the Lancashire Fusiliers and a bastard child was the result so I am informed."

"That may be," agreed Malone, seeing there was no way of avoiding it. "I met the lady in question on board ship where she had just lost her son to disease. But I see it as no business of yours or any other for that matter."

"She works for me, Malone of course it concerns me. You are enamored of this girl?"

"She is no girl, sir and we are friends, no more than that."

"You should know I don't usually keep track of my staff's dalliances, particularly below stairs serving maids but in this case our mutual acquaintances in Dublin may not be too pleased with such a liaison?"

"This does not affect our business here, Mr. Croker."

"I hope not but I fear you are treading on thin nice."

"My concern alone."

Croker sunk his beard to his chest and nudged the papers on the floor with his toe, "I have enough to trouble me elsewhere at present, believe me these

TONY MASERO

are trying times. Just be sure that you finish with
Grady that is all I care about."

Malone rose to leave. "As to that, the wheels are
in motion."

"Is that all you have for me?"

"One more thing, I shall need a pistol. Small,
pocket sized. The French do a nice model, a .50
caliber flintlock."

"That should not be too much of a problem, I'll
see what I can do."

"Very well, then I'll say good night to you, Mr.
Croker."

Croker fluttered fingers in farewell but he was
already lost in thought about other matters.

––––––––

On the Thursday afternoon, Bridget hurried down
the driveway eager to meet Malone who awaited her
in a hired Hansom cab. She did not notice Fogarty,
who that morning had taken a saddle pony from the
stables on the pretext of a ride and was in fact
watching hidden in the trees along the winding drive.

With a happy greeting, Malone held open the
doors to the Hansom cab and helped Bridget up
into the seat beside him. She sat with hands in her
lap, a twinkle in her eye and still dressed in her ubiq-
uitous black skirts and shawl.

Without ado, Malone rested his hands on hers,
kissed her mouth and told the driver to move on.
They were so engaged with each other that any
glance behind would have shown the mounted

Fogarty some yards away following them at a distance.

Bridget met Malone's gaze and he saw there a hint of excitement and a glow of nervous passion.

"Take me somewhere," she said with an air of boldness.

It was on Malone's lips to ask her where when the import took hold and he understood her meaning without words.

With a call to the cab driver, Malone ordered him to change direction and head for the hotel where he had moved. With Croker's advance in his pocket and feeling flush he had left the seedy room of his original arrival and taken full board at three dollars a day in Keefers Grand Central Hotel.

The hotel was a mighty place and stretched from the numbers 667 to 677 on Broadway and was a large six-story building with some eighty-five rooms and a pillared porch walkway along the entire front. It stood near to the Elevated Railroad and had three lines of hire carriages waiting parked at the door. All of it enabled Malone with an easy and rapid escape route if so needed.

To avoid any difficulties on moral grounds Malone had Bridget walk on through the foyer while he collected his key. He showed her to his nicely appointed room and without a word being spoken between them he drew all the window drapes and brought a musky darkness to the room.

Both knew what they were about and a thread of anticipation ran through them.

"Will you help me?" asked Bridget as she

TONY MASERO

fumbled with the buttons down the front of her
bodice and with a smile, he crossed over to oblige.

They embraced and kissed eagerly, hungry for
each other now. As their clothes were rapidly thrown
aside below them in the foyer, Fogarty was asking in
which room was his business associate Mister
Malone lodged as he had urgent papers that must be
delivered there before the day was done. Then with
the knowledge safely tucked away and a satisfied
smirk on his face Fogarty left the hotel to collect his
horse.

Meanwhile in the darkened room, Malone and
Bridget enjoyed each other, finding that there was
instantly an easy and relaxed relationship between
them. No embarrassment appeared and an impa-
tient Malone covered the pale and slender form of
his love with rapid intensity. He kissed her breasts
and held her small waist in his broad hands, lifting
her to himself. She, gasping with delight as he
entered, threw her arms around him and dug into
the hardened muscles of his back pulling him willingly to her.

Gradually, Malone felt the wire that bound his
hardened heart begin to unwind. A feeling of an
elastic release began to free the tensions of his
imposed task as if such things had no place in the
world he occupied now. As they rocked together on
his bed with the softened light from between the
curtains falling in thin streams across their naked
bodies Malone marveled that he should find such joy
with this tender woman. What light there was in the
room molded itself across Bridget's limbs and he

patrolled each part of her body as if an explorer discovering new lands.

When culmination streamed from him he knew a flowering that opened inside himself as if a summer flower opening its petals and he expired that beauty in a dizzying crescendo that left them both complete and exhausted.

Afterward, Bridget rested her head upon his shoulder and whispered, "And now you may tell me where we were supposed to be going?"

He turned to look at her. "To some fine shop, I intended to buy you new dresses."

She frowned, "You did not."

"I did indeed."

Suddenly she reprimanded him, "You will never do that, Malone. I will be no kept woman I'll have you know."

"Ach! It was meant as no such thing."

She relented at his innocence. "I know but there is no need for such things. I am content with all we have here."

Malone smiled and touched her lips with his forefinger. "You are a proud woman, Bridget Reilly."

"Not so proud I have given myself to a wild Irishman with blood on his mind."

Malone shook his head. "Do not think on such things."

"I know what goes on in Croker's house, the comings and goings at all hours and that wretched Fogarty creeping around spying on everything."

"He has troubled you? If he does, you will tell me."

"There is nothing I cannot handle with a hypocrite like that."

"He is a louse, that's to be sure but if he bothers you, I will see him off. Count on it."

"I am more concerned with your labors for Boss Croker, I fear he will drag you into one of his nefarious activities."

"I will tell you this, my orders are from the Brotherhood and not from him."

"There is corruption here, Malone. Evil and wicked men, I've seen their faces when they come to call. They live for no cause at all except for money and power."

"You will know how it is, Bridget. I am a soldier committed to a just cause, I wish only for independence for our country. Sometimes one must dig in the dirt to achieve that."

She clung to him in a sudden firm grasp. "Leave it, my love, come away from this cursed duty. This is a big country and here we can disappear if we so have a mind."

Malone shook his head. "No, there is no worse crime than betrayal, it is a sin not forgotten or forgiven by those I serve."

"I too knew a soldier once," she said coldly. "So I know of betrayal and all the despair that follows, believe me. But now I have found you and for once the light shines in my life again, I would not give it up for anything."

He held her close then and kissed her again to stop her words and the afternoon folded away into gentle embraces and warm oblivion.

She calls to me, my fairest rose
To cast aside my hidden cape
And take a path where no one goes
To make myself a different shape

But I have found within her arms
A place that gives the best of all
Caught in a net full of those charms
I pray I'm saved before I fall.

CHAPTER SIX

J oseph E. Grady had arrived in town.

Word arrived for Malone along with the pocket-sized pistol he had requested. He spent the next few days staking out the area and caught his first sight of Grady when he took an early morning walk around the tree-lined Lower Manhattan Square that housed city hall.

Thankfully Grady had avoided his more extravagant attire but it was still a colorful collection with a more common frock coat in bright green with clashing large plaid pants and the rest was composed of a silk top hat and colorful cravat with a slender walking cane in his gloved hand. He wore long bushy white sideburns and a clean-shaven chin but the hair under his hat was long and reached down over a freshly pressed collar. The face was fleshy and Malone detected willful sagging evident in his over-weight body under a paisley vest.

Grady ambled dreamily at a relatively slow pace and was easy for Malone to keep in sight. As they moved through the other strollers Malone was marking out the lie of the land and deciding where best to make the strike.

The roads were wide and quite often populated with walkers as well as carriages and delivery carts. It all allowed Malone a clear view of his victim with space all around that kept any collateral damage to others at a minimum. A single back shot from the large caliber pistol to head or spine would bring Grady down and probably kill him instantly, it only remained for Malone to plan his successful escape route. The trees about were good cover and with the loud retort of the pistol he knew from experience there would be surprise and shock before onlookers took any action.

He needed to find the place that best suited his purpose and on consideration the great steps leading up to the columned entrance of city hall seemed a likely spot. From there he could quickly disappear amongst the trees opposite.

The building towered above with shaded windows and four great Union flags flying from the rooftop. If his escape across the road was blocked he saw an alternative route alongside the structure where a narrow walkway led to swathes of green lawn and more trees.

Grady paused to talk to a small child flower seller hawking her wares from a basket he bought a posy from the girl and continued on his ambling way, casually sniffing at the flowers occasionally. A beggar crossed his path and Grady diligently searched in his purse to offer a few coins to the man. The seemingly inoffensive millionaire was obviously the charitable sort, Malone decided, but then he could afford to be so.

It was to be a pitiable act against one so harmless and it needled at Malone. Yet he could not afford to think like that, his directive was firm and to be an effective assassin there was no room for empathetic sympathy. The act would call for cold objectivity and single-mindedness or the hand would shake and the resulting act is ineffective.

It would be on the morrow as there seemed little point in delay, the sooner it was done Malone could pull away from under Croker's shadow. What he would do about Bridget was another matter and it troubled him as he made his way back to the hotel.

She had no wish for him to complete his charge and Malone worried about how she might react once the deed was done. Could he take her with him back to Ireland? That was another consideration. He guessed that her reaction to that particular alternative would be negative, not only for the sore memories the country held for her but also as his service in the Brotherhood would undoubtedly call for more acts of danger in the future.

But he knew above all else that he did not want to lose her, that was the strongest motivation in his thinking but how he would handle it he had, as yet, no idea.

———

The next day dawned with the kind of gray overcast sky that made all the stone buildings in the city gleam with a white glow. The city awoke to its normal backwash of indistinct noise like the hazy buzz of a hive and with the same kind of busyness the city started the day. Along the docks small armies of longshoremen marched to their daily tasks while above them men began to labor on the great span of the developing Brooklyn Bridge. Ships on the Hudson boomed their horns and steamers chugged out black smoke to join the smoke already rising from the factories and warehouses populating Lower Manhattan.

Malone was up early, he made sure the priming in the pistol was ready and kept it in the deep pocket of his overcoat. Then he walked rapidly to where he would station himself in wait for Grady as he took his morning perambulation.

Malone stood among tree shadows in the parkland opposite the wide road that passed before the neo-classical façade of the city hall. There were comparatively few pedestrians about, some hurrying as if they were on their way to work, other early walkers strolling with their dogs. But the roadway itself was busy with produce carts and horse drawn market vehicles ready to deliver their orders before the day began and the rattle of their wheels and the clop of horses were the only noise.

Then Malone saw him.

Grady wove his way at the same relaxed pace he enjoyed along the sidewalk before Malone and he left the cover of the shadowy trees to take up station behind the man. He would shoot close, he decided, a bullet delivered not more than a few feet from Grady's back to be certain of a killing shot.

There was a sudden loud noise from further

down the street with men shouting incoherently and Malone looked in that direction but could see nothing out of the ordinary. He approached at a faster pace now, eager to have the matter done with and ready to race away after it was finished. Malone's blood was up and a cold wire of thrill ran through him as his hand fastened on the pistol's grip in his pocket with his thumb levering back the flint hammer. He prayed there would be no misfire but the evening before he had oiled and worked the mechanism to see that it behaved perfectly so he expected no problem.

Just then Grady turned sharply left and ambled out into the roadway, ready to cross over before the tiered steps outside city hall. Malone prepared to follow when he glimpsed from the corner of his eye the sudden movement of a wagon fast approaching.

It was a white-painted, high sided and covered ice wagon delivering blocks of ice from the icehouse to residential houses for refrigeration purposes. The bolting horse between the shafts was rolling its eyes wildly and racing down the street in panic. Way back behind the speeding van, men were bawling and running after the runaway with little chance of stopping the animal.

As the dreamy Joe Grady stepped out into the road he was unaware of the heavy wagon coming toward him. Malone froze for a moment on the sidewalk as he estimated the trajectory of the vehicle heading for his prey before an automatic cry of warning burst from his lips.

The panicked horse barreled into Grady spilling him under its hooves. He cried out once sharply, the sound barely audible under the rattle of the wagon. The horse stumbled and then ran on and was quickly followed by the wagon wheels and the combined weight of fifty and hundred pound blocks of ice inside. The wheels bounced over the rolling figure of Grady and crashed down as the fleeing animal swerved away. It spun across the roadway with the wagon tilting on its side as it followed the maddened animal's flight.

At full tilt the horse ran into a lamppost and with a rending crash the wagon coming behind collided with the animal knocking it to the ground. The splintered wagon burst open and in a great shower of exploded chippings like a rain of hail it skated blocks of ice from inside and they slid haphazardly in every direction across the roadway.

Malone was quickly over to the fallen figure of Grady but it was obvious he was quite dead with his portly body crushed, his head twisted at a strange angle and with blood pouring from multiple gashes and abrasions.

A crowd gathered quickly around the fallen man as the sweating driver and his mate came pounding up uttering despairing curses. Across the way the horse was screaming terribly, its neck stretched long as it thrashed in an attempt to lift itself but both forelegs were broken and the animal only rolled in the harness tangling itself further in its wild desperation.

With cold deliberation Malone stepped away from the crowd and strode across to the suffering beast. Drawing the pistol from his pocket he did not hesitate but delivered a finishing shot that instantly put the creature out of its misery. The gunshot was only one more noise amongst the loud sounds of uproar and passed unnoticed.

Breathing heavily, Malone stepped away and before he was noticed he rapidly slipped down the walkway beside the city hall and across the lawn to disappear amongst the trees.

As he moved off the irony of it did not escape him, set to perform a murder the task had been done for him and the ball intended for Grady had sent his equine killer to its rest. The business was over and bizarrely not by any hand of his.

Malone found a nearby café and ordered himself a coffee and brandy to allow the furor outside to die down and his nerves to settle. Thoughts rolled around his mind as he steadied his nerve and tried to plan the next move.

He decided to send a message to Croker immediately and apprise him of events before he did anything else. He hoped Croker would invite him to the house for a full report and there he might see Bridget and they could arrange a time to decide on their future together.

There was no immediate response and Malone walked back to his hotel and waited. He waited throughout the day checking the front desk constantly but no message came and by evening Malone was beginning to wonder if Croker were away on business somewhere.

Next morning he took a Hansom out to the

house and knocked on the door. The usual manservant who eyed him distantly and raised inquiring eyebrows answered it.

"May I help you, sir?"

"I need to see Croker."

"I'm sorry Mr. Croker is not in at present."

"No? Is he away?"

The manservant offered a polite smile. "He is unavailable, sir."

"You mean he's here but he's not seeing me, is that it?"

"I cannot comment on that."

"How about Bridget? I'd like to see her."

"I fear Mrs. Riley has left our employ."

"*What?*" burst out Malone. "What do you mean —left your employ?"

"I mean she has gone, sir. Taken her belongings and left."

"Holy Michael! What the hell is going on?"

Fuming, Malone pushed the manservant aside and forced his way into the foyer.

"*Croker!* Where the devil are you?" he bellowed.

There was no answer from the silent house and Malone grasped the manservant by his lapels and pulled him close.

"Where is he?" Malone shouted into the man's face angrily. "Take me to him or by God, I'll box your ears for you."

"Sir, sir, please," whined the servant, wriggling in Malone's grip. "Mr. Croker cannot be seen."

"Listen, you ninny," roared Malone. "Get him or it'll be the worse for y—"

"Mr. Malone, *Mr. Malone!*" the call came from

the stairway and Malone turned to see Croker standing there with a portfolio of papers under his arm. "What is the meaning of this?"

"I wrote you, do you make no reply?"

"You mean about Joe Grady's unfortunate demise?" said Croker blithely. "Yes, I had heard. There seemed little point in continuing, our business is finished surely?"

Malone detected the dismissive tone in his voice and for a moment he was thrown by the indifferent response.

"Then what's this about Bridget? Why had she gone? Did you fire her?"

Croker spread his hands innocently. "Good heavens, no. The woman has decided to part ways with us, that is all. Now will you release poor Chalmers, I'm afraid he does not take rough handling too well."

Only then did Malone realize he still had the servant grasped in his fist and he quickly pushed the man away.

"That's better," said Croker, seeing that Malone had recovered himself and he could safely continue his descent down the stairs. "Now, as I say, we are done, Malone. I shall write our mutual friends that the mission is successfully completed even though you had no hand in it and therefore I feel no obligation to them. Having said that I shall pass on report that you have carried out your work most satisfactorily. There." He shrugged. "Will that do?"

Malone drew a breath and asked in a calmer voice, "Will you tell me where Bridget has gone?"

"I have no idea." He turned to the manservant.

TONY MASERO

"Do you know anything about Mrs. Riley's where-abouts, Chalmers?"

"No, sir, I am afraid I do not."

"She left no message, no word?"

Croker shook his head negatively and waved the portfolio in Malone's direction, "Now if that is all, sir, I have much work to do so I trust you will excuse me."

> *The pretty bird has left me*
> *Has taken flight and flown*
> *Without a word to see*
> *She's left me on my own*
>
> *Have I sinned so badly*
> *And caused such awful pain*
> *That she must part so sadly*
> *And seen no more again.*

CHAPTER SEVEN

Malone pounded the streets desperately searching for Bridget.

It was a foolish task in such a busy and volatile city and with no clear direction for his search. Frantically he explored the places they had visited together but to no avail. His mind was in uproar over the fact that she would disappear so quickly and he feared that his determination to complete the task she so disapproved of had given her reason to leave. Still he could not believe that she would do such a thing without some explanation or a least a simple word of farewell. It seemed so out of character.

He was on the verge of giving up after an exhausting day when on returning to the hotel he found an envelope waiting for him at the desk.

"We have matters to discuss. If you would see the Riley woman again come to Vinegar Hill outside Arbuckle's Yuban warehouse at ten of the clock tonight."

Malone pondered over the slip of paper for some time. Who and why—he wondered but at least it explained Bridget's disappearance. There was something amiss here and he racked his brain thinking who might be behind it and he considered that there was a possibility that maybe his masters in the Irish Republican Brotherhood had disapproved of his behavior in some way or that perhaps their allies in New York the organization known as Clan na Gael had some call on him for a service. But none of that explained why they would use Bridget in such a manner. It was someone with a grudge he was sure of it and the only person he could think of on that score was Damon Fogarty.

If Fogarty was behind it, then the meeting would have one purpose only and that would mean a bad result for Malone. He still had the pistol so at least there was some means of defense and if it meant Bridget's safety then it was a meeting he could not avoid so he would be there.

————

The docks at that time of night were deserted apart from the occasional night watchman but generally those ancients stuck to their cubbyholes or gathered around a hot stove. Tall buildings in dark brick rose around the unlit alleyways and cobbled streets and without streetlights the whole area was enclosed in shadow. An unpleasant smell arose from the waters of the East River that spread its tainted miasma of oil and waste and raised a thin mist that seeped eerily through the empty gantries and moored sailing vessels with their spiders web of rigging and tall masts. The stinking river vied with the pleasant aroma that came from all the coffee beans stored in the warehouse and it brought a strange conflict of odor to the night. Along the wide road outside, parked cargo wagons and carts stood in quiet isolation amongst the overhanging gloom of the warehouses and above all stood the solid blocks of the almost finished suspension towers for the Brooklyn Bridge that rose skeletal against the night sky.

Malone had arrived early and stood with hands sunk deep in the pockets of his overcoat inside the deep shadows alongside the storehouse. Yuban's was part of the massive Arbuckle's enterprise and it was a four-story building that stretched along twelve city blocks with a facade pockmarked with arched openings and half-painted brickwork. The painting was a large hoarding advertising the tinned brand of its famous coffee and it glowed pale in the poor light. Across from the buildings water could be heard lapping against the dock's pilings and with it the lowing of tugs and steamers out on the river that sounded mournfully through the deserted streets.

There was a chill in the air that came from the mist and seemed to permeate Malone through his coat. He wrestled his shoulders against the damp night air and moved from one foot to the other on the cold stones underfoot.

Then he heard them coming, footsteps loud on the cobblestones and more than one of them.

Malone moved out of the shadows and saw four silhouetted figures coming toward him. One of them carried a lantern and by its light Malone saw that

Fogarty was in the lead with the two heavyset fellows he had seen with him on that first day. Between them they brought a slighter form and with a sudden clutch at his heart Malone recognized Bridget.

At sight of Malone, Fogarty brought his group to a stop some twenty yards away.

"There y'are," he greeted cheerfully.

"What is you want?" growled Malone.

"Oh, just a word or two. Appears you are cut free of the Boss right now, is that not so?"

"Will you let Bridget free?"

"To be sure, in a moment or two."

He is happy, Malone thought, pleased with himself and content to have me where he wants me.

"Unfortunate you tried that," said Malone and then louder, "Are you all right, Bridget?"

"Not so bad," she replied.

"Has he hurt you at all?"

"Of course not," butted in Fogarty. "Not at all, would we harm one of the female gender? No, sir, we are gentlemen all. It is you I have a bone to pick with."

"Then release her from those two apes, if you will."

"You've a fine tongue on you, haven't you, Malone. But now you don't have any protection from the Boss, it's just you and me now."

"So what do you propose, is it fisticuffs you're thinking of?"

"I think not, you're too big a fellow for the likes of me."

"Well you have those dummies to back you up, I

should have thought you were bold enough with them behind you."

Fogarty shook his head. "I wish you wouldn't refer to my colleagues in that manner. They're fine boys and will not take kindly to harsh words."

"Well, what is it you want from me then?"

"A pound of flesh is all. You see you have treated me poorly, Malone. Looked down your snotty nose at me as if I were some ill formed no-account. Well, now you are on your own and I'm thinking that the Boss would sooner be rid of you and all the confidences you hold."

"You come with Croker's blessing, is that it?"

"Not so much but I believe he will shine on me with a kinder light if I prove myself of good use."

"You're a poor fool, Fogarty. Croker has no illusions about you, he sees you like the toady you are and you'll not change his mind."

"That's to be seen, isn't it now?"

With that Fogarty pulled a pistol from inside his coat and pointed it directly at Malone's face. A broad grin split Fogarty's face and the light from the lantern gave it an almost demonic gleam.

"So that's it," said Malone, his hand inside his pocket wrapping around the grip of his pistol. "It's bloody murder you've in mind."

"No!" cried Bridget. "Do not."

"Ah, there speaks the soft words of love," said Fogarty. "Do you hear it, Malone? Let it be the last few glad words you hear on this earth."

With that he levered back the hammer of the flintlock. "Will you say your farewells to your beloved?"

Only Malone saw the dark shapes emerging from the mist behind Fogarty and his bodyguards. They moved silently and speedily like ghosts and ran full flight to come up behind the three men. Carrying long night sticks they struck without pause felling the two bodyguards and then with a strike to the back of the head they brought down Fogarty, who folded quietly to the cobbles with the sound of a blow that's smack echoed through the docks with all the sharp impact of hard wood hitting bone.

Released from their grip, Bridget ran swiftly across to Malone who held her tightly in his arms.

"Thank God you're safe," breathed Malone into her hair as she clung fast to him.

"Mr. Malone?" said one of the strangers, tugging at the peak of his flat cap.

"I am and who the devil are you?"

"I'm Corporal Liam Ferguson, we are of the Clan na Gael and himself, Captain Carruthers sent us word from Dublin to watch over you. We've been your guard for many a day but this seemed the best time to interfere."

"I'll say," agreed Malone. "In the nick of time indeed."

"The Brotherhood keeps a close eye on our agents over here and this one here." He pointed his stick at the unconscious form of Fogarty. "Is not the best of fellows, he has a way of tale telling to people whom he shouldn't. The man's an informer, he likes to play both sides of the coin."

"That doesn't surprise me."

"Well he'll be no concern of yours any longer."

Already the other men were dragging the unconscious bodies away toward the river.

"What will you do with them?"

"Oh, they'll be going back to Ireland," said Liam with a half smile and a glint in his eye. "Thing is they'll have to swim the whole precious way."

———

"But you can't go back," cried Bridget.

They stood together in his hotel room. She quivered with relief at her rescue and anger at his decision but Malone was quiet and determined.

"I must," answered Malone. "They will be waiting on me and if I do not show, well you've seen what they can do."

"They will never let you come back to me."

"No, I will explain. I'll have good cause, say we are to be married and almost tell them the whole truth if not all of it. That way we'll have a chance."

"Dear God, this is crazy, Malone. I wish you would not do it."

"Believe me, I know of what I speak. It is best this way and then maybe we may run. I'm thinking California, they say that is a fine place."

She shook her head. "It must be like a prison, this blessed cause you speak of."

He snorted a laugh. "Not so you'd notice, it's a thing you are born into, Bridget. It's laid on you when you enter this world."

"Like a ball and chain," she observed skeptically.

"Maybe but it only lives because we believe in it. If nobody did, it would fade away and if we will fight such a war it has to be on level ground so the rules that keep it alive are fierce."

"And you will turn your back on all that?"

He turned her head toward him gently with a finger to her chin. "I shall," he promised with a kiss.

———

Three weeks later he was standing in the small smoke filled cellar of the Gallaher Ale House before the imposing figure of Captain Damian Carruthers. It was a dank smelling little drinking house in Oxmantown to the north of Dublin with ancient timbered walls that suffered from damp rising from the nearby waters of the River Liffey.

The captain stood behind a simple empty table with the green and golden sunburst flag of the Brotherhood stretched on the wall behind him. A few of his lieutenants occupied the rest of the room sitting and drinking or smoking their clay pipes. They were all subdued as they waited to see how the returned Malone was to be treated.

"Nice to see you back again." Smiled Carruthers, extending his left hand and shaking Malone's.

Carruthers was a handsome man, a square jawed figure with dark curly hair and thick eyebrows. His eyes were of the piercing variety and held the aquamarine blue more often found at the bottom of icebergs in Arctic seas. Right now he fixed that penetrating gaze on Malone.

The captain was a strongly built square shoul-

A BREAK IN THE CLOUDS

dered fellow and Malone had only respect and admiration for the man but there was one anomaly that he found faintly disturbing. Carruthers had no right hand it having been blown off by a musket ball when he was still a child and in a hunting accident. He did nothing to disguise the loss preferring an empty sleeve to any wooden prosthetic and this he would wave about when giving instruction like a bird flapping its wing. It seemed to Malone an unnecessary demonstration of the man's capabilities that were good enough without resorting to such flamboyant displays.

Despite that Malone liked the man and took direction from him easily.

"So tell me," said Carruthers. "What's the craic and how did it go?"

"Not at all as expected but with the same result after all. The mark, a fellow called Grady was causing Croker some difficulties by funding an opponent of his. So I followed our boy and was about to bring him down when he stepped off the pavement and straight under the wheels of a runaway wagon. Killed him instantly."

Carruthers huffed a laugh. "Holy Jesus! Who'd have believed it?"

There was a collective chuckle of approval from the others in the room.

"Still Croker got his result albeit not by my hand."

"So he did, so he did, Malone. Well it's good to have you back, m'boy. There are many things here that need attending…"

"One thing, Captain," said Malone, holding up

a finger. "I have met a fair *cailín* over there and would marry her."

"Really? You hear that, you fellows," said Carruthers, a broad smile on his lips. "Bless me, Malone. I would never have thought it of you, congratulations."

An appropriate collection of cheers and hand-clapping from the company echoed Malone's proclamation and Carruther's approval.

"So tell me about this girl. Is she Irish?"

"Indeed she is, there is one thing though I must advise you of."

Carruthers nodded expectantly.

"She had a child off a British officer not by her choice I hasten to add, it was more forced on her as it were."

"Bastard!" hissed Carruthers; only too ready to believe how the hated enemy would behave.

"Thing is that folks here saw it as an unworthy association and reviled her for it. So she left for the Americas for a different life free of such base accusation."

"It can be an unfortunate thing amongst our vengeful folk when appearances are deceptive," sympathized Carruthers. "She has a name?"

Malone was prepared for this and had chosen to use the family of some of his distant relatives. If Carruthers made a cursory check, he would find the family lived there and hopefully would press the issue no further.

"She does indeed. She is a pretty lass called Niahm Mulvane of County Limerick."

"So you'll be going back to wed, is that the matter?"

"I shall if you will permit."

"To be sure, Malone and good luck to you but then will you be returning here after the deed?"

Malone smiled evasively. "We intend a honeymoon before considering that."

Carruthers studied him suspiciously with his piercing eyes. "Like I say we need you here, I hope it will not be for long."

"Always ready, sir. You just have to call, if you can find me, that is."

And so tis done
The die is cast
I'll leave no run
Of words to last

With eyes set west
On hope we'll ride
Forget the rest
As we two hide

And what will be
When we are gone
My love and me
To sing our song

A LOOK AT: TONY MASERO COLLECTION VOLUME ONE

WESTERN AUTHOR TONY MASERO TAKES YOU ON FOUR THRILLING WESTERN ADVENTURES IN THIS AUTHENTIC AND HARD-HITTING COLLECTION!

Texas 1914. Clelland Fellows is riding back across the border with blood on his hands and a promise to keep. Leaving one war behind, he finds another one waiting. There is a killer on the loose, and this ex-soldier must take up arms and return again to the chaos that still reigns across the Rio Grande.

"The Western world Masero describes is both romantic and sordid, as much Eastwood as Wayne; breath-taking scenery as a backdrop for stupidly violent men living in filth—physical and moral."

Asa Feathers has served hard time as a frontier warrior and is ready to call it quits. His life has been one long battle of fighting Indians and outlaws. Now, he's ready for some peace and quiet. Rape, murder, and robbery are the hallmarks of the Cane gang, and they will stop at nothing to achieve their vengeful ends.

Grab your copy now and discover why Tony Masero is a master of the violent Western that won't let up! This collection includes *Diehard, In the Devil's Grip, The Last Hunt,* and *The Vengeance of Ender Smith.*

AVAILABLE NOW

ABOUT THE AUTHOR

Tony Masero grew up in a deprived and grey post-war London, where the only relief from bomb craters and food rationing were colorful Western books and movies. The pictures on the screen displayed wide sunlit spaces, glorious forests, breathtaking mountain ranges, and—most importantly—adventure and a great sense of freedom. His love of that early thrill has subsequently inspired many of his own books. Living far from the Wild West and any kind of armed culture, he made up for it by practicing longbow archery in the forests of southern England.

At the age of three, Tony's father, a renowned woodcarver, placed a pencil in his hand, an act that resulted in a later career as a Designer and then Illustrator. Working in the international advertising and publishing world, Tony produced a great deal of art for book covers, and through the research involved in their creation is where his interest in writing began.

Research is important in his own books, and many of Tony's tales are based around some historical incident or characters that truly existed. From there, imagination takes flight and, for a person with a visual frame of mind, his books are often imbued with a natural pictorial quality and full of human characteristics that are true to us whatever our origins.